Hope Deferre

Hope Holla e at thirty-one be y, and they find it ironic that she is giving advice about love as the newest columnist for *Agape Today*. Ben Porter writes an irate letter in response to one of Hope's columns. Regular correspondence is sparked and soon deepens. But Ben doesn't know how to find Hope when she declines to meet him in person.

Wait for Me by Terry Fowler

Cathy Burris meets with an accident, which puts her in the lap of an old school acquaintance. Champion of the underdog, she holds Austin Collins's bullying in the past against him, even though he does seem to be trying to show her how he has changed. Her tendon injury doesn't keep her from answering magazine letters with advice on love. One regular writer intrigues her. Could he be. . . ?

Mission: Marriage by Aisha Ford

Melanie Taylor has a heart for helping people and used to dispense advice freely until she ruined her best friend's romance and completely embarrassed herself. The job for *Agape Today* seems perfect for her, letting her remain anonymous while still working as a nanny. Could her advice to a shy young man help her open the door to a relationship with her employer's aloof brother?

I Do Too by Pamela Kaye Tracy

Shelby Tate prides herself in her career climb to managing editor of *Agape Today* magazine, but she is without an advice writer. . .again. If only Sebastian Maitland, owner of the magazine, would let her hire a married person for the job. When Sebastian tells her to write it herself, her pride takes a tumble. Shelby's new role is about to change her ideas about career. . . and men.

Dear Miss Lonely Heart

Four Stories of Love Within the "Advice Column"

Aisha Ford
Terry Fowler
Linda Lyle
Pamela Kaye Tracy

BARBOUR PUBLISHING

ISBN 1-59789-289-0

Published by Barbour Books, an imprint of Barbour Publishing, Inc., P.O. Box 719, Uhrichsville, Ohio 44683, www.barbourbooks.com

Printed in the United States of America.
5 4 3 2 1

Dear Miss Lonely Heart

Hope Deferred

by Linda Lyle

Chapter 1

Hope Hollaway placed the bouquet of roses on the grave. Virginia Hollaway Adams was at peace at last. Hope took a few steps away from the grave before a voice halted her steps.

"Hope! Wait up."

She watched her sister Faith struggle across the wet grass in her stiletto heels. Looking down at her own flats, Hope shook her head at the teenager's lack of common sense. Faith wouldn't be a teenager much longer. The reality was hard to believe. It seemed like only yesterday when Hope had moved back to take care of her sisters after her father and mother were killed in a car accident.

"Where's Charity?" Hope asked as Faith closed the distance between them.

"She left with Harry and Paula."

Harry and Paula Madison had been her anchor during the last ten years, lending support just when she thought she couldn't go on. They had been her parents' best friends and neighbors since before Hope was born. They would be waiting at home to give whatever help they could. Their help and God were the only two things she could count on in times of trouble.

"I thought you were going to ride home with them." Hope brushed a stray curl behind her ear, running a hand over the short bob to smooth it back in place.

"I wanted to talk with you, so I sent Charity on with them to open the house."

"Oh." Hope didn't like the sound of this. "What did you want to talk about?"

"Not here," Faith replied, motioning toward the grave. "Let's talk in the car." They walked to Hope's blue Sable in silence. Hope measured her long strides to match Faith's shorter steps. At five foot ten, Hope didn't need high heels. Besides, they just got in the way on days like today. She waited until they were on the road before starting the conversation again.

"Okay, so what's up?"

"I wanted you to know that I made a decision about college."

"Great! Are you going to Johns Hopkins or the University of Maryland?" Hope asked, lighting up at the prospect.

"UCLA."

"UCLA!" Hope fairly screamed out the letters. A car blared its horn as she swerved into the next lane. She got the car under control and then tried to manage her anger.

"I guess telling you in the car wasn't such a good idea," Faith said, her face pale from the near collision.

"What is wrong with you? You know we can't afford for you to live away from home and go to college. There are plenty of schools right here in Baltimore."

"I know. That's why I applied for a scholarship."

"What scholarship?" Hope asked.

"I was afraid of how you would react if I told you that I wanted to go to UCLA, so I applied without telling you. I also applied for financial aid. I knew that if I didn't get it, I would never be able to go. I thought I'd wait until I heard from the committee before I told you. That way, if I didn't get in, there wouldn't be a big fuss. Besides, you had Aunt Gina to worry about."

"So you wait until *now* to tell me?" Hope took a deep breath. "How are you going to pay for living expenses?"

"Sheena and Christy moved to California last year. They have a small apartment with room for one more."

"Sheena and Christy? So that's where this is coming from."

"It's not just them, Hope. I want to go to film school, and I want to get away from here," she added under her breath.

"What's wrong with home?" Hope asked, slowing the car as she turned into the driveway. She put the car in park and switched off the ignition. Still, Faith didn't answer. "I asked you what was wrong with home."

"You are!" Faith blurted out.

"Me?" Hope felt a stab of pain in her chest.

"I love you, Hope, but you've got to let me live my life. You need to get a life of your own."

"I have a life, thank you very much," Hope replied.

"Hope, you were only twenty-two when Mom and Dad died. You've spent the last ten years raising me and Charity. Then, just when we were getting able to take care of ourselves, Aunt Gina got sick."

"So?"

"So, you never take time for yourself. When was the last time you went out?"

"I don't know. I wasn't counting." Hope felt her cheeks flush at the mention of her dating life. It had been the object of controversy in the family, and the neighborhood, for that matter, for as long as she could remember.

"It's been over a year, and even then, you didn't give the guy a chance. You dumped him after the second date. Kevin was really into you."

"First of all, it's none of your business. Second, there was no chemistry between Kevin and me. That's why I quit dating him." She took another deep breath. "What does this have to do with you going to California?"

"I want to be out on my own, take care of myself." Faith got out of the car and headed for the house.

The rambling Victorian home had been in the family for years. Thankfully, it had been big enough for the girls and their aunt Gina. The house would seem empty without the older woman's laughter and stories. With a sigh, Hope stepped from the car and followed Faith inside. Mourners were already arriving. She would have to wait until after everyone left to finish her conversation with Faith.

Hope greeted friends and relatives as she made her way toward the kitchen. She found Charity in the dining room, rearranging the table to accommodate the ever-increasing collection of casseroles and desserts. Charity gave Hope a wan smile as she walked into the kitchen. Paula was already in an apron, doing dishes.

"You don't have to do that."

"You know me. I can't stand dirty dishes." Paula looked her directly in the eye. "Faith told you, I see."

"You knew!"

"She came to me a couple of days ago. She needed an open mind."

"And I don't have an open mind?" Hope sputtered.

"Not when it comes to the girls." Paula turned back to the sink. "You've got to let them go sometime."

"I know," Hope said with a sigh. "I just didn't think it would be so soon."

"Hope?" Charity called quietly from the doorway. "Can we talk?"

"If it's about your sister, then no. I need to think about it for awhile." Hope pulled the aluminum foil off of yet another casserole dish.

"It's not about Faith."

Hope looked up to see Charity's solemn expression. Something big was up—something more than Aunt Gina's funeral. "Sure, Sweetie. Why don't we go to my room, where it will be quieter?"

The sisters made their way through a maze of people to the stairway. There were even people in the upstairs hallway. Hope tried to smile, but her nerves were tied in knots. After opening the door to her room, she let Charity go in first and then closed and locked the door firmly behind her.

"Now, what's got you so serious?" Hope asked, trying to lighten the situation.

"I need to tell you something. I kept waiting for the right time, but there's never been a right time."

"Go on."

"Bob asked me to marry him," Charity stated bluntly.

For a moment Hope stood rooted to the spot in confusion. Married? Charity and Bob? "When did this happen?"

"A couple of weeks ago."

"I see."

"Hope, you know I love him, and he's a good man, a Christian." Charity stopped at Hope's raised hand.

"I know. It's just a shock."

"Then you're not upset?" Charity asked, her eyes hopeful.

"No, I'm happy for you. It will just take a little getting used to."

Charity crossed the room and wrapped her in a hug. Hope held on a little longer than was necessary, but she was afraid to let her go. Finally, she released her sister with a small sigh.

"I'm going to go tell Faith."

"Okay." Hope nodded and motioned Charity out of the room. As soon as she was gone, Hope closed the door and clicked the lock. She sank onto the chair at her desk and laid her head on her arms, letting loose the torrent of tears that she had dammed up all week. She cried for her parents, Aunt Gina, and the way her sisters would soon leave her alone with an empty nest. Despite her arguments to the contrary, she knew going to California would be good for Faith, and she couldn't ask for a better brother-in-law than Bob, but it all came too close together. The house would be so empty without her sisters and Aunt Gina.

When the tears abated, Hope raised her head and stared at the advertisement circled in the magazine *Agape Today*. It was for a job as a love advice columnist for "Dear Miss Lonely Heart." Charity had laughingly given it to her and dared her to apply since she was so fond of giving her sisters advice. As a joke, she had sent off the application. Now, a job didn't seem like such a bad idea. The upkeep on the house and property taxes were getting to be more than she could handle. The sisters had been living off the inheritance from their parents and took in Aunt Gina when she became ill. Hope could sell the house as they had discussed earlier and give each girl her share of the money. That would help Faith with college expenses and give Charity a nice wedding. There would probably be enough left to help Hope move to an apartment in the city. Now all she had to do was get a job.

Hope took in a deep breath and brushed the last of the tears from her eyes. A job would have to wait until later. Right now, she had a house full of guests who needed her attention. She glanced at the ad one more time. Maybe a new start wouldn't be such a bad idea. Wiping the thought from her mind, she unlocked the door and walked downstairs with what she hoped would pass for a serene expression.

Chapter 2

Thinking back over the last few weeks, Hope finally felt a little excitement mixing with the feelings of loss. She had talked with the girls and Paula and Harry about selling the house. They all agreed it would be for the best. She hated to let the house go, but it wasn't practical to keep it. Paula and Harry knew a young man by the name of Benjamin Porter who was looking for an older house to restore. He was coming by this afternoon to do a walk-through and, with any luck, to make an offer. The sound of the doorbell announced Mr. Porter's arrival and set Hope's heart skipping. She took a deep breath before turning the knob, but it did nothing to prepare her for what waited outside her door. From Harry's description, she had pictured someone fresh out of college. She had pictured wrong.

The guy who stood in front of her was all man. Probably in his mid to late thirties, he was six foot five with dark wavy hair that made her want to run her fingers through it. He would never have to worry about male-patterned baldness. His bright blue eyes pierced the fog in her brain and jolted her back to reality.

"Ms. Hollaway?" he asked, one eyebrow raised in question.

"Yes, I'm Hope Hollaway." She tried not to stutter, but

those eyes were hard to ignore, especially when they were staring you down.

"I'm Ben Porter. I believe Mr. Madison made arrangements for me to tour the property."

"Yes, I was expecting you. Please, come in." Hope stepped back and motioned him into the foyer. "I hope you will ignore the mess."

He gave a brief nod but didn't answer. With a practiced eye, he surveyed the hallway and the foyer as well as the stairway. Hope followed his gaze, waiting for a comment that never came.

"What would you like to see first?"

"How about the kitchen?"

Hope led him into the room and watched as he turned the faucet on and off and looked under the sink. He muttered under his breath but still said nothing. She spent another thirty exasperating minutes as he toured the house without saying a word to her until he asked to look around the grounds.

"Help yourself. When you're finished, I'll meet you in the drawing room."

He nodded and disappeared out the front door. With a sigh, Hope went to the kitchen and placed two mugs and a carafe of coffee on a tray along with some sugar and a creamer. Maybe this would warm up his personality, she thought. She smiled as she carried the tray to the drawing room. Before she could sit down and pour a cup of the steaming liquid, Tight Lips was back.

He took the offered seat but declined the coffee. Somehow she wasn't surprised. Any expectations she might have harbored were squashed like a June bug under a boot by his next words.

"I've been looking for the perfect house to restore for my future bride. This is it." The finality in his tone shocked her almost as much as the statement itself. He was engaged. He wanted to buy this house. One out of two wasn't bad.

As Ben walked to his car, his smile broadened. He had been praying for a wife and a home to fill a void in his life. Maybe God had just answered both prayers at once. It was everything he had dreamed about, and the house wasn't bad either. Hope Hollaway was tall, but not skinny. Her black hair had caught his attention first, but her eyes had almost left him speechless. They were as black as her hair and mirrored his every expression. A man could get lost in those eyes and never want to come back.

Ben started the engine and took one last look at the house before pulling away. The house, the woman, it was perfect. He had the house. Now all he had to do was win fair maiden. *Fair maiden? I've been watching too many medieval stories lately.* He dismissed the fanciful thoughts and focused on the job ahead.

Since Harry was the family lawyer, he took care of the sale of the house, leaving the girls to handle the contents. Hope was resigned to the notion that she would never see Ben Porter's beautiful blue eyes again. She had also grudgingly agreed that Faith was making a good decision. Faith's portion of the inheritance would be enough to cover her living expenses so she wouldn't have to work a full-time job and go to school. Charity and Bob decided since they had been dating for two years and the sale of the house was imminent, a quick wedding was in order. The sudden turn of events left Hope a little shaky since her future was still so uncertain. She started packing and praying that God would open a door for her before the sale of the house was final.

Three days later, Hope stood to stretch her aching back and survey her handiwork. Most of the closets downstairs had been cleaned out. Three large boxes had the name of each girl written in permanent ink, one had the name of a local charity, the other simply said "trash." She heard the familiar *swoosh* of mail sliding through the slot onto the floor. That was one more thing she would have to take care of very soon. She made a mental note of it, then stooped to pick up the pile of envelopes. One in particular caught her eye. Dropping the rest of the stack onto the foyer table, she ripped it open.

Hope read the letter for the third time before she actually comprehended what it said. She got the job! She felt a little thrill. It had been almost a year since she quit her job at the *Baltimore Sun* to take care of Aunt Gina. Even then, she had only written copy or done fillers. This would be her first real job as a writer—even if it was as an advice columnist.

The letter from *Agape Today* came as both a shock and a relief. Shock because they had hired her, sight unseen, and relief that she had a job, sort of. The agreement stipulated there would be a three-month trial period. Obviously, they were desperate for someone to fill the position.

Putting down the acceptance letter, Hope picked up the newspaper to start looking for a place to live in the city. She circled a few ads and checked the phone book before making a couple of calls. Within an hour, she had several appointments for viewing apartments scheduled for the next day. Hope hung up the phone with shaking hands. Everything was changing so fast, it was hard for her to keep up.

It suddenly occurred to Hope that she needed to call the magazine to confirm that she was accepting the job. The conversation was brief and to the point. She talked to Shelby Tate, the editor, and made an appointment to be at the office for orientation in two weeks.

The next two weeks flew by in preparation for the move and Charity's wedding. The couple opted for a small, but elegant service at their church and a long honeymoon in Hawaii, courtesy of Bob's parents. Still, there were a lot of details to take care of before the big day. Before Hope could turn around, it was time for her trip to D.C. She left early on a Monday morning, weaving in and out of the beltway traffic. She was relieved to find the office building where *Agape Today* had its headquarters.

It didn't take her long to find the office of the editor, Shelby Tate. Hope walked into the reception area with what felt like Mexican jumping beans in her stomach. The receptionist's smile eased her fears a little.

"I'm here to see Shelby Tate. I'm Hope Hollaway."

"Oh, yes, Ms. Hollaway. We've been expecting you."

Hope followed her directions and found the door open. She tapped lightly, waiting in the hall until the editor motioned for her to come in.

"I've got to go now. I have someone in my office."

"I'm Hope Hollaway. I believe you were expecting me." Hope held out her hand, and the other woman took it in a surprisingly strong grip.

"Yes. You have no idea how excited I am to see you. We've been scrambling to answer the letters ever since our last columnist up and married on us without a word of notice." She motioned toward the chair across from her. "As you can tell from the sign, my name is Shelby Tate."

"Ms. Tate, it's good to be here."

"Call me Shelby. We're pretty informal around here. Now

that we've got the niceties over with, let's get to work. We have a lot of ground to cover if we're going to get the column done for the next issue."

For the next several minutes, Hope's new supervisor outlined the rules, regulations, and procedures. Hope would work out of her home by mail and fax machine. Someone in the office would forward the letters to Hope, who would then choose three letters to respond to that covered the major question groups that arose. Hope would then fax or mail the letters she had chosen with her responses.

"Clear as mud?" Shelby asked with a smile. When Hope only nodded, Shelby continued. "I know it is a little confusing at first, but it's really very simple. I'm sure you'll catch on quickly."

Shelby took her down the hall to a cubicle in one corner of the office. "That will be your work space whenever you need to come in. Several of our columnists use it on occasion."

Hope looked around at the plain space, devoid of any personal articles. She was glad she would be working from home. Sitting down in the office chair, she turned to Shelby.

"Now what do I do?"

"Since we're close to a deadline, I thought it might be best if we go ahead and finish this month's column, and then you can take the letters home for next month."

"Okay. Where do we start?"

"Well, I've already picked out the letters for you to respond to, so you don't have to worry about that this time. All you have to do is answer them in 250 words or less." Shelby handed her three letters. "I'll leave you alone and let you get started. If you need any help with the computer programs, let me know."

Hope nodded, and Shelby returned to her office. Hope hadn't expected to start work so soon. It was overwhelming.

She took a deep breath and reminded herself that she could do all things through Christ. With determination, she turned to the letters at hand.

The first two were comparatively easy to answer. It took her the rest of the morning to work out rough drafts for them. The last letter jumped out at Hope, and she found herself empathizing with the writer.

Dear Miss Lonely Heart,

Is chivalry dead? Two weeks ago, I went out with a guy from work. When he took me home, he didn't even put the car in park. He was gone before I even reached the door. The next week, I went on a blind date with the friend of a friend. The guy not only didn't open the car door, but he also walked into the restaurant in front of me, letting the door slam in my face. What's a girl to do?

Damsel in Distress

Hope read the letter several times before picking up a pen and jotting down a reply.

Dear Damsel,

Chivalry is a lost art. It might not be dead, but it's about to breathe its last. Although I wouldn't go on a second date with either of those two, I wouldn't hold my breath waiting for a knight in shining armor. If you can find a guy who will at least wait until you get to the front door and won't let the door hit you in the face, then I'd say you're doing well.

Miss Lonely Heart

Hope typed up the last letter and added it to the folder. She glanced at her watch and realized that she would have to hurry if she was going to miss the rush hour traffic. When she took her replies to Shelby Tate's office, the editor had gone to a meeting. The receptionist took the file and told her that Shelby would be in touch. After catching the elevator just before the doors closed, she leaned against the wall and let out a sigh. She hadn't realized how much work giving advice could be, but was happy that she could do the job. The clicking of her heels across the tiled foyer held a ring of confidence she hadn't heard in a long time.

Ben drove by the house again and made some notes in his notebook. There were several things he needed to order so he'd be ready to work as soon as the final papers were signed. He was disappointed to notice that Hope's car wasn't in the driveway. Frowning, he made a few more notes, then headed home.

He checked the mailbox when he reached his apartment. There was the usual assortment of bills and junk mail. At the bottom of the stack was the latest issue of *Agape Today*. He unlocked the door and walked over to his desk. Dumping the mail in his in-box, he began flipping through the magazine. He stopped at the advice column. It was usually good for a laugh, but one letter and response now irked him. Women today were so unpredictable. One minute they wanted a man to treat them like a princess, and the next they acted like he'd offended them by opening the door. This writer had some nerve! It was about time they got a man's opinion on this subject, and he was just the man to do it. He pulled out his computer keyboard and typed out a quick reply.

Satisfied with his work, Ben printed the letter and addressed an envelope. He put the stamp on it with a little more pressure than necessary and walked it down to the mailbox at the corner. He closed the lid with a grim smile. Venting his aggravation left him feeling calm and relaxed. He whistled a tune as he walked back to his apartment.

Chapter 3

Hope looked at the nearly empty room and pushed back the tears that threatened to spill over. Charity had already moved all the furniture she wanted to the apartment she and Bob were renting. The wedding was in three days. Irritable and overly emotional ever since the funeral, Hope found herself snapping at Faith and Charity for the smallest reasons. She had to get a grip. The moving van would be here for her things tomorrow. She had found a cozy apartment in a quiet neighborhood. The rent was affordable and the upkeep was significantly less than the house, but she was going to miss the creaking stairs and high ceilings. Logically, she knew that they needed to sell the house, but hearts rarely listen to logic. The sound of the doorbell jerked her out of her reverie. She opened the door with a sense of *déjà vu* as a pair of deep blue eyes stared back.

"Ms. Hollaway, I wanted to take some measurements, if it is agreeable with you."

Hope opened the door wider and motioned for him to come inside, then closed the door behind him. He looked around at the empty rooms and frowned.

"Something wrong, Mr. Porter?"

"It doesn't seem right for a house like this to be so. . . empty."

Hope was surprised to hear such depth of feeling beneath the no-nonsense attitude. "I was just thinking the same thing. Would you care for some coffee to warm you up?" For an instant, she saw his guard come down and his face relax.

"That would be nice. Thank you." He motioned toward the stairs. "Is it all right if I go upstairs?"

"It's fine." She shrugged and gave a weak smile. "My sisters are gone right now, and almost everything is packed up anyway."

He nodded and disappeared around the corner of the landing. She stood there staring for several minutes at the spot where she last saw him. Giving herself a mental shake, she turned resolutely and marched to the kitchen. She was grateful that making coffee gave her something to do.

She prepared the tray before she realized that there was no couch to sit on in the drawing room or really in any room in the house. Every spare space was filled with boxes or suitcases. Each sister had chosen a room and gathered the furniture and knickknacks that she would be taking with her. The dining room was filled with items to be sold or stored. Most of the things were just too big for an apartment, like the extended dining table and buffet, which included twelve chairs and a china cabinet. Every single chair held a box. She walked through the room, running her hand along the worn surface of the table.

"It's a beautiful set."

Hope jumped at the sound of his voice.

"I'm sorry. I didn't mean to startle you."

"I guess I wasn't paying attention." Hope walked back toward the kitchen entrance and motioned for him to follow.

"We'll have to have coffee in the kitchen. I don't think there's a free seat in the house."

"I know what you mean." He smiled for the first time, and Hope felt like the breath had been sucked out of her chest. She had thought his eyes were beautiful before, but add the megawatt smile, and they lit up like stars. "My place looks pretty much the same."

"Coffee?" She had meant to sound bright, but all that came out was a croak. She cleared her throat, feeling the heat rise in her cheeks.

"Sounds like you might be catching a cold."

The note of concern in his voice melted her knees. She pulled out a chair from the nook and sat down. He followed suit, taking the chair directly across from her. His closeness sent her pulse speeding. It was disconcerting to realize that she had no real control over her reaction. It had been a long time since she had even thought about a relationship. Relationship? What was she thinking? The man was engaged.

While Hope filled their mugs, she tried to regain control of her wayward thoughts and focus on how to carry on a conversation without sounding like an idiot. She was relieved when he took the lead.

"If I may ask, what are you going to do with the dining room set?" He carefully measured two spoons of sugar into his coffee and stirred.

She was again struck by his meticulous and polite nature. She stifled a giggle as she pictured him in a butler's uniform with a starched shirt, then reddened as she realized he had asked a question.

"I'm sorry. What did you say?"

"I asked what you were going to do with the dining room

set, but it's really no business of mine." He dismissed the question with a wave of his hand.

"Oh, that's okay. It's a really good question because, to be honest, I don't have a clue what to do with it."

His head jerked up in surprise. "You mean you're not taking it with you?"

"Charity and I don't have room in our apartments, and Faith will be living with two other girls in California. Even if she had room, it is too far to move such big pieces." Hope shrugged and then dipped two spoons of sugar into her cup and stirred. The spoon made a clinking noise, bringing a frown to his face. She put down the spoon, and his face relaxed.

"Ms. Hollaway, I have a proposal for you."

"Call me Hope."

"Hope?" He smiled. "That's a beautiful name."

"Thank you." She began sipping her coffee to hide her embarrassment.

"Well, Hope, I was wondering if I could buy the set from you. Then you wouldn't have to move it anywhere."

"That would be wonderful. The set really goes with the house. . . . However, I will have to check with my sisters before I can make a deal."

"That's fine. I totally understand."

"I'll ask them as soon as they get home."

They drank their coffee in silence. He downed the rest of his in an uncharacteristic gulp and stood up.

"I should probably be going now."

"Okay. I'll walk you out."

He followed her to the front door, but turned back before leaving. "Is it all right if I call tonight about the furniture?"

"Sure. They should be home in time for dinner. Why don't

you call after seven?"

"Seven. I'll talk to you then." He gave a curt nod, then trotted down the stairs. Hope watched until he got into a worn pickup truck and pulled away. After closing the door, she leaned back against it and sighed. How could she be so stupid as to fall for a guy who was already taken?

Ben smiled as he walked into his apartment. He surveyed the rented furniture, glad that it would soon be gone. A few more weeks, and he would be living in the house of his dreams. Things were moving along just as he had planned. The topper had been being able to buy the dining room set. It belonged in that house. He could just see the dinner parties they would have. There was never just him in his dreams. There was always a wife, although her face was often blurry. Somehow her features had become more distinct with each passing day. Dark hair and dark eyes complemented a pale complexion and a dazzling smile. Yes, things were all going according to plan.

Hope heard the mail drop onto the floor in the hall. She picked it up with a sigh, remembering that she still had to have her mail forwarded. Flipping through the stack, she pulled out a thick envelope from the publisher. She scanned the magazine with a smile before taking the rest of the mail to the kitchen table. Putting off the inevitable, she sorted the mail into stacks. Then, she picked up the large envelope and opened it. She poured a pile of letters onto the table. With an opener in hand, she began emptying the envelopes, sorting the notes into categories as she went.

After thirty minutes, Hope stood and stretched before pouring another cup of coffee. Sitting back down, she opened the next letter, almost dropping it into the scalding liquid when she read the contents.

Dear Miss Lonely Heart,

I take offense to your stand on chivalry. If chivalry is dying, then feminism threw the final blow. Just last week, I held the door open for a young lady who informed me that she was more than capable of opening a door for herself. How can a guy be a gentleman when women don't know how to act like ladies?

A Wounded Knight

Hope read the letter in shock. How dare he criticize her? He obviously didn't know what he was talking about. In a fit of pique, Hope scrawled out a quick reply.

Dear Knight,

The test of a true gentleman is the way he behaves in even difficult situations. Anyone can behave nicely when trying to impress a girl, but a real gentleman treats everyone the same, no matter how she or he behaves.

Miss Lonely Heart

She signed the letter with a flourish, then put her reply with the letter. It would never be published, but it made her feel better. She finished the last of the letters just as Charity and Faith came through the door. Looking at the clock in dismay, she realized it was after six and she hadn't even started dinner. With a groan, she stacked the letters and carried them upstairs to her room.

Back downstairs, the memory of the stinging reply was

soon forgotten as the girls worked together to prepare the meal. To Hope, it was like old times. She tried to capture every moment in her mind because this would be their last real meal as a family in this house. Soon they would all go their separate ways. Hope pushed back tears for the second time that day.

"Girls, I just want to apologize for the way I've been acting lately. I didn't mean to be so snappy."

"It's okay, Hope. We're all a little stressed about moving out, but it will be all right," Charity said.

"Yeah, Hope. I haven't exactly been perfect myself." Faith popped Hope with the end of the dish towel.

"You better watch out, little sister. You're not too big for me to handle," Hope warned, grabbing another towel.

"Hey! You're supposed to be the grown-up here," Faith said with a grin.

"Well, I'm tired of being the grown-up," Hope said as she twisted the towel.

Some good-natured squeals erupted as Hope chased Faith around the kitchen. After a few minutes, Charity yelled above the noise, "Time out. Dinner's ready."

With teamwork, dinner was on the table in a matter of minutes. Charity prayed a lovely blessing over the food and that the new owners would be as happy here as she and her sisters had been while growing up.

The prayer reminded Hope of Mr. Porter's request. As they ate, Hope filled them in on the new owner's visit and his request. The girls quickly agreed that the proposal solved the problem.

They had just finished clearing the table when the phone rang. Hope was surprised that even the sound of his voice could have such an effect on her.

"Ms. Hollaway? I mean, Hope?"

"Yes?"

"Did you discuss my proposal with your sisters?"

"I did, Mr. Porter. They think it's a perfect solution."

"Great." He named a more than generous price, and Hope quickly accepted. "Hope?"

"Yes?"

"Please call me Ben."

"Okay, Ben. It'll be all yours as soon as the wedding is over."

"Wedding?"

"Yes, the wedding is next weekend. Then we'll be out of your hair."

"Oh." It sounded like he choked on the word.

"Are you all right?"

"I'm fine," he assured her.

"Well, then I hope you enjoy the furniture and the house as much as we have. Have a nice night."

"You too." It sounded like he wanted to say something else, but instead he gave a clipped good-bye and hung up. Disappointed, Hope returned the phone to its cradle and helped the girls finish the dishes.

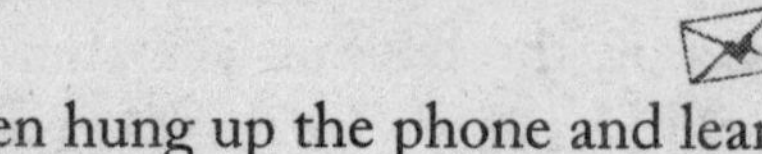

Ben hung up the phone and leaned against the wall. All of his plans were in ruins. Why hadn't Harry said something about a wedding? Everything was ruined. He slumped into the nearest chair and propped his chin in his hands, resting his elbows on his knees. What was he supposed to do now? He looked around the room as if the answer were in front of him. His glance fell on his Bible. Maybe it was in front of him. He picked up the well-worn book and flipped through its pages. It fell open to Proverbs chapter nineteen. The twenty-first verse caught his attention. "Many are the plans in a man's heart, but it is the LORD's purpose that prevails."

Ben bowed his head and asked for the Lord's forgiveness. He had been making his own plans instead of letting God be in control. Hope was a beautiful woman, but she obviously wasn't the right one for him. God would send him a wife when He was ready. In the meantime, he had a house to renovate.

As he sat with the Bible in his hands, it occurred to him how long it had been since he had attended worship service at church, let alone Sunday school. He had put off looking for a church when he had moved into the area because the transition had kept him busy. Now, he had no excuse. There was no time like the present, but which church should he visit first? A sudden inspiration struck him. He picked up the phone and called Harry Madison.

"Harry, I was just wondering if you could suggest a good church in the area."

They talked for several minutes about the details, then Ben hung up the phone. With that taken care of, he busied himself with packing. At the very least, it would give him something to do with his hands and maybe he could forget about a certain dark-haired beauty.

Chapter 4

Hope wiped away a tear as Charity walked up the aisle on Bob's arm. Her little sister was a married woman. Hope shook her head and took the arm of one of the ushers, following Charity out the double doors of the church. The rest of the evening was a blur of pictures and greeting guests. Before she had time to enjoy any of the festivities, it was time for Charity to throw the bouquet. Hope tried to hide behind a flower arrangement as all of Charity's unmarried friends gathered at the foot of the stairs leading to the balcony.

"Where's Hope?" Charity asked.

"Behind the flowers," Faith said.

Hope made a mental note to pay Faith back later. She gritted her teeth into a semblance of a smile and moved to the edge of the crowd, pulling Faith in front of her. Charity grinned, then turned her back to the group. She tossed the flowers over her shoulder. In what seemed like slow motion, Hope saw the bouquet soar over the crowd, straight toward her. The last thing she wanted was to catch it, but some inner reflex sent her arm shooting out to grab the prize anyway. The guests applauded while her sisters looked like two cats that had just eaten a bowl of cream. Luckily for Hope, the attention was soon focused on the happy couple as they prepared to leave. Hope made her way through the throng to Charity's side.

"I'm happy for you, Sis."

"Thank you, Hope." Charity motioned around the church. "I don't just mean for the wedding. You've always been there for me and Faith."

"You're my sisters. I'll always be here for you."

Faith joined the other two in a group hug. Tears flowed down their cheeks. Hope held them both close for a moment, then released them.

"Come on, girls," Harry called. "This is supposed to be a happy occasion."

"It is, Harry," Hope replied, wiping the tears from her face. "Get out of here, you lovebirds." Hope shooed them toward the door. "Everyone's waiting on you."

After another quick hug, Charity grabbed Bob's hand and they made a mad dash for the car. Hope remained in the church and was struck by the sudden stillness. She was reminded of all those years of laughter, teasing, and yelling. She was going to miss it all. A little piece of her was jealous of Charity, riding off into the night with her prince. They were so young. Suddenly, she felt old and forgotten. Where was her Prince Charming? Shaking off the melancholy, Hope went down to the fellowship hall and started cleaning.

At midnight, Hope unlocked the door to her new apartment. Flipping on the light switch, she tried not to notice the silence. She looked around the room and sighed. Everything was as the movers had left it two days ago. Boxes were stacked in every corner. She hadn't even had time to make her bed. The apartment was warm and stuffy, so she adjusted the thermostat. The hum of the heat pump was comforting after the pressing silence of just a moment before.

Hope looked around at the mess, unsure of what to do next. Faith was staying at a girlfriend's house tonight, so she was on her own. For the first time in ten years, there was nothing that had to be done, no one to cook for, and no problems to solve except her own. A sudden urge to cry almost overwhelmed her. Shaking it off, she moved toward the nearest box. The ringing of the phone startled her, but it took three rings for her to find the phone. Finally, she grabbed the receiver and said, "Hello?"

"Hope?"

"Charity? What are you doing calling me while on your honeymoon?"

"I just wanted to call and let you know that we arrived at the hotel okay."

"Liar," Hope said softly. "You called to check up on me, didn't you?"

"Well," Charity hesitated. "I wanted to make sure that everything was okay in your new place. That's all."

"It's sweet of you to worry, but I'm the big sister. I can take care of myself." Hope put assurance in her voice that she didn't feel. "It's great having the bathroom all to myself, and I can watch anything on television that I want to. I'm footloose and fancy free."

"I'm so glad," Charity said with obvious relief.

"So, quit fretting. I'll be fine." Hope twisted the cord between her fingers. "You just go enjoy your honeymoon."

"All right, I will," Charity said. "I'll call you when we get back. Love you."

"Love you."

The click at the other end of the line almost sent her into

tears again. She went into the bedroom and opened her overnight bag. In minutes, she had unpacked her toiletries and changed clothes. After several minutes of digging, she finally found the box with her linens. By one o'clock, she had the bedroom in decent shape with the bed made and a path cleared to the bathroom door. She turned on the nightlight before turning out the lamp and crawled under the covers. Despite her fears of living alone, Hope slipped quickly into a deep sleep.

The next few days were filled with unpacking her apartment and arranging for Faith's things to be sent to California. Right in the middle of unpacking, Hope received a phone call from *Agape Today*.

"Hope? This is Shelby Tate. How's the move going?"

"As well as can be expected. I'm surrounded by what seems like a thousand boxes, and every time I unpack one, two more appear."

"I know the feeling," Shelby said with a chuckle.

"What can I do for you, Shelby?"

"Well, I hate to push you when you are in the middle of moving, but I would really appreciate if you could get your letters in a week earlier this month. Some of the staff will be going out of town to a publishing conference, so we need the magazine to be ready ahead of schedule."

"Actually, I'm just about finished."

"Great! That will make my life so much easier."

"I'll get them in the mail to you tomorrow, if that's okay."

"That would be great. You're a trooper, Hope. Got to go."

Hope said good-bye and hung up the phone. The only problem now was finding the box that had her office items. It took all afternoon to find them. To save time later on, she moved all the boxes to the spare bedroom where she was going to set up her own home office. She found the packet of letters in the last box.

"Typical," she muttered to herself.

"Talking to yourself?" Faith asked from the doorway. Hope jumped and then put her hand to her heart.

"What do you mean, sneaking up on me like that? Haven't you heard of knocking?"

"Why knock when I have a key?" she asked, dangling the offending key in Hope's face.

"I gave you that for emergencies or in case I'm not at home—not so that you could give me a heart attack."

Faith simply grinned and sat down on the one chair in the room. "What's going on in here?"

"I'm looking for the letters to send to the magazine. They moved up the deadline."

"Wasn't that nice of them?" Faith asked. "Didn't they know you were moving this week?"

"Yes, but that's neither here nor there. I've already finished the letters. I just need to find the replies so I can mail them." With a grin of victory, Hope pulled out the missing letters and waved them over her head. "Here they are."

"Great! So, now you can help me with my stuff."

"What stuff? You're not leaving until next Saturday."

"I know, but if I can get everything packed up tonight, Jake said he would take it with Sheena's stuff, and I won't have to pay for shipping."

"Sheena's brother is driving to California?"

"Yeah. Jake said he's always wanted to take a road trip across the country, so he's leaving in the morning. He should get there before I do."

"Well, hurray for Jake." Hope grabbed the packet and an

envelope, quickly stuffed the papers inside, and stuck a preprinted label on the outside. "Let's get going."

Later that evening, Hope and Faith staggered into the living room of her apartment and collapsed onto the couch. They had dropped the package in the mail and packed the rest of Faith's belongings, except some of her clothes and toiletries, into boxes. Jake had come by at seven o'clock with the moving truck. It took the three of them close to an hour to finish loading the truck. Hope was beyond exhaustion.

"I'm starved," Faith complained.

"Me too." Hope looked at the half-unpacked kitchen and groaned. "There is no way I'm going to cook tonight."

"No need." Faith stretched for the telephone without getting up and dialed a number. "I'd like a large pizza with everything on it and a two-liter bottle of Dr. Pepper."

Relieved, Hope relaxed onto the couch. She straightened up. "I don't have any cash. Maybe I can hurry to the ATM before the pizza gets here."

"Relax, big sister. I've got it under control." Faith pulled a couple of twenties from her wallet and waved them at Hope. "I'm buying tonight."

"Well, that's a switch." Hope sank back into the couch. "There are some perks to you girls growing up, after all."

Faith grinned. "I told you so."

"If I weren't so tired, I'd wipe that silly smile off your face."

"Oh, yeah?" Faith teased.

"Yeah."

Hope pulled a pillow from the couch and a pillow fight ensued. The doorbell interrupted their tussle. Faith grabbed her wallet and bounded to the door. She paid the deliveryman while Hope got the glasses ready.

They ate picnic-style on the floor since Hope hadn't unpacked the dining room yet and the table was covered with boxes. They reminisced about old times while they ate, then talked about Faith's plans for the fall. Afterwards, Hope put the remains of the pizza into the refrigerator, box and all.

"Aren't you going to take the leftovers out of the box and put them in a storage container?" Faith asked, feigning shock.

"First of all, I don't know where any of my containers are at the moment. Second, I really don't care."

"Well, all right, Sis. You've finally learned how the rest of us live."

Hope shook her head and walked back into the living room. She hated to see Faith go. They were having such a fun time remembering the good old days, and there wouldn't be too many more of these times together.

"Hey, why don't you stay here tonight, and I'll beat you at Monopoly."

"You're on, but I'm the one who is going to win."

Hope smiled as Faith searched for the board game in a stack of boxes. One thing was for sure. Faith would never change, and that was just fine with Hope.

Ben sorted eagerly through his mail, hoping to find a response from the writer at *Agape Today*, but he only found the newest edition of the magazine. He flipped it open to the advice column to see what she had to say today. As he scanned the letters, he was shocked to see his included. Her reply was just as curt as his had been and cut him to the quick. What she said about being a gentleman all the time struck a note in his spirit. The Bible said it wasn't what people did to you that mattered, but how you treated others.

There was more to this columnist than he had anticipated. Something about her witty reply made him want to know her better. He turned on his computer and typed up a quick response. When he mailed the letter this time, he sent it out with a prayer that she would answer. With a smile, he strolled back to his apartment. *You never know what a day will bring*, he thought as he closed the door. *You never know.*

Chapter 5

With Faith's help, Hope managed to finish unpacking by the weekend. She tried to make every moment count since Faith would be leaving soon. She dreaded the thought of being alone again but kept it to herself. There was no need to make Faith feel any guiltier than she already did about leaving. No matter how much Hope hated to admit the truth, it was time for Faith to try her wings.

"Hey, why the long face?" Faith asked as she folded a pair of shorts.

"Nothing. I guess I was just concentrating too hard. Which picture do you think will look better over the couch? This one?" Hope held up a large painting of a lighthouse with a stormy sea in the background. "Or these two?" She held up two smaller prints with the same ocean theme.

"I like the big one. Then, you can put the two smaller ones on the short wall near the door," Faith replied.

"Good idea. What would I do without you?" Hope joked.

"You'll be just fine."

Hope turned and looked at Faith. Her tone belied the cheerful expression. She should have known it was impossible to hide her feelings from her sister. Faith had always had a way of seeing past her mask of self-sufficiency. Maybe that was why it was so much harder to let her go than it had Charity. Besides, Charity would be living across town. Faith was moving to the other side of the country.

"Don't worry about me."

"I can't help it. I feel like I'm leaving you all alone." Faith frowned as she stacked the folded shorts into an open suitcase.

"I won't be alone. Charity will be just a few miles away." Hope put her hands on her hips. "What happened to all that noise about needing to be out on your own, about me needing to get a life of my own?"

"I don't know. It just doesn't feel right somehow."

Hope crossed the space between them and put her hands on Faith's shoulders. "Listen, little sister. I'm quite capable of taking care of myself. I've been doing it for a long time." Hope raised her hand before Faith could argue. "I know it will be hard at first—change always is—but you were right when you said we needed to move on."

"I guess so." Faith's head drooped forward and she kicked at the carpet with the toe of her shoe. Hope lifted her chin with one finger.

"You're having a case of cold feet, just like Charity did the day before the wedding."

"Charity was nervous?" Faith's eyes popped open. "She seemed so steady and sure of herself."

"You didn't see her the night before the wedding. She came into my room in a panic, afraid she was doing the wrong thing. We all have moments like that. The key is to just keep going and not let fear run our lives."

"Are you afraid, Hope?"

"Yes, but I'm excited too." Hope turned to the stack of

laundry still to be packed. "Now, let's get packing."

The next few days passed rather quickly. By Saturday, Faith had regained her sense of adventure and was itching to get moving. Hope took her sister to the airport, still wishing Faith would change her mind—but she didn't. Once Faith left, Hope headed for the parking deck. It was time to start her new life, whatever it may be.

As soon as she walked into her apartment, she sifted through the mail. She had been waiting for the latest issue of *Agape Today*, which should have arrived in the morning mail. It was buried in a pile of sales papers. Flipping open to her column, she quickly scanned the page. Her mouth dropped open when she read the final letter. It was from the Knight along with her scathing reply. How did that get in there? Grabbing the phone, Hope dialed Shelby Tate's number with shaking fingers.

"Shelby Tate."

"Shelby, this is Hope Hollaway."

"Hi, Hope. Great work."

"Thank you, but I'm afraid there was a mistake."

"A mistake?" Shelby's voice lost its cheerful lilt at the mention of the word. "What mistake?"

"The letter from the Knight. It wasn't supposed to be published."

"But you included a reply with it. A very good one, I might add," Shelby said, chuckling.

"I only wrote the reply because I was a little miffed at getting such a negative response. I didn't mean for it to be printed. I have no idea how it got into the envelope."

"Don't worry. It'll be great. The readers will love it."

"Are you sure?" Hope asked.

"Positive. Otherwise, I wouldn't have printed it."

"Well, if you think it's all right. . ."

"I do. Now, I've got to go. Don't worry about a thing. Bye."

Hope replaced the receiver in its cradle after Shelby hung up. Shaking her head to clear the cobwebs, she looked at the phone for several minutes and sat down on the couch. She read the article over again. With a sigh, she closed the magazine. Seeing the letter reminded her of the day she had gotten it. Ben Porter had come by, and it was the last time she had seen or spoken to him. He had sent a check in the mail to cover the cost of the dining room set. Since all the papers had already been signed regarding the sale of the house, there had been no reason to call him.

Hope tried to erase all thoughts of Ben Porter out of her head. There was no sense in thinking about a man she would most likely never see again and who obviously had a girlfriend. Pushing both Ben Porter and the Knight from her mind, she concentrated on paying her bills and balancing her checkbook.

Neither man crossed her mind over the next few days as she set up her new office space. Once Faith was off on her own, Hope went on a shopping spree, buying a new desk and other office supplies. Busy assembling and organizing her desk, she didn't have time to think about either of them until the next stack of letters arrived from the magazine.

Normally, the letters were just stuffed into a large envelope in random order. This time, one of the letters was marked with a sticky note from Shelby.

Hope,

Thought you might want to read this first. Your answer will make a great addition to the normal three letters.

Happy Writing!
Shelby

After opening the letter, Hope glanced at the signature line and felt her heart start jumping when she recognized the name, the Knight. She took a deep breath before reading.

Dear Miss Lonely Heart,

You do have a point about being a gentleman at all times; however, do you have any suggestions on how to deal with such situations? I'm interested to know your opinion.

A Penitent Knight

Hope reread the note several times, trying to think of a reply. There was something familiar about the Knight's turn of phrase, but she couldn't place where she had heard it before. Despite herself, she smiled because he had written back. It was silly to feel a little thrill at seeing his handwriting again, but she felt it nonetheless. She thought about it for several days before she replied.

Dear Knight,

I think that you should just be a gentleman in all situations. If a woman doesn't appreciate your efforts, then move on. Jesus Himself said to "turn the other cheek."

Miss Lonely Heart

Hope printed her reply with a smile. As she added it to the other responses, she wondered if he would write again. No matter. It was fun while it lasted. With a sigh, she turned back to sorting the letters into groups and filing them away. Just as she was about to sink into a funk about her lack of social life, the phone rang.

"Hope?"

"Charity? When did you guys get back?"

"Well, we actually got back a few days ago, but we've been running ever since. Between unpacking, doing laundry, and going grocery shopping, I've barely had time to breathe."

"Now you know how I've felt all these years."

"I don't know how you did it all."

"You'll catch on soon enough." Hope could hear Bob whispering something in the background and Charity hushing him. "What's up? Are you two already fighting?"

"Not really. Bob just wanted me to ask you something."

"What?" Hope prodded.

"Well, you see, he has this friend. . ."

"Not a blind date?" Hope squealed.

"It won't really be a date. It'll just be dinner at our new apartment. You're my sister and he's Bob's best friend. It's not like you two will be alone or anything," Charity pleaded. "You don't have to stay late if you don't want to. Just come for dinner."

"Charity. . ."

"Please. I'll make your favorite meal."

Hope twisted the phone around her finger. She had been praying in her quiet time every day that God would open up doors for a new relationship. Maybe this was an answer.

"All right."

"Great!" Charity exclaimed. "You won't regret it."

"I'd better not," Hope warned.

"How about tomorrow night at six-thirty?"

"You work fast, don't you?" Hope asked, smiling in spite of herself.

"No time like the present. Besides, I don't want to give you time to back out." Hope could hear Bob laughing in the background.

"Okay, six-thirty is fine."

They chatted for a few more minutes before hanging up. Hope prayed she wasn't making a mistake. Blind dates had always turned out badly in the past. She hoped that tomorrow night would be an exception. *Who knows? This might be the man of my dreams.*

Chapter 6

Hope dabbed a drop of perfume on one of her wrists, then rubbed it against the other. She hardly ever wore perfume, but she made an exception tonight. The scent was a Christmas gift from Faith that had never been opened. She hoped it lived up to its advertising tonight. Grinning at herself in the mirror, she made a final inspection. The burgundy pantsuit accentuated her dark hair and eyes as well as flattering her figure. For the first time in ages, she felt attractive. She hummed a tune as she walked through the apartment, turning off lights and securing windows. Tonight was going to be special. She could feel it in the air.

An hour later, seated across from Bob's best friend, Chuck, Hope was beginning to have second thoughts. Over dinner, the two men had talked nonstop about baseball, a sport she loathed with a passion. On top of that, his voice reminded her of a guy in high school who teased her mercilessly. Every time he opened his mouth, she cringed and had to suppress a shiver of disgust. When dinner was over, Hope was anxious to help Charity in the kitchen if only to get away from that voice.

"So. . .what do you think?" Charity asked, her face beaming. "Isn't he cute?"

"He's all right, I guess." Hope looked into the living room. From a distance he was nice looking, but that voice drove her insane.

"What's wrong with this one?" Charity asked, folding her arms over her chest and slouching in defeat.

"What do you mean *this* one?"

Charity tugged her farther into the kitchen and pulled the kitchen door closed. "Keep your voice down."

"All right." Hope carried the stack of plates she was holding to the sink.

"What's wrong with Chuck? He's nice looking, has a good job, and goes to church. What more do you want?" Charity asked, counting off his good qualities on one hand.

"Well, for one, he sounds just like Andy Martin."

"Andy Martin?" Charity gaped. "That kid from high school? What's he got to do with this?"

"Every time Chuck opens his mouth, all I can think of is Andy Martin."

"That's the worst excuse you've ever come up with."

"Excuse? Excuse for what?"

"For not dating a guy."

"What are you talking about?" Hope rinsed the plates and dropped them into the dishwasher with a bang.

"You know what I'm talking about. You do this every time."

"Do what?" Hope asked as she dumped handfuls of silverware into the rinse water.

"Find reasons not to like a guy. You never even give them a chance, just like Kevin."

"Not this again." Hope took a deep breath, pushing down the bitterness that threatened to erupt.

"You didn't give him a chance, either."

Hope continued to load the dishwasher in silence. She could feel Charity's eyes boring into her back.

"Stop it."

"What?" Hope asked, whirling around in frustration.

"Stop doing my dishes. This is my house and my dinner party," Charity said, her lips a thin line. It was the same look she got whenever Hope tried to help her with her school projects. "I can take care of myself and my house."

"So can I," Hope said between clenched teeth.

"Then why did you run Kevin off?"

"Why do you keep bringing him up?" Hope asked, frustration rising to the boiling point. "Why do you and Faith insist on dragging up ancient history?"

"Because we love you and we worry about you." Charity crossed the room and encircled Hope in her arms. "We want you to be happy."

Though tempted to be angry, Hope knew they only wanted the best for her. They had no idea what it was like to be alone. Maybe she should just tell the truth now and get it over with. Sighing, she shrugged free of Charity's embrace and wrapped her arms across her chest.

"I didn't want to tell you girls this, but I guess it's time I gave you the facts."

"What are you talking about?"

"It's about what happened with Kevin." Hope walked around the kitchen to give herself time to think through what she was about to say. "Kevin was a nice guy, and I liked him, but I dumped him for a good reason." Hope paused.

"Which was. . . ," Charity prompted.

"He told me that he wanted to keep dating me, but he wasn't going to be tied down by two teenagers and an invalid.

He suggested I send you girls to foster homes or distant relatives so that I could have a life of my own."

Charity was silent for several minutes. "Why didn't you say anything before?"

"I didn't want you to think that you were a burden."

Charity crossed the room and finished loading the dishwasher in silence. When she turned around, Hope could see a hint of tears in her eyes. In a few steps, she crossed the room and wrapped her sister in a big hug.

"I'm sorry, Hope. I didn't realize how much you had to give up to keep us together."

"It was worth it," Hope said firmly. "I guess we'd better get back in there."

"Yeah, but you don't have to stay long if you don't want to. I think Chuck and Bob are going to watch a baseball game tonight."

"I think I feel a headache coming on," Hope said, putting a hand to her temple.

"Me too," Charity said. They both laughed at the same time. "Come on, I'll see you to the door."

Hope grabbed her purse from the bedroom and walked to the front door. The two men were immersed in a game on the television. She waved good-bye to Bob.

"Leaving already?" he asked.

"Yeah. I have a headache, and I have a lot to do tomorrow."

"Oh. Well, feel better soon," Bob mumbled, turning back to the television. Chuck didn't even bother to look up, for which Hope was grateful.

"Good luck," Hope whispered to Charity on her way out the door.

"Thanks," Charity said.

Hope waved good-bye before turning down the hallway. The evening had started out so well. She had such high expectations, only to be let down again. This was exactly the reason Hope gave up on dating. That and the fact that other than Kevin, no one asked her out in the last five years. With a sigh, she got into her car and drove home. By the time she got there, she really did have a headache.

"Guess that's what I get for lying," she mumbled aloud.

Overwhelmed by a wave of fatigue, Hope got ready for bed even though it was only eight-thirty. After finishing her nightly routine, she sat down on the bed and leaned her head against the wall. She couldn't stand another roller coaster like tonight. Her heart just couldn't take any more letdowns. How many times had she met a guy, only to have him want to be just friends or run away when he found out she had guardianship of two sisters? It just wasn't fair. Just as her pity party was getting under way, her Bible on the nightstand caught her eye. Picking it up, she opened it at random to Proverbs.

She read several lines before Proverbs 13:12 popped out at her, so she read it again. "Hope deferred makes the heart sick, but a longing fulfilled is a tree of life." It was like it was written just for her. She was heartsick, yet the second part of the verse gave her hope for the future.

"God, I know I haven't been all that I should be," she prayed aloud, "but I need Your strength right now. It's hard for me to believe that You have someone out there for me. I need a word from You."

Tears were streaming down her face as she uttered the last words. Too much had happened in her life lately. She couldn't handle it all. When she had the girls to take care of, she at least had a purpose. Now that they were on their own and there was no giant house taking up all of her energy, she didn't know what to do.

"Lord, help me. I don't know what You want me to do. I'm thankful for my job and for enough money to live on for now, but I need a purpose. Show me Your will."

Hope allowed the tears to fall for a few more minutes before wiping her eyes on a tissue and blowing her nose. She'd needed a good cry. Exhausted, she turned out the light and snuggled beneath the covers. Tomorrow was a new day, and it would be soon enough to think about her future. Closing her eyes, she dreamed of a green tree with long limbs full of luscious fruit. Just as she reached out to grab a piece, she woke with a start.

A look at the clock revealed that she had only slept for an hour, but it seemed like forever. Something about that tree struck a note in her unconscious. Maybe she was reaching for the wrong thing. Why couldn't she try freelance writing? She had plenty of time and opportunity as well as a few contacts from the paper. It had been something she had wanted to do for years but had never had time to pursue it. Well, now she had nothing but time on her hands. With a purpose in mind, Hope rolled over, but sleep was a long time in coming.

Chapter 7

Hope awoke with a sense of purpose, but when she sat down at her desk, she was at a total loss as to how to start. After several minutes of staring at a blank computer screen, she stopped and looked around the room as if there were an answer floating in the air. The only thing she saw were two packed boxes. With a sigh, she pulled them toward her and began to sort through the contents. It wasn't writing, but it was better than sitting there like an idiot.

The first box contained an assortment of office supplies and a few pictures, which she quickly took care of, but the second box held old writing textbooks and college papers she had written. At the bottom was a portfolio from her journalism class. She pulled it out and dusted it off. It had been years since she had looked at any of this. Flipping through the pages, she smiled at the memories they evoked. The last entry caught her eye, so she stopped to read the entire piece.

It was a personal profile that she had written about a local professor. Hope pulled the pages from the notebook and carried them to her desk. She had recently read that the same professor had a book being published. If she did a little research and updated the piece, it might sell as a companion piece to go with a book review. Since she didn't have anything else to do, she began typing the information into the computer. She spent the rest of the afternoon looking for more current leads and information on the Internet.

The ringing of the phone startled her. She looked up and realized she had been writing for two hours. She hit the save button as she grabbed the phone.

"How's my favorite girl?" a deep voice asked.

"Harry?"

"Well, who did you think it was? Don't tell me you've gone and snared a man already?" he teased.

"No, I just wasn't expecting a phone call. What can I do for you, Harry?"

"You can have lunch with me and Paula. We haven't seen you in what seems like forever." Hope could hear the sadness in his voice. "We miss you girls."

"We miss you too, Harry."

"Well, how about lunch in Little Italy on me?"

"Done. Our usual spot?" Hope asked.

"You got it, Kiddo. See you in twenty minutes."

"I'll be there."

Hope arrived twenty minutes later on the dot. Even though she had been on a roll with the piece she was writing, it was nice to get out of the apartment and talk to people. The apartment was too quiet without Faith around, and since she worked at home now, there was no place in particular to go.

She saw Harry and Paula in their usual booth in the corner. The owner, Mr. Martinelli, and Harry were old friends, so they never had to worry about making reservations. Weaving her way between the tables, she quickly joined them. She slid into the booth across from the older couple and smiled.

"It is so good to see you guys," Hope said.

"You too, Sweetheart." Paula reached over and squeezed Hope's hand. "It's been too quiet without all of you girls."

"Well, I wouldn't say quiet," Harry said with a frown. "Ben's been hammering, sawing, and drilling constantly since he moved in."

"That's true," Paula said.

She patted Harry's hand and smiled up at him. His expression softened, and Hope felt another moment of envy. Would she ever have what they had? Paula turned back to Hope.

"Ben's really fixing up the house. It's going to look just like it did in the old days. I'm glad you sold it to him."

"I'm glad too." Hope tried to smile, but her heart wasn't in it. It had been a lifelong dream to fix up the old house, but there was never enough time or money. Now, someone else was living her dream. Her cheeks warmed when she realized Harry had asked her a question. "I'm sorry. What did you say?"

"I asked how you were keeping yourself busy these days."

"Well, unpacking and getting Faith off took up most of the first couple of weeks. Today, though, I pulled out some of my old journalism notes from college." The waiter came to their table, giving her the perfect opportunity to change the subject.

"So, what's good today?" Hope asked, smiling at the waiter.

"Everything, of course," he replied, returning her smile. He held the look a little too long, causing blood to warm her cheeks. She looked at Paula.

"What are you having?" She meant to sound calm, but her voice came out as a squeak.

"I'll have the fettuccini Alfredo."

"Make that two," Harry added.

"Sounds good to me too."

"That's three fettuccini Alfredos. I'll be back shortly with your breadsticks and sauce." The waiter gave a little bow and beamed at Hope before turning on his heel.

"It looks like you've got an admirer," Harry said, grinning broadly.

"Never mind," Hope mumbled, becoming suddenly engrossed in the dessert card.

The lunch would have been perfect, if not for the unwanted attentions of the waiter. He took every opportunity to stop at their table and stare at Hope. It was beginning to unnerve her. Paula and Harry caught her up on all the news from the neighborhood and their family, which kept her from thinking about a certain dark-haired carpenter living in her house. She shook her head as the thought went through her mind. It wasn't her house anymore.

"Something wrong?" Paula asked.

"No, just trying to clear my mind."

"I hate to leave so soon, Sweetheart, but I've got a meeting in about fifteen minutes." Paula looked at her watch. "I'll have just enough time to get there if the traffic's moving."

"I was just glad to hear from you," Hope said. They exchanged hugs at the door of the restaurant before going their separate ways. As Hope turned toward her car, the waiter appeared at her side.

"Excuse me, you left your carryout box."

"Oh. Thank you." Hope prayed that she didn't look as flustered as she felt. The waiter's dark eyes seemed to penetrate her thin, protective shell. His obvious admiration left her feeling vulnerable.

"By the way, my name is Joey." He held out his hand. She hesitated before accepting it. His handshake was warm and firm.

"I'm Hope."

"That's a beautiful name." He shifted his weight. "Just like you."

"Thank you," Hope mumbled, unsure of where to look.

"I'm on break. I thought that maybe we could get to know each other."

At Hope's tentative nod, he motioned toward a bench near the entrance. After they were seated, he turned toward her and smiled. They chatted for a few minutes about the weather, Mr. Martinelli, and the restaurant. Hope began to relax.

"You know what I do for a living," he said, motioning toward the building. "How about you? What do you do?"

"I write a column for a Christian magazine."

"Oh."

Hope could tell by the look on his face that he wasn't thrilled with her job choice, at least not the Christian part. He chatted for a few more minutes, but she could tell he had lost interest.

"Well, I'd better get back to work." Without a wave or a backward glance, he disappeared into the restaurant.

With a sigh, she headed for her car. A good man—especially a Christian man—was hard to find these days. An image of Ben Porter flitted through her mind. He seemed like a good guy, but she knew very little about him, except that Harry thought highly of him. On a whim, she turned left out of the parking lot and drove toward her old neighborhood. She was curious to see what improvements Ben had made on her old house.

Ben looked down the street from his perch on the ladder. He almost fell off when he saw a familiar blue Sable round the corner. Trying to get a grip on his feelings as well as the ladder, he made his way to the ground just as Hope pulled up in front of the house. He waved, motioning for her to get out.

"I didn't mean to disturb you," Hope called from the car.

Disturb him? Who was she kidding? He had done nothing but think about her despite his vow to do the opposite.

"I'm thankful for the break. Why don't you come in and look around?"

"I'd like that."

He took her around the outside, then held the door open for her as she entered the foyer. Her little gasps of delight made his heart soar. He watched closely for any signs of censure, but she seemed totally thrilled with the work he had done.

"I love it. It's as I always imagined it would be," Hope whispered. She looked at her watch and her eyes widened. "I've been here way too long. It's going on five o'clock."

Surprised, he looked at the hall clock. As if on cue, it began to chime the hour. Without thinking, he blurted out, "Why don't you stay for dinner?"

His inner voice warned him that he was playing with fire, but he couldn't resist the opportunity to get to know her better. She paused for a moment, and he thought she would refuse. "I wanted your opinion about some changes I made in the kitchen and master suite. You would actually be doing me a favor. I need a woman's opinion."

"Well, if you really need my help. . .I guess I could stay for a little while."

"Great!" Ben motioned her toward the kitchen.

As he closed the door an hour and a half later, he was more interested than ever. Over dinner they had talked about growing up, their testimonies, and how difficult dating was now. She was everything he had ever wanted and then some. She even agreed with him on the tile he had chosen for the bathroom and kitchen. *Why were all the good ones already taken?* He pushed away from the door and turned toward the dinner dishes that waited to be cleaned.

That evening, Hope sorted through her mail. She opened an envelope from *Agape Today* to find another letter from the Knight. It was just the one letter, which piqued her curiosity. Ripping it open, she unfolded the paper, her heart racing in anticipation.

Dear Miss Lonely Heart,

I don't know why I'm writing this. I only know that I feel compelled to write you personally. Since I don't have your address, I'm sending this to the magazine with hopes that it will be forwarded to you.

Your column intrigues me, and I would like to begin a correspondence with you. If that is agreeable, please respond. If you don't, I'll understand. If you do, please tell me more about yourself.

Sincerely,
A Lonely Knight

Hope sank into the nearest chair with a contented sigh. He wanted to write to her, not for advice, just to her. Holding the letter to her chest, she smiled and chewed on the inside of her lip. She was about to get up and write a response when another thought crossed her mind. What if he was a psycho or something? Grabbing the envelope, she looked at the address. It was a post office box in Washington, D.C. If she used the magazine's address, he wouldn't have any way of tracking her down because they didn't use her real name in *Agape Today*, and the magazine never gave out personal information.

She was anonymous in a way. The thought gave her a feeling of freedom. She grabbed a pen and paper from her office and sat down. She told him she would be glad to correspond with him and stopped with the pen in midair. Somehow, she wanted to tell him everything, but that didn't seem appropriate. Sifting through all the possible subjects she could mention, Hope finally decided to tell him about her writing.

After finishing the letter, Hope put it in one of the magazine's business envelopes and copied down his address. She put the addressed envelope in another business envelope addressed to the magazine with a note for them to mail it from *Agape Today*. Pleased with her plan, she dropped the letter in her outgoing mail before returning to her home office.

Chapter 8

Hope soon discovered writing was hard work. The first day, the words had flowed onto the page without effort, but the next day she only finished part of the research. It didn't help matters that her mind kept straying to a certain faceless knight. She kept trying to conceive of what he looked like and what might happen if they met. An imaginary knight was easier to deal with in many ways.

On Sunday Hope was totally distracted by thoughts of a knight in shining armor. She went through the motions of singing and even turned her Bible to the text for the sermon, but she couldn't remember a song they had sung or what the subject of the sermon had been. What she did remember was seeing Ben Porter slip into the back of the church. She spent the afternoon watching old movies on cable, but her thoughts kept straying to the Knight and Ben Porter. She had to forget about him. He was engaged and busy preparing a home for his future bride.

How pitiful was she, spending her Sunday afternoon pining after two men she didn't even know? One was a man she only knew from his letters, and the other was already taken. She could not blame her mood on any one thing. It was the accumulation of too many Saturday nights spent at home in front of the television. After Kevin, she had given up on ever having a relationship as long as the girls were still at home. Now that Faith and Charity were out on their own, she couldn't help but think that maybe she had been alone because no one wanted her. She held the tears back as long as she could, and then the dam burst. She cried, her body shaking with every sob.

After the tears passed, Hope dried her eyes and blew her nose. She needed someone to talk to, but she couldn't share this with Faith or Charity. They would just brush it aside and tell her how special she was. That's what sisters did. They couldn't relate to what she was going through because Charity met Bob in college and Faith had a string of boyfriends. Hope needed to talk to someone who knew where she was coming from.

"What about the Knight?" a quiet voice whispered.

Before she could lose her nerve, Hope typed out all her doubts, concerns, and frustrations about being single and over thirty. Once she started, all the anger and bitterness poured out. Every pitying glance and contradicting advice she had ever received came out. She ended with an apology for complaining to him and then printed and quickly signed the note. Hastily, she put the letter into an envelope and addressed it. She would never mail the letter. It was too personal, yet writing it all down was a form of release. Sighing deeply, she leaned the letter between her keypad and monitor. Tomorrow, she'd toss it in the fireplace and burn it.

The next day, she returned to writing her article. Hope was halfway through revising a tricky paragraph when the doorbell startled her. Hitting the save button, she walked to the door and looked through the peephole. With a smile, she unlocked the door and pulled it wide open.

"Charity!"

"Hey, Sis. I was in the neighborhood and thought I'd stop by and see what you've done with the place."

"That's right. You haven't been here since I finished unpacking." Hope pulled Charity into the apartment and gave her a hug before shutting the door. "Look around," she said, waving with her arm.

"You've done a great job, but then you always were the domestic type," Charity said with a sigh. "I can't seem to do anything right."

"What's wrong?" Hope asked, motioning for Charity to sit down.

"I don't know. You made everything look so easy. I thought it would be fun to play house permanently, but it's a lot of work. How did you ever take care of the house? Our apartment is bad enough."

"Now you know why I gave up the old place. When I had you girls to help with the cleaning, it was pretty tough, but I knew I couldn't handle it alone—especially not with all the repairs that needed to be made."

"Hope, did I ever tell you how much I appreciate all you've done for us?"

"Yes, and it's okay. I loved the years we had together."

"Me too." Charity looked around the room. "I guess I'd better get going." She picked up her purse and rose.

"It's lunchtime. Why don't you stay and eat with me?"

"Really? That would be great." The relief on Charity's face made Hope question her sister's presence in the neighborhood.

"What's really bothering you?"

Charity's smile faded. "Is it that obvious?"

"Only to me. What's up?" Hope put her arm around her

sister's shoulders and led her to the kitchen. Hope pulled out a barstool for Charity, then went into the kitchen and pulled out leftover stew from the night before.

"I don't know. I just feel so overwhelmed." Charity raised her arms in the air in frustration.

"Overwhelmed by what?"

"I. . .I burned dinner last night," Charity wailed.

"Is that all?" Hope stifled a giggle.

"It was humiliating," Charity whined. "Bob tried to be sweet, but I could tell he was disappointed. I'm just worthless in the kitchen."

"Sweetie, everybody has bad days. I've burned my share of dinners."

"You're just saying that to make me feel better," Charity said, crossing her arms on her chest.

"I promise. When I first took over the house, all I could do was open cans of soup and heat them up." Hope reached across the nook and took Charity's hands in hers. "You'll learn. Just give yourself time."

"If you say so. . ."

"I say so. Besides, what's wrong with Bob? He did work for a caterer."

"You mean get Bob to cook? I thought that was the wife's job."

"Who said?"

"I don't know. Everybody?"

"Well, you and Bob aren't everybody. Why don't you work together in the kitchen? I'm sure he won't mind. He's probably waiting for you to ask." Hope ladled the stew into two bowls and set one in front of Charity. Then, she poured tea into two glasses.

"You think so?"

"Yes, I do. Now, eat your lunch before it gets cold, then I want you to go home and talk to your husband."

"Yes, Mommy." Charity grinned and picked up her spoon. "This is delicious. Where did you get the recipe?"

"Bob."

With a groan, Charity continued eating. After they finished lunch, Charity made a closer inspection of the apartment while Hope put away the leftovers and loaded the dishwasher.

"Oh, Charity?" Hope called.

"Yeah," she said, sticking her head around the office door.

"Could you do me a favor? I need to mail a couple of things and the postman has already been by. Would you take them by the post office on your way home?"

"Sure. Where are they?"

"They're on my desk, next to the keyboard. You're a lifesaver. I don't want to have to pay late charges on my credit card."

"I'm at your service," Charity said, giving a mock salute. As she came out, she put the stack of envelopes into the front pocket of her purse.

"Next time remember that you don't need an excuse to come by and see me. If you want to talk, come on over or call me. Okay?"

"Okay." Charity reached out and gave Hope a quick hug. "I'll see you later."

Hope closed the door and locked it before going back to the kitchen to finish cleaning up. Fifteen minutes later, she went back to her desk and sat down. She started to type, but felt that something wasn't quite right. Then, she remembered the letter to the Knight. Pulling up everything on her desk, she searched frantically for the missing envelope, but it was nowhere to be found. She grabbed the phone and dialed Charity's number.

"Please be home," she begged out loud.

"Hello?"

"Charity? This is Hope. When you were in my office, did you see an envelope with the magazine's letterhead?"

"Yeah. It was between the keyboard and the monitor. Don't worry. I got it too."

"You mean you mailed it?" Hope squealed.

"Well, yeah. You had it addressed just like the others. I stuck a stamp on it, so don't worry—it'll get there."

Hope moaned.

"What's wrong?"

"There was a little problem with it." Hope prayed her sister wouldn't ask any more questions. It would be too embarrassing to explain both the Knight and the letter.

"Oh, well, I'm sure it'll be fine."

"Yeah, you're probably right," Hope mumbled.

"I've got to go. Bob's home, and we need to have that talk, soon. Bye."

Hope hung up the phone and sank into her office chair. How could she be so stupid? She should have put the letter in a drawer somewhere or burned it. Now there was no turning back. At least he was a total stranger who she'd probably never see. The thought brought a tinge of disappointment. Taking a deep breath, Hope turned back to the computer and tried to pick up where she left off, but the letter was never far from her mind.

Ben recognized the handwriting the minute he saw the envelope. He ripped into it like a child opening a Christmas present. It was the second letter in only a matter of days. He sank into the nearest chair to read. The words were like an echo of some of his own thoughts. There was something compelling about this woman. He felt like they were on the same wavelength. He hurriedly typed out a reply and put it in the mail. One day soon, he wanted to meet this woman. He was becoming more certain of that fact every day. The only question was, how was he going to pull it off?

Chapter 9

Hope's worst fears were realized a few days later when she received a letter from the Knight. She opened the envelope with trembling fingers and discovered that he had read both letters.

Dear Miss Lonely Heart,

I know exactly how you feel. I don't know how many well-meaning friends and relatives have tried to give me advice or set me up with someone they think is perfect. The worst part is when they assume I'm afraid of commitment. I think that is more a problem for men than women. My best friend is always parading women in front of me as if women were candy in a candy store and I only have to pick the right flavor. Love is more complicated than that. It hurts when people say they understand what I'm going through, when in reality, they don't have even the least grasp on the concept of being single today and over thirty.

I hope we can continue this correspondence. It's nice to know there is someone out there I can share my problems with who understands.

Sincerely,
Your Knight

The last line sent a thrill from the roots of her hair to her little toe. Her knight. She lifted a prayer to God to thank Him for knowing what she needed ahead of time. She read the letter again and again before finally folding it and putting it back in the envelope. It was a relief that someone finally understood how she felt.

For the next couple of months, the letters came almost weekly. Sometimes Hope chafed at the delay of sending the mail through the magazine, but other times she was glad of the anonymity. It was hard to open herself up to people. At least through the letters, she didn't feel like she was being judged. She and the Knight shared their hopes and dreams, discovering that they had many in common. They both wanted a family and felt the pressure of time constraints. They both loved old houses. He often wrote about the house he was working on at the moment. Originally, he had intended to remodel it and then sell, but now he was growing attached and wanted to find someone to settle down with and make it a home.

They shared the same religious background and beliefs. He wrote many a letter asking about her opinion on different issues. It was easy to tell from his letters that he was an intellectual as well as a romantic. When she mentioned that they might start e-mailing to speed up response time, he was adamant that they write letters. He said he liked to feel the paper and see her handwriting and know that she had touched the same paper he held.

After she received that letter, Hope realized she was falling in love with a man she had never met. There was a niggling doubt that maybe he wasn't who he said he was, but somehow, deep in her heart, she believed he'd be the same in person as he was in his letters. She just wondered if she would ever have the courage to meet him and find out.

As the months passed, the column became part of her normal pattern. There was always at least one funny or bizarre letter to keep things from getting boring. The trial period had long since expired, and Shelby seemed pleased. Hope had even gotten some fan mail, praising her for her timely and Christlike responses. After one such letter, Hope had been convicted to pray over every letter and response. Unfortunately, she had not been so diligent in the beginning, but God knew her heart and had helped her through. She was praying over the newest batch of letters when the telephone rang.

"Hope?"

"Shelby. What can I do for you?"

"Well, I'm in the process of planning a meeting with all of our columnists to discuss how we can improve our circulation numbers. I just need to know if you can make it on April fifth."

"Let me check my calendar. I don't think I have anything scheduled. Hold on just a moment."

Hope put the phone on her shoulder and rifled through her desk drawer. She finally found the calendar in the very back. She flipped it open to April.

"April fifth is fine. I'll put it down."

"Great! You need to be here by nine and expect to stay late. We'll provide lunch and dinner, if necessary. Any questions?"

"Should I bring anything?" Hope asked.

"Just your suggestions."

"Okay. I'll see you on the fifth."

"Bye." Hope heard the click before she had time to say good-bye. One day, she was going to beat her to the click.

March flew by as Hope put everything she had into the article. She had set April fifth as the finish date solely because it was the only date that came several months before the release of the professor's book, giving her plenty of time to pitch her idea to the editor. The last week of March she worked until late in the evening, struggling to find the right words. Then, on April Fool's Day, she typed the last word and printed it out. It was finished. Hope worked the rest of the day on a query letter. She knew the editor's preferences, which gave her an edge on the competition. When she was convinced that she had done her best, she printed out the letter and put the package in the mail. Only time would tell. As her journalism teacher always said, "You've got to keep moving forward." She pulled out her portfolio and started looking for a new article idea.

Two days before the meeting in Washington, Hope made a list of suggestions for Shelby, then tried to relax and enjoy herself. She took a long bubble bath and gave herself a manicure. She even took long walks around the neighborhood and watched spring breaking out. Still, time dragged on until the night before her meeting in Washington when the answer finally came.

A business envelope with the *Baltimore Sun*'s logo was waiting in her mailbox. With trembling fingers, she broke the seal. She had sent a nine-by-eleven envelope with an SASE, so there was a good chance that it wasn't a total rejection. Holding her breath, she unfolded the pages and let out a gasp when she read the final word: *sold.* She had just sold her first real article to a serious paper.

"I can't believe this." Hope leaned against the back of the sofa unable to comprehend what she'd just heard. "I'm going to be in print." Hope had to shake herself out of the coma she was falling into and read the letter again. Hope set down the letter, then did a little dance across the room. She had to call and tell Faith and Charity. A look at the clock told her she needed to call Faith first. After a half-hour of hearing Faith squealing in delight, Hope finished the call and dialed Charity's number.

"You're kidding!"

"No. I'm not. I just got the letter."

"We're going to celebrate," Charity said. "I'll be over in a few minutes."

"Wait! It's not set in stone yet. I haven't even signed an agreement."

"Agreement or no agreement, we are celebrating. I'm on my way."

True to her word, Charity was ringing the doorbell in less than fifteen minutes. She held up a bottle of sparkling white grape juice and fresh pastries from the bakery on the corner.

"Eclairs, my favorite," Hope said as she took the box from Charity.

"Only the best for you." She held up the bottle. "Bob and I got this as a housewarming present a few weeks ago, but we've never opened it. It's been chilling the whole time, so it should be just right."

"Are you sure Bob won't mind?"

"Positive. It was his idea."

"I knew I always liked him," Hope said as she pulled two of their grandmother's crystal glasses from the cupboard.

"You've never let us drink out of those," Charity said, a hand to her throat.

"I think it's high time we did. You girls are really women now, and it's time I started treating you like adults."

"I'll second that, and I'm sure Faith would make three if she were here."

"Cheers."

They clinked glasses and laughed until almost midnight

about anything and everything. They had finished off the pastries and two glasses of grape juice by that time.

"I've got to get home, and you've got to get to bed, young lady," Charity said, pointing a finger in Hope's face.

"Yes, Ma'am."

Hope said good-bye to Charity at the door and put away the grape juice and glasses. By the time she was ready for bed, she was exhausted. Not even the sugar could keep her awake tonight. She dropped off to sleep, dreaming of a knight on a white horse reading her article and smiling.

Chapter 10

Hope found a parking space near the magazine's office building, which was lucky, considering the lack of spaces available. She had left home early in case she ran into any traffic snarls or parking delays. As it was, she was twenty minutes ahead of time. She checked herself in the mirror and smoothed her hair into place. Now she had time to call the publisher in New York before the meeting. Grabbing her cell phone, she dialed the number Paula had given her the night before. Within minutes, she'd scheduled a meeting for Monday morning. Looking in the mirror one more time, she couldn't help smiling at her reflection. Things were looking up.

When Hope stepped off the elevator, she wondered if she shouldn't get back on it. A gentleman with his back to her was giving the receptionist a hard time. She gave Hope a warning look, so Hope ducked into the nearest office and peeked out between the blinds. She had no trouble understanding what the man was saying, and there was something familiar about the voice.

"I need to speak to Miss Lonely Heart," he was saying.

"I'm sorry. I've already told you, it is our policy not to reveal the name, address, or phone number of our columnist."

"But it's very important that I speak to her."

Hope strained to see the man's face, but a rubber plant obscured her view. She was afraid to step out. Something about the receptionist's look told her to stay put until the man was gone.

"I'm sorry, Sir, but I can't do that. If you don't leave, I'll have to call security."

"No need for that," he said. Turning briskly on his heel, he headed for the elevator and then stopped. "May I leave a message?"

"Of course." She handed him a pen and notepad.

Even from where she was standing, Hope could tell that his penmanship was neat by the precise way he moved the ballpoint. Despite herself, she was intrigued.

"Thank you," he said. The words were polite, but they sounded brisk even through the glass. Once again, he turned toward the elevator. As soon as the doors closed, Hope stepped out into the foyer.

"What was that all about?" Hope asked.

"Another weirdo, I guess." The girl shrugged her shoulders.

"Does this happen often?"

"Every once in a while." The receptionist handed her a folded piece of paper. "I don't think he wanted me to read this."

"I'll take care of it," Hope said with more confidence than she felt. Her heart beat a staccato rhythm as she walked back to the cubicle. She wanted to read the note before the meeting started and that looked like the closest thing to privacy she would get today.

Hope was relieved to find the cubicle empty. She sat down, sliding her chair into the corner so that no one would notice her. With trembling hands, she opened the letter.

Dear Miss Lonely Heart,

I was informed that you would be in a meeting at the magazine headquarters today. I felt it was a divine appointment as I am also in the city today. I want to meet you in person. I know this is strange, but I promise I am neither insane nor mean to do you harm. Can we meet at the coffee shop on the corner at the metro stop near the Capitol Building? I will be there from 11:30 to 1:00 P.M. I'll sit at the end of the counter. Please come.

Your Knight

Hope took a moment to catch her breath. She had almost met her knight. He had been standing right there, and she had been hiding in another room. Still, she didn't know the man. He might really be a stalker, but something deep inside said that he was the real deal. There was only one way to find out. She would sneak down there during her lunch break and check him out from a distance. If she still felt secure, she would introduce herself. At the least, she could put a face to the nameless knight once and for all.

The meeting went well, but Hope had a hard time concentrating on the subject at hand. Her mind was on a certain knight, sitting only a few blocks away. She turned the pen through her fingers before finally settling down to take notes. By eleven-thirty, she was fidgeting in her seat. At a quarter before twelve, Shelby called a break.

"Let's meet back here at one-thirty," Shelby said.

Hope grabbed her belongings and stuffed them into her bag. While other writers stood around in small groups to chat, she headed for the door. She thought she had made a clean break until she heard Shelby's voice calling her.

"Hope. Where are you going? We're about to order lunch."

"I have an errand to run. I'll be back in about thirty minutes." Hope tried to smile calmly at Shelby, but the woman seemed to see through her.

"An errand?"

"Yeah. It won't take long." Hope prayed that she wouldn't ask her what the errand was because she wouldn't lie to her, but it would be so much easier if she could just leave without answering any more questions.

"What about lunch?"

"Just order me a roast beef sandwich, chips, and a cola."

"All right," Shelby said after a short pause. "Just make sure you're back here in plenty of time for the meeting. I need your input."

"Don't worry. I will be," Hope said. She released the breath she had been holding as Shelby went back into the conference room, then Hope took off for the elevator.

Hope managed to get out of the building without being stopped again. She had passed the metro station as she was coming in, so it didn't take long for her to find it. Grabbing a ticket from the machine, she made her way down to the tracks. A train was just pulling in to the station. Stepping on, she was oblivious to the lunch crowd pushing its way onto the small car. Glancing at her watch, she realized that it was almost twelve-twenty. By the time she got to the coffee shop, she would only have about ten minutes before she had to start back or else miss lunch altogether.

The train pulled into the station at twenty-five after the hour, and Hope disembarked on shaky knees. She had no trouble spotting the building because it was the only coffee shop in sight. Hope waited until a group of people were walking in together and joined them. With her eyes straight ahead, she sat at the counter and ordered a cappuccino. While she was waiting for her order, she scanned the room. What she saw at the end of the counter made her mouth drop open.

"Miss, here's your order."

"Excuse me?"

"Your order's ready," the clerk answered.

"Oh. Thank you," she said, distracted by the dark-haired man at the end of the counter. Heart racing, she walked slowly across the room, taking care not to spill her coffee, and sat down one stool over from the man. He kept looking toward the door. This couldn't be right. Finally, she worked up her nerve and spoke.

"Looking for someone?"

He turned sharply and stared. She hadn't been mistaken. It was Ben Porter.

"Hope? What are you doing here?"

"I could ask you the same question," she said, taking a sip of the hot liquid.

"I guess I'm waiting for a miracle," he said with a sad smile.

"How's that?"

"Nothing." He moved over to the stool next to hers. "What brings you to town?"

"I came in for a meeting."

"I didn't realize that you worked in D.C."

"Well, I actually work from home, but the magazine I write for is here in the city."

"Really? Which magazine?"

"You've probably never heard of it. It's a small Christian magazine."

His head snapped to attention, and she knew that it was

true. She was looking at her knight. What had happened to the fiancée? Had they broken up? Was he coming here on the sly? The questions zipped through her mind like lightning. She had to know the whole truth, but she was going to take this one step at a time.

"I might. What's the name?"

"Agape Today."

Hope had to contain a smile as Ben's mouth fell open in disbelief. He was beginning to understand.

"You're not. . ."

"Miss Lonely Heart," she finished. She held out her hand. "The Knight, I presume."

He took her hand and wrapped his own around it. He sat silent for several minutes, but he never let her hand go.

"I can't believe this," he said, shaking his head.

"It was kind of a shock for me too." Hope cleared her throat. "I was especially stunned because I was under the impression that you were engaged."

"Me?" His brow furrowed in confusion. "Why would you think that?"

"You said you wanted to buy the house for your bride."

"I was speaking about the future. I'm not, and have never been, engaged."

"Oh." It was the only thing that came to mind.

"While we're talking about shock, what does your husband think?" he said sharply, dropping her hand.

"What husband?" Hope stared at him.

"You mean you didn't get married?" he questioned, eyeing her suspiciously.

"I don't know what you are talking about. I have never been engaged."

"But, you said that you would be out of the house as soon as the wedding was over."

"Not me—Charity," Hope said, then lowered her voice. "Why did you think it was me?"

"I don't know. I just assumed the oldest would be getting married first. Since the youngest sister was going to college, I figured the middle sister was too young to get married."

"I think twenty-one is old enough to get married," Hope said dryly.

Ben stared at her for several minutes. To break the contact, she looked down at her watch. She jumped down from the stool.

"I've got to go. I've barely got enough time to get to the meeting." Grabbing her purse, she looked back over her shoulder. "I'm sorry."

She rushed out the door and practically ran back to the station. Tapping one heel on the floor, she looked at her watch every fifteen seconds. Luckily, the metro wasn't crowded, and she made it back to the building with five minutes to spare. Her stomach growled, but it would have to wait until later for lunch. She slipped into her seat in the conference room just as Shelby was about to take the floor again. Shelby gave her a look but didn't comment. Hope was just about to relax when a commotion started outside.

"Just a moment." Shelby stepped out of the room. When she opened the door, Hope recognized Ben's voice. With a groan, she tried to sink lower into her seat, but there was no way to avoid a scene.

"Hope, can you come out here for a minute?" Shelby asked.

She stood up and walked slowly toward the door. Didn't he know he could get her fired? Shelby motioned her into her office and closed the door.

"That guy out there says he knows you."

"That's Ben Porter. He bought our family home."

"What's he doing here?"

"I'm not sure," Hope said, looking at the toe of her shoe as it made rings in the carpet.

"Well, I think you'd better talk to him. I'll get the meeting started."

"I'm sorry, Shelby."

"Just get rid of him and come back to the meeting."

"I'll only be a minute."

Hope followed Shelby into the hall. As soon as Shelby had closed the conference room door, Hope turned toward the reception area. Ben was waiting rather impatiently next to a security guard.

"Ben, what are you doing here?"

"I needed to see you, Hope."

"I see you're acquainted," the security guard said dryly.

"Yes, Sir. I'll take care of this," she replied. As soon as the guard returned to his post, Hope turned on Ben. "Are you trying to get me fired?"

"No, I just needed to talk to you. You left the coffee shop so fast, I didn't have time to tell you why I wanted to meet you today."

At that moment, Hope felt the receptionist drinking in the whole scene. She looked at Hope with questioning eyes, but Hope only shook her head and motioned for Ben to follow her. She went into Shelby's office and closed the door behind him.

"What?"

"I want to see you again. I'm tired of talking through letters. I want to get to know you face to face."

"I think that could be arranged," Hope said quietly, her

hands folded over her chest.

"Good. How about tonight? I could meet you here after the meetings and we could get dinner before you leave the city, to avoid rush-hour traffic." He stepped closer, reaching out to tuck an errant strand of hair behind her ear.

"That would be nice." Hope could hear her voice wavering. She felt his breath on her cheek.

"I'm glad that's settled. Now, one more thing. . ." He paused.

"What?"

He raised her chin until their eyes met. He closed the distance and kissed her softly on the lips. "I've been wanting to do that since the first day I met you," he whispered.

"Me too."

He smiled and backed away. "I'll see you at five o'clock."

"If we're finished."

"If you're not, I'll wait."

Hope watched as her knight walked down the hallway and disappeared around the corner. *Sometimes fairy tales do come true,* she mused as she returned to the meeting.

Epilogue

Hope signed the letter of resignation with a sigh. She had liked the job at *Agape Today,* but rules were rules. Only single people could write the column, and Hope's single days would soon be over. As she was putting the letter in an envelope, Ben came into the office.

"Finished?" Ben asked.

"Yes." She sealed the envelope and addressed it.

"Are you sorry?"

"Why would I be sorry when I'm getting a knight in the bargain?"

Ben grinned and pulled her into his arms. After a long kiss, he released her. "Better not have too much of that before the wedding."

"You're probably right."

"When does Faith come home?"

"After her last final on April thirtieth."

"So, we'll have a June wedding, just like in the fairy tales," Ben said with a grin.

"Just like in the fairy tales," Hope repeated.

LINDA LYLE

Linda hails from her native state of Alabama. She is single but very thankful for a close Christian family in which she is the youngest of five. She is an avid reader who at age thirteen decided she wanted to try writing a story, and before she knew it, she had one hundred pages written. She put writing aside to focus on her education, but she took every writing course she could and experimented in writing short stories and journalizing ideas. She finished her first book less than a year before it was published. Linda is very happy to be able to write wholesome and entertaining fiction that portrays her Christian values.

Wait for Me

by Terry Fowler

Chapter 1

"Can you take me to the hospital?"

Cathy Burris braced herself for her brother's acerbic outburst. Will wasn't known for his patience or tact. No doubt, disturbing him on a busy workday would surely earn a comment.

"What happened?"

His question carried an undercurrent of concern, and she roused herself from her shocked state and managed a trembling reply. "I fell in the street and hurt my knees and leg pretty badly. I can call a cab if you're busy."

"Don't be ridiculous," he chastised. "You wouldn't call if you didn't need me. Where are you?"

She gave him the address. "In front of the building. I'm using my cell phone."

"Should I call an ambulance?"

"No, Will," Cathy said quickly. She didn't want to make a big deal of such a stupid accident. "I can wait."

"I'm on my way."

Only minutes later, Will wheeled her into the emergency room. Cathy fumbled through her bag in search of her insurance card while Will gave her name to the triage nurse. The woman took her vitals and completed the necessary paperwork.

"Wait over there," the nurse instructed, pointing the way to an area filled with people.

Cathy tried to shift in the chair and moaned when discomfort shafted through her.

"She's in a lot of pain," Will told the nurse.

"We'll get to her as quickly as possible."

Will pushed her over to an empty space along the wall.

The flimsy tissue was stained red with blood from the abrasion on her knee. "Will, can you see if they have a gauze pad or something?"

After he left, Cathy leaned over to examine the damage. Sitting up, she knocked her arm against the chair and winced when it began to throb. Only then did she notice the puffiness about her wrist. *Girl, when you do something, you do it good,* she thought grimly.

Will returned with wet paper towels. "Here, see if you can clean that up a bit. I brought some dry ones too. How did this happen?"

"I jumped off the sidewalk and my foot gave way. I think I sprained my wrist when I tried to stop the fall."

He shook his head. "Why were you there, anyway?"

She dreaded this part. "A job interview," she mumbled.

"What did you say? A job?" he asked, almost in disbelief.

"Well, yes. I don't plan to spend the rest of my life doing nothing."

"What sort of job? I thought we agreed you'd stay with Dad."

His tone set Cathy's nerves even more on edge. "News flash, big brother: Dad doesn't need a baby-sitter. The job is as an advice columnist for *Agape Today* magazine. I can work from home."

"Advice? What kind of advice?"

"Catherine Burris."

Saved by the nurse. Cathy thanked God for the interruption. The injury had her too emotional to deal with Will's reaction to her new career choice.

"Push me over to the desk, Will. My hand hurts."

The nurse directed him to wait outside before wheeling Cathy back to a curtained cubicle. "Take off your stockings, and lie on the bed."

What is left of them, she thought, grimacing as she aimed the shredded ruins at the trashcan. Sheer hosiery didn't stand up well against asphalt streets.

She climbed onto the gurney, wincing with each shift of her body. The nurse returned. "We're going to send you for X-rays. Then the doctor will examine you."

As she followed the technician's instructions, Cathy worried over how her injuries would affect her new job. She had just told the editor she wanted to start work immediately. Would this require her to give up before she got started?

"Please, God, let my injuries be something uncomplicated," she whispered.

After the films were finished, the technician wheeled her back to another cubicle.

A white-coated doctor entered the room, his head lowered as he read her chart. "Catherine Burris? I had a friend named Burris in high school who had a sister named Catherine." He looked up. "Cathy?"

Austin Collins. She'd know that voice anywhere. Twenty years hadn't been hard on her brother's best friend from high school. He was as handsome as ever. Maybe more so.

Standing about six feet, his body showed the benefits of the athletic endeavors of his youth. His chocolate brown hair needed a trim, and his sea green eyes were as gorgeous as ever. Eschewing a full beard, Austin had opted for a moustache and well-trimmed goatee that made him appear more distinguished.

"Hello, Austin. I didn't realize you were a doctor."

"I didn't know you were home."

They spoke simultaneously, each voicing their surprise.

"I left the military recently because of Pop's medical problems. I had my twenty years in."

The teasing grin disappeared as he asked, "Mr. Burris is sick? I've really been out of touch. How's Will?"

"Fine. He's in the waiting area."

"Great. We need to catch up on old times. I've been meaning to call your dad and ask about Will."

Cathy felt hurt that he wouldn't ask about her too. That he wouldn't really shouldn't be a surprise to her. She'd been invisible to Austin Collins all those years ago. Why would he see her now? "He's been in Washington for a couple of years," she said. "He requested a transfer when Mom passed away."

"Oh. I'm sorry to hear of your loss. You were two lucky kids. I moved back about six months ago. Listen at me, rattling on with you lying here in pain. You fell?"

Cathy explained how the mishap occurred and braced herself for his comments. Unless Austin had developed a bedside manner, he was likely to be as bad—or worse—than Will. The two of them had often teamed up on her.

"I can't believe I did something so silly."

He shrugged. "Accidents happen. Let's see how bad it is."

His long fingers probed delicately at her abraded knee, then moved along her leg.

At sixteen, she'd had a huge crush on this man. In truth,

Cathy left home because of Austin Collins.

"Looks like you might have torn your Achilles tendon."

"Is that bad?" she asked. It sounded bad. Anything torn, particularly in the human body, couldn't be good.

"I'm referring you to an orthopedic surgeon. He'll be able to tell you more. Now let's see your wrist."

She rested her hand in his.

"It's a sprain. I'll have the nurse wrap it for you. I need to clean your knee and hand to make certain there's no debris in the abrasions."

"Thanks, Austin."

"It's my pleasure. I can't tell you how good it is to see you again."

Somehow, Cathy just didn't believe him.

Austin Collins had Cathy Burris on his mind when he pulled the curtain closed behind him. She was still a lot of woman contained in a very neat package. Not tall—around 5'4"—she'd never been an exceptional beauty, but she had enough spunk for six women. Her chestnut brown hair appeared to be in the growing-out stage—probably for the first time since she'd joined the military. No doubt she'd been an impressive sight in her uniform.

Will's baby sister had been the bane of their teenage years. The Burrises were firm believers that the older brother should look out for his sister. She constantly tagged along, generally made a nuisance of herself, and tattled on them when they mistreated her, which Austin figured they probably did more often than they realized. He couldn't say how many times he'd heard Cathy scream, "Wait for me!" when they attempted to elude her. Probably millions.

She'd often referred to him and Will as insensitive jerks. Granted, they were a bit more macho than the average guy, but it took strong self-esteem to move forward in the world.

Only a couple of years in age separated them from Cathy, but when they were sixteen and on the football team, they didn't want a fourteen-year-old girl tagging along.

He told the nursing staff where he'd be and walked into the waiting area. Scanning the area, he spotted his old friend sitting along the far wall. His high school pal hadn't changed much. "Will, buddy, long time no see," he called as he approached.

"Austin?" Will jumped from his chair. They clapped each other on the shoulder and hugged. "Man, I didn't know you were back in Washington."

"About six months now. Been meaning to get in touch, but this place keeps me on a tight leash. I've only got a minute. How about we get together soon and catch up on old times?"

"Sounds good. I want to introduce you to my wife and children." Will extracted his wallet from the inside pocket of his suit and opened it to the photo he always carried. "That's Merry, my wife. This is Trey, and that's Bella."

"Wow. You still know how to pick them."

"What about you? You found your perfect woman yet?"

The strangest thought filtered through his head. Austin shook it away. "I just saw Cathy. She's looking good too."

"She hasn't changed much," Will warned.

Austin understood immediately and grinned broadly. "Still championing the underdog?"

"Trying to make me see the error of my ways."

"I always admired her for that," Austin admitted.

"Don't tell her I said so, but I did too."

They laughed together.

"When's your next night off? You can come over for dinner. Meet the family. I'll invite Pop and Cathy to join us."

"Friday?"

"How about seven?" Will extracted a business card from his gold monogrammed holder and jotted his home address and phone number. "How's Cathy?"

"I'll let her tell you; she'll be out shortly. Patient confidentiality, you know."

Will clapped Austin on the shoulder again. "We call it client privilege. Good thing Cathy called me to bring her. Otherwise, we might not have run into each other until the next class reunion."

"Not so good for Cathy, but I'm glad to see you both. I've got to run. I'll be in touch."

Chapter 2

How poetic that the one person in the world whom she would never consciously seek out had reappeared in her life on today of all days. And again, not under the most auspicious of occasions. At least he hadn't made fun of her to her face. No doubt he would get a good laugh with his coworkers later, though.

Why couldn't she give Austin the benefit of the doubt? Because he and Will were very much alike. Handsome, popular star athletes who had all but run the school. Cathy hated the way they ignored the less popular kids. Their superior attitudes irked her.

Granted, Will seemed different now. He was a good provider for his wife and children. When their mother died, he'd readily agreed he should be the one to come home.

She couldn't help but wonder about Austin. Was he married? Did he have children?

The young man she remembered had his pick of beautiful girls. No doubt, becoming a doctor made him even more popular with the ladies. She hadn't noticed a wedding band on his finger. In a way, it bugged her that she'd looked.

Cathy long ago convinced herself Austin was not the man

God intended for her, yet the moment she laid eyes on him, she felt the immediate attraction.

"Ready?"

The question jerked her back to the present. She looked up at the nurse and nodded. The woman gave Cathy her orders—a referral appointment with an orthopedic surgeon and a prescription for pain pills—before wheeling her out into the waiting room.

"Everything okay?" Will asked.

"I'll know more when I see the orthopedic doctor."

The plate glass doors slid open, and Will pushed her off to the side and parked the wheelchair. "Wait here. I'll get the car."

"I'm not likely to be running any races while you're gone," Cathy mumbled when he ran off.

He pulled his Volvo to the curb and left it running as he came around to help her into the passenger seat. "Did you call Pop?" he asked, glancing at her before he put the car in gear and started out of the lot.

"I didn't want him to worry."

Will nodded. They both knew their father had a tendency to fret about his little princess. His heart attack so soon after their mother's death scared them both. They were dedicated to keeping their father healthy and happy.

"Did you drive downtown?"

"I took a cab."

"I'll drop you off at home."

"Can we pick up my prescription first? I'm going to need something for the pain."

Will stopped by the drugstore the family had used for years and ran inside to retrieve her medication. He returned with a sack full of items.

"Here. Mr. Mike thought you might need gauze pads and tape. He said to tell you he hopes you feel better soon. Oh yeah, there's some antibacterial ointment and an ice bag too. He said it'll help with the swelling in your wrist."

The gesture brought tears to Cathy's eyes. "Thanks, Will."

"No problem, Pest. Now tell me about this job."

As always, Will amazed Cathy with the ease with which he navigated the long, uneven lines of heavy traffic.

"It's a freelance position. Doesn't pay much, but I'm looking forward to getting started."

He swung out around a double-parked car. "What prompted them to offer you the job?"

"They gave me three letters and asked me to write responses. Then they hired me."

"What sort of letters?" he asked curiously, shifting his gaze from the street to her for a second. "Are you the next etiquette expert?"

"No, it's an advice column."

He gave her a sharp look. "What sort of advice? You'd better be careful in this sue-happy society. Some nut will bankrupt you."

She ignored the legal advice and said, "I'm pretty sure we're protected by the magazine."

"So are you going to tell me what kind of advice you'll be offering?"

Cathy took a deep breath. "The name of the column is 'Dear Miss Lonely Heart.' "

" 'Dear Miss Lonely Heart'?" Will repeated. "You're advising people on love relationships? Oh, that's rich." He started to laugh.

"I've had relationships," Cathy protested.

"I'll hand it to you. You've got the Miss Lonely Heart bit down cold. Except for that crush on Aus, I don't think you've ever been serious about any man. Plan to rekindle the flame now that he's back?"

"You'd do well not to bring that up again." Cathy's tone was flat and cold. She'd tried to forgive Will for the part he'd played in telling Austin how she felt about him, but she still felt betrayed and hurt.

"Come on, Cath. It's water under the bridge. You're not a teenager anymore."

"Drop it, Will. You never understood how embarrassed I felt."

"Aus looked good, don't you think?"

No way would Cathy admit to Will that Austin had aged well. "He hasn't changed much."

"I invited him to dinner Friday night. Think you and Pop can make it?"

Cathy hated to cook and never refused any meal she didn't have to prepare. Besides, Will's wife, Meredith, was a great cook.

"If I can walk, we'll be there."

"I'll pick you up, if you want."

"We'll manage. What time?" she asked as Will pulled into the driveway.

"Seven. Stay put. I'll help you inside."

Minutes later, Cathy sat with her leg propped up on a footstool.

"Are you sure you're okay?" her dad asked, placing her pain pills and water on the nearby table.

"She's fine, Pop. Stop worrying."

He looked to his daughter for reinforcement.

"I'm okay." No way would she tell Pop her knee and hand

hurt like crazy. "I'll live to fight the streets again."

"Hey, Pop, guess who we ran into at the hospital?" Will asked.

Their dad shrugged and shook his head.

"Remember Austin Collins? He's working at the hospital emergency room."

"How's he doing? I haven't seen Austin in years."

"Looks great. Said he's been back in Washington for about six months now. He wants to see you too."

"The years have really flown. Seems like yesterday all of you were running in and out of the house, slamming the screen door behind you. Now he's a doctor, you're a lawyer, and Cathy's a retired master sergeant."

"Life does have a way of moving on. I've got to run." Will tapped Cathy on the head. "Call if you need anything."

She nodded and leaned against the chair back. What a day.

Chapter 3

After her accident on Monday, Cathy found the week slowed to a crawl. The days with nothing to do but sit around seemed long and unending. The pain pills knocked her out, and the waking hours were spent reading and watching television.

She didn't see the orthopedic doctor until Friday, and Cathy decided not to contact the magazine until after she'd seen him. No sense in mentioning the situation until she had a better idea of what the future held.

Her sister-in-law came by on Friday morning to drive her to the doctor's office.

"You didn't have to do this," Cathy protested when Merry came into the family room.

"Why not? You're always doing stuff for us. Since you came home, you spend as much time with our kids as we do."

"But you had to take off from work."

"They'll survive one day without me."

Like her husband, Meredith was an attorney. Unlike Will, Merry worked in the public defender's office. She and Cathy shared the need to help those less fortunate than themselves.

"I'm praying that this is nothing. I suppose Will told you

about the new job?"

"Yes. I warn you, Cathy, you haven't heard the end of that."

"I know. Let him have his fun."

Merry's smile was apologetic. "I think it's great."

Cathy grinned. "Me too. I've subscribed to *Agape Today* for years. When they started the column, I read the letters and thought about what I'd say. I never dreamed I'd be the columnist offering advice. It doesn't pay much, but it's not about money. I want to help people, to make a difference in this crazy world."

Merry nodded her understanding. "You'll do a fine job. You always do. Ready?"

Cathy stood. "I hope this stupid accident doesn't force me to quit before I get started."

"We've been praying too," Meredith said. "And I've got the prayer circle at church going full force."

Cathy shared a smile with her sister-in-law. "That should do it. Those people have sent up many a powerful plea to the Lord."

After they were seated in the van, Meredith looked over her shoulder and backed into the street. "What was that address again?"

Cathy dug the paper out of her bag and read off the street number and name.

"I know that building. Lean back and take it easy."

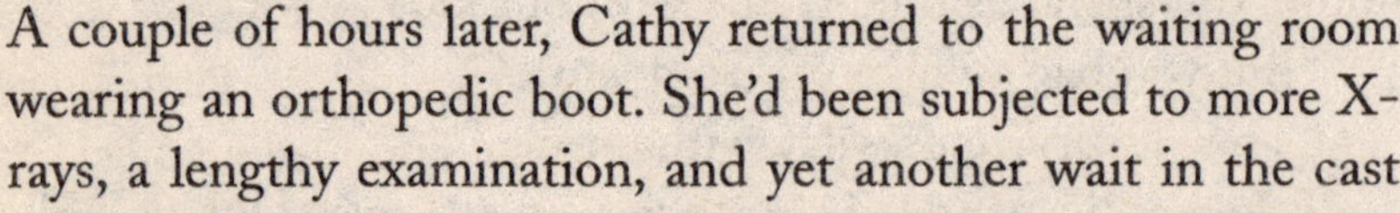

A couple of hours later, Cathy returned to the waiting room wearing an orthopedic boot. She'd been subjected to more X-rays, a lengthy examination, and yet another wait in the cast room to be fitted.

After checking out, she walked into the lobby and sat down beside Merry. "It's official," Cathy announced almost tearfully. "My Achilles tendon is torn. The doctor wants me to wear the boot for a couple of weeks to see if it starts to repair on its own. If not, he'll have to do surgery."

"Oh, Cathy, I'm sorry," Merry exclaimed, reaching down to grab her bag. She pulled out tissues and placed them in Cathy's hand. "What does surgery entail?"

"I don't know. He says it's outpatient. They operate, and I go home the same day. I'll probably have to wear a cast once they make the repair."

"How is this going to affect the job?"

"I'm not sure," Cathy said, disappointment weighing heavily. She'd so hoped the news would be better. "I plan to call my editor when I get home and tell her what's happened."

"Sit here while I get the car."

"I'll hobble on out with you and wait. I might as well get used to this moon boot."

"Is that what it's called?" Merry asked.

"No, but it's about as unwieldy as a space suit."

"Look on the bright side—you don't have to use crutches."

"Good thing. I'd probably fall and break my neck."

Cathy appreciated Merry's efforts to cheer her up but abhorred the thought of being restricted in any way. She hated burdening her family. She loved doing for others but didn't like needing their help for herself.

Merry opened the door and helped Cathy into the van. "Comfortable?"

Wearied by the short trip from the office, she nodded. Merry shut the door, going around to climb in behind the wheel.

Cathy thought about what she would say to Shelby Tate when she called. How would the woman react to the news?

"Tell me about this friend of Will's."

Surprised, Cathy glanced up at Merry and said, "Extremely

handsome, popular, Mr. Personality—just like Will. He and Austin have been friends for as long as I can remember."

"Will says he's not married and that you liked Austin."

"Did he tell you what he did?"

Merry nodded.

"I never felt comfortable around Austin after that."

"Why?"

Cathy shrugged again. "He never said a word."

"Nothing?"

"No 'You're a nice kid but—' No 'drop dead.' Nothing. At least he didn't laugh in my face. Just kept treating me like Will's little sister."

"Men can be so blind at times. So how do you feel about him now?"

"I don't know."

"Are you still attracted to him?"

"I don't want to be."

"Why not?"

"It took me twenty years to get over Austin Collins."

"I'm thinking maybe you're not over him, after all."

Cathy looked at Merry in stunned silence.

"We're here," Merry announced, pulling into the driveway.

"Thanks for the ride."

"What's a sister-in-law for?"

"I'll probably call on you again soon."

Merry nodded. "Good. Let us take care of you for a change."

"I don't have a choice."

She went around to help Cathy out. "See you tonight?"

"We'll be there. What should we bring?"

"A healthy appetite and a smile will do just fine. Stay off that leg as much as possible and call us if you need anything.

Promise?" Merry asked as she hugged her good-bye.

"Between you, Will, and Pop, I'll be an invalid by the time my leg heals."

"No chance of that. I'd better get moving. I gave Melanie the afternoon off."

"Give the kids a hug for me and tell Melanie hello."

Will and Merry had found a jewel in Melanie Taylor. The young woman had come to work for them as a part-time and summer baby-sitter while she attended the University of D.C.

From the moment they met, Cathy bonded with Melanie; and when possible, they attended the theater and did other fun things together. She knew from past conversations that Melanie missed her family and friends in St. Louis, and Cathy feared she would return home soon.

If it happened, Cathy was more than willing to help out with Trey and Bella. Hopefully, it would be a while yet. Running after a couple of kids with this boot or a cast on her leg wouldn't be possible.

Cathy waved good-bye to Merry before letting herself into the house. Hearing the whine of her dad's woodworking machinery in the garage, she decided to make her call. She made slow progress up the stairs to her bedroom. Dropping onto the side of the bed, she removed Shelby Tate's business card from her nightstand drawer.

Reluctantly, Cathy reached for the pink princess phone and dialed the number. The direct line to the editor's office soon had Shelby Tate on the phone.

"Hello, Ms. Tate, this is Cathy Burris."

"Cathy, call me Shelby," she invited, her tone brisk but friendly. "What can I do for you?"

"I'm afraid I have bad news."

"Don't tell me you're not taking the column?" The woman sounded almost frantic.

"That's going to be your decision. When I left your building, I stepped off the curb and tore my Achilles tendon. Right now, I'm wearing an orthopedic boot; but if it doesn't work, I'll need surgery."

"I'm so sorry."

Cathy detected sincerity in the woman's words. "I just saw the orthopedic surgeon today. I'm obviously not going to be as mobile as when I accepted the position."

"You didn't hurt your hands, did you?"

"I sprained my wrist, but it's much better," Cathy said.

"Then I don't think we have a problem. You were going to work from home anyway, and with fax and computer, you won't need to come to the office. We can mail or messenger the letters to you."

Cathy felt a weight lift from her shoulders. "I'm so glad. I didn't want to let you down."

"I appreciate that. I think things will be just fine. We're all terribly impressed with the way you answered those letters and look forward to working with you."

"I can't tell you how thankful I am that this won't make a difference. I really want to write the column."

"Good. Gotta run. My new boss is shouting my name. He is such a bear. Stay in touch and let us know how you are progressing."

"Thanks again."

Cathy replaced the receiver and fell back on the bed, smiling happily.

"Thank you, Lord," she praised. "Help me be worthy of this task You've set for me. Fill my head with the advice that will help these people as You would have them be helped. Never let me feel that I, alone, am capable of doing anything without Your help.

"Now, Lord, I ask You to help me face Austin Collins tonight. Help me to overcome the embarrassment of the past and to be the creation You gave life and breath to. Amen."

Only God could help her through tonight. From the age of sixteen, when she'd stopped seeing him as Will's buddy and began thinking of him on a romantic level, Cathy fought the burgeoning feelings. She'd known there was little likelihood she could attract a guy like Austin.

At least her head had known, but her heart was filled with hope. She'd tried to keep it a secret, but Will quickly tuned in on her feelings. The day she overheard him joking with Austin about the crush his little sister had on him, Cathy wanted to die.

All that summer, she'd avoided Austin. Any time he came to the house, she made a point of staying in her room or going off with her friends. When their paths did cross, Austin continued to treat her like a kid sister. Cathy felt even more heartbroken because he never acknowledged her feelings for him.

Finally, Will and Austin went off to college. She still saw Austin when they came home, but he never said a word about what Will had shared with him. She accepted that he could never care for her romantically, and in her senior year, a recruiter visited the school. Cathy made the decision to put even more distance between Austin and herself.

Her parents tried to change her mind, but Cathy knew she had to escape their protection. They already talked about her attending the same college they'd gone to. *The same college as Austin.* The air force became her only hope of escaping Austin and the embarrassment she felt every time they ran into each other. Leaving her family, friends, and home had not been easy, but she'd never regretted taking the step.

Now Austin was back. He still saw her as Will's thirty-eight-year-old kid sister, but she felt okay with that. Cathy had long since realized there was no future for her and Austin Collins.

Chapter 4

When Cathy and her father walked into Will's living room that night, Austin greeted them and immediately vacated the armchair. "Cathy, sit here. Will told me about your diagnosis."

She waved him back. "I'll sit over here."

"This chair is more comfortable," he insisted, gently taking her arm and guiding her. "You need to put your leg up."

The comfortable chair was her favorite part of Merry's Country French décor. Cathy gave in, and Austin waited until she settled her leg before sitting on the edge of the ottoman.

"Hopefully, this boot will do the trick. I don't look forward to the prospect of surgery."

"Who does?" He smiled and reached over to pat her hand.

Will entered the room, carrying a tray. "Stop playing doctor, Aus." He thrust a small plate in his friend's direction along with a cocktail napkin. "Merry said to eat some of these hors d'oeuvres while she finishes dinner."

"I'll see if I can help," Cathy said.

Will and Austin blocked her way.

"Merry sent strict instructions you're to stay off your leg," her brother said.

"I'm not an invalid," she complained.

Will grinned. "Wish I had a photo of you doing a nosedive into the street."

Cathy ignored him. "Where are the kids?"

"In their rooms. Can you believe they preferred cartoons to two guys sitting around discussing the old days?"

Cathy shook her head at the thought of grown men talking about high school while a pair of small children looked on. "No doubt. It was pretty boring even then."

Will grimaced playfully at her. "What do you want to drink?"

"Iced tea would be great."

He glanced at their father, who watched their exchange from the sofa. "What about you, Pop?"

"Make that two."

Will disappeared into the kitchen. Cathy took advantage of her father's question-and-answer session to learn what Austin had been doing for the past twenty years.

"After I finished my training, I worked in a needy rural area for a few years."

"That must have been a different world," Pop commented.

"Definitely. Gives you a real appreciation of how good we have things in the bigger cities. At times in my childhood, I felt deprived, but I didn't have a clue what deprivation was until I saw how some of these people lived."

Cathy couldn't help herself. Her curiosity demanded a response. "What made you decide to go there?"

"I had a contract to fulfill. The government paid a big chunk of my tuition in return for a few years of my time. In the long run, it seemed more feasible than spending years paying off college loans."

Cathy considered this was the Austin she knew. For him,

the decision had been a means to an end, not an altruistic act.

"Between the football scholarship and the contract I signed, I'm relatively debt free. There was no other way I could pursue my dream of becoming a doctor. My father couldn't afford it, for sure."

Cathy attempted to digest his words along with the crudités. She'd never considered that Austin's father couldn't afford to pay his college expenses. He'd hung out with the rich kids in high school, and she'd just assumed he could attend any school that struck his fancy.

"How is your dad?" her father asked.

"He died ten years ago."

"I'm sorry to hear that. We lost contact when he moved away. Ronald was a good man."

"The best."

"Was he sick?" Cathy remembered Austin's father as a man who never had a lot to say. He rarely attended school events.

"He died in his sleep." Austin's smile disappeared. "The doctors think he had a heart attack, but we don't know for sure. I think he just gave up on life once Mom passed away."

Cathy wondered if the man had died of a broken heart. From the few times she'd met Austin's parents, Cathy remembered his mother as the livelier member of the couple.

"Dinner's served," Merry called from the dining room. She greeted the family and asked about Cathy's leg.

Cathy pushed her leg off the ottoman. "I'm about as speedy as a turtle, but I'm getting there."

"Slow and steady wins the race," Merry reminded.

They all laughed and moved toward Merry's beautifully arranged table. Her brother had married the perfect woman. If Merry hadn't opted to be an attorney, she could have had a career as an interior designer.

They sat and joined hands to say grace. Seemingly comfortable with that family tradition, Austin took hold of four-year-old Trey's hand.

Will carved the pot roast and served the plates as they were passed to him.

Merry leaned closer to Cathy as she passed the plate and asked softly, "Did you call the editor?"

Cathy nodded, not wanting to get Will started on the subject. "Everything's okay."

She reached to position the plate in front of her niece, adding the side dishes the little girl wanted. A bread lover like her father, Bella immediately began eating her dinner roll.

The conversation meandered through a number of topics before Will managed to bring up her new position.

"Did Cathy tell you about this new job of hers?" Will asked Austin, hardly able to restrain his laughter. "She's taken a position as a freelance advice columnist. Get this: She's advising the lovelorn." He laughed gleefully, enjoying his hilarity at her expense.

Cathy looked up from cutting Bella's meat.

"William Burris," his wife called sharply.

"Ah, Merry, it's so funny. Cathy's the only woman I know of who stayed in the military for twenty years and didn't snag a guy."

Cathy's face fired red-hot. "Excuse me," she mumbled. "I've lost my appetite."

Moving as quickly as her booted foot would allow, Cathy stopped in the center of the kitchen, not sure where to go next. The dining room was no longer an option. Being embarrassed in front of the family was one thing, but she refused to be made a joke of in front of outsiders.

The garden beckoned, so she opened the French doors and stepped carefully onto the stone patio. Crossing over to the stone bench in the far corner of the garden, she sat. Feeling sorry for herself, she allowed the tears to spill over down her cheeks.

"Cathy?"

She looked up in surprise when Austin stepped out of the kitchen door. Not wanting him to tease her more, she swiped her cheeks.

He approached tentatively, as if uncertain how she'd react. "Are you okay?"

She sniffed and nodded. "My dignity is in shreds, but otherwise, I'm fine."

"Your dignity is fine. Will didn't come out of that conversation looking too good, though."

Austin sat beside her on the stone bench, passing her the handful of paper towels he'd grabbed from the kitchen.

Super absorbent, no doubt, Cathy thought, considering he'd brought her enough toweling to dry up a neighborhood of women on a crying jag. She mumbled her thanks and tucked her hair behind her ears. "I love my brother, but I'm so tired of him making jokes about my life. Will, the star athlete. Will, the overachiever. Mr. Perfect. People never make jokes about Will because everything always goes perfectly for him."

"I think his dinner party is a bust."

His tongue-in-cheek comment made Cathy giggle.

"And I imagine Merry will have a few choice words to share with him after we leave," Austin added.

"I don't know how she stands him."

"She loves him. Will's Will. He doesn't realize how sharp his tongue is. I remember more than one time back in high school when it sliced through my tough hide."

"He's an excellent husband and father," Cathy admitted.

"And friend and brother," Austin added, his gaze holding hers in the low wattage of the garden spotlights. "He'd give you the shirt off his back, if you needed it."

"That's true."

Austin reached for her hand. "I think the new job sounds great. What made you decide to try writing a column?"

She glanced at their hands and eyed him suspiciously.

"I'm not trying to be funny. I really want to know. I'm a lot more mature than you remember."

Cathy didn't know what to say. She wanted to believe him, but too many memories of the young Austin blocked the way. "People have always come to me for advice," she said with a slight shrug. "I figured I might as well get paid for it."

Austin nodded. "Will always called you the public defender of the playground. You fought a lot of battles."

"I hated the class distinctions. I just wanted kids to enjoy their time in school instead of getting caught up in being a member of the right group. Look at the mess in the schools today—students killing each other because someone hurt their feelings or didn't treat them the way they want to be treated. The world would be so much better if life wasn't a popularity contest."

"Some people need the class distinction to make them feel worthwhile."

"Being a big man on campus was pretty important to Will."

"And me," Austin admitted. "Popularity is not totally a bad thing, Cathy. College recruiters look for the brightest and the best for scholarships. I didn't make the pros, but football helped pay for my degree."

"Did you choose medicine for the status aspect?"

A frown crossed his face. "You think so?"

"No, I think you wanted to help people. If status had been important, you wouldn't be in the emergency room. You'd be in one of the high-dollar practices. Thanks, Austin."

His frown creased his forehead. "For what?"

"Putting the situation in the proper perspective. Will doesn't mean to be a jerk. Sometimes he can't help himself."

"Got your appetite back yet? Your sister-in-law's pot roast is the best I've ever tasted."

Cathy laughed at his obvious hint. "I wouldn't want to deprive you of the best roast you've ever had."

Austin stood and pulled her to her feet. "You need to eat to keep your strength up. You're still a tiny thing."

"I'm five foot four of lean, mean fighting machine."

"Yeah, right," he said in a teasing tone. "Let's go eat Will's pot roast. He can eat crow."

Cathy laughed again. "Lead the way."

Chapter 5

The invalid role was not a good fit for Cathy. Two weeks passed slowly as she sat and watched the house revert to her pre-homecoming state. Pop was a clutter bug. He never returned anything to its proper place and allowed household chores to back up in favor of his woodworking projects.

After twenty years in the air force, the discipline and routine she'd learned were as much a part of Cathy as the oxygen she breathed. The structure had taught her the importance of organization, minimalism even. She didn't need stuff cluttering her life.

The doorbell rang, and Cathy didn't bother to move. *Let Pop get the door.* She didn't want another lecture on how she needed to rest her leg if she hoped to get better.

"Look who's here," her father announced as Austin followed him into the family room. "Entertain him while I check things in the kitchen."

Their old town Alexandria, Virginia home wasn't exactly close to the hospital. "What brings you out our way?" Cathy asked after inviting him to take a seat.

"I thought I'd check on my patient."

Confused by his comment, Cathy pointed out, "I'm not your patient."

"Sure you are," he insisted, grinning broadly. "Just because I passed you on to a specialist doesn't mean I didn't treat you first."

"Yeah, I can see you convincing the hospital to let you treat patients like that."

Austin chuckled. "Okay, you win. Will and I golfed this afternoon, and he says you're about as miserable as you can get."

"You have a pill for miserable, I suppose?"

"Just what the doctor ordered," he countered playfully at her skeptical response. "I thought maybe we'd order a pizza and play a rousing game of Monopoly."

"Oh, please—too much fun will kill me."

Austin grinned. "Cut the sarcasm, or I'll think you're related to Will."

Cathy looked at Austin closely, searching for any indication of why he was there. Dressed in shorts and a sport shirt, he'd evidently exchanged his golf shoes for sandals after leaving the greens.

"Isn't it hot out there for golf?"

Austin leaned back and stretched his arms over his head. "Typical August weather. We spent as much time as possible under the shade of the cart canopy."

"Who won?"

"Me. Who else?"

His confident air and the defeat of her competitive brother brought a smile to Cathy's face. "I'm sure Will loved that."

"He demanded a rematch. I told him he's too cutthroat for his own good. So what do you say about the pizza?"

Cathy shrugged, indicating the kitchen with her thumb. "Ask Pop. He's been in there all afternoon. Said something about making a big pan of lasagna. I think he believes pasta is some sort of cure-all. We've had it every night this week."

"There's a cure for what ails me in your dad's lasagna," Austin agreed eagerly. "Think I could wrangle an invite?"

"Consider yourself invited."

He adjusted his body against the sofa cushions and glanced at the program she watched. While channel surfing, she'd stopped on the landscaping program.

"You like to garden?" he asked.

"I never had more than a few potted houseplants. I thought maybe once I got everything sorted out in the house, I'd check into reviving Mom's gardens, but you know the story."

He nodded. "When do you see the doctor again?"

"Saw him this morning. He scheduled surgery for the thirteenth of September."

A deep, heartfelt sigh issued from Austin. "I'm sorry, Cathy. I know you didn't want that."

"Definitely not. Now I get to go the whole route: surgery, cast, probably this boot again, then therapy."

"Your surgeon is one of the best," he reassured.

"I've heard that. That's one plus in all the negatives."

"Let's talk about something else," he suggested.

"So how did you and Will manage to get a day off during the week?"

"I have to work this weekend. Will's his own boss. Must be nice."

"He works pretty hard. I keep telling him he needs to spend more time with his children while they're small and want to spend time with Daddy."

"Where do the years go? It's so hard to believe it's been twenty years since I saw you last. Out of all of us, I'd say you're the lucky one. You're already retired."

Thinking of herself as retired at thirty-eight always struck Cathy's funny bone. "After the first couple of enlistments, it seemed smart to stay on. Now I can pursue my own interests."

"Any letters arrive yet?"

She eyed him curiously, wondering about his interest in her job. "No. Any day now, I imagine."

"I'm glad the column didn't fall through."

Her father returned and served Austin the ice water he'd requested. "Dinner's almost ready."

"Set another plate, Pop. Austin needs a pasta fix."

"Good thing I chose the big dish," her father said with a knowing smile.

She recalled Will and Austin's appetites as teenagers. "I want my serving first."

"Hey, I'll have you know I'm not a pig."

"Can't prove it by me. I've seen you and Will wipe out one of those big dishes in seconds."

"Must have been Will. I'd never eat like that."

Cathy's eyes grew wide with disbelief. "I've seen you in action. At least Pop will have help with the dishes tonight."

"Sounds like a fair trade to me."

"Mail came," her father said, passing Cathy a bundle of envelopes. "I'd better set that extra place."

"Oh, joy. I've been preapproved for three credit cards today," Cathy announced as she thumbed through the junk mail. "Not bad for a retired person." The larger white envelope on the bottom of the stack caught her eye, and Cathy pulled it out. "It's from *Agape Today*." She ripped open the flap and peered inside. "Letters," she exclaimed with delight.

Austin's smile encompassed his entire face. "Why don't you

check them out while I help your dad in the kitchen?"

"Thanks, Austin." She appreciated his sensitivity as she scanned the note Shelby Tate had clipped to the twenty or so envelopes.

Cathy,

Hope you're feeling better. Here's your first batch of "Dear Miss Lonely Heart" letters. After you read and choose the ones you plan to answer, write your responses and fax the information to the office. We have a list of referral agencies we forward to the other letter writers. Be sure to keep the deadline date in mind. Call if you have any questions.

Cathy flipped through the envelopes, counting them and longing to start reading. *Just one little peek,* she thought. No, she decided, fighting the urge. She didn't have time right now to give any of the letters the attention they deserved. She certainly intended to read and pray for those who had written them.

Austin appeared in the family room door. "Ready to eat?"

She nodded, beginning her struggle to get to her feet. Austin moved quickly and offered a hand.

"Thanks."

"How were the letters?" he asked.

Cathy glanced at the envelope on the end table. "I'm saving them for later."

Dinner was interesting. Austin shoveled in lasagna, all the while entertaining them with stories about his work. "We slap bandages on our kids the moment they get a scratch. They use remedies you can't even begin to imagine."

"My mom did a lot of that when we were growing up," Bill

said. "She didn't believe in paying the doctor for every little ailment. Can't begin to tell you how many old wives' remedies she used. Bet you never taped a penny to a puncture wound."

Austin shook his head. "Can't say I have."

"So were you glad to get back to modern medicine?" Cathy asked.

"Yes," Austin admitted. "Technology is wonderful in helping me make my diagnoses."

As she listened to him talk, Cathy looked for the teen she remembered from years past. The young man who believed life consisted of football and girls. Maybe he wasn't as obvious now, but Cathy felt pretty certain he still existed. Austin Collins couldn't have changed that much.

"Something wrong, Cathy?"

He startled her with the query. "No, just thinking."

"You're eager to get to those letters, aren't you?"

Cathy decided to leave what she'd been thinking unsaid. "Pop, this lasagna is great."

"Best I've ever had," Austin agreed. "Why don't I help with the dishes and say good night."

"You're a guest," Bill protested. "I'll do the dishes."

"But I invited myself. Least I can do is wash a few dishes."

"Maybe next time. I'm glad you stopped by for a visit. It's been too many years since you last sat at my table."

"I got so homesick when I first went off to college," Austin admitted with a sheepish smile. "I missed my family and all of you so much."

Cathy halted her slow return to the family room, twirling slowly to look at him. "Then why did you go?"

Austin's gaze locked on her. "It was something I needed to do."

Chapter 6

Maybe one day I'll tell Cathy the real reason I decided to go away to college, Austin thought as he unlocked his apartment door. Would she be surprised to learn the truth? He thought so. Sometimes it surprised even him.

Shoving his gym bag off the sofa, he caught sight of the pile of mail that needed going through. Pity he couldn't get as excited about the bills and junk mail as Cathy was about that envelope she'd received today.

Austin pictured her sitting in the middle of her bed with letters spread all about her, joyful at the happy letters, her heart aching as she read of others in pain. Cathy invested quite a bit of herself into caring for others. Most people didn't care enough, but he suspected she cared too much.

He thought about this need to spend time with her. Years ago, he'd been too worried about what his friend would think to pursue Will's little sister. He doubted Cathy had a clue about how he felt then. Or now. She seemed so intent on distancing herself from him. Hopefully, he could make her understand.

The legal pad and pen on the table caught his attention and sparked an idea. Why not? What would one more letter hurt? The first one should have been in the batch she received today. He wanted to be sure this one got into her next batch from the magazine.

Something he needed to do. Austin's earlier words lingered in Cathy's head as she prepared for bed. Why had Austin felt the need to separate himself from the people who loved him? To go to a place where he knew no one? Surely he could have found some underserved area locally.

Cathy switched on the lamp by the bed, casting the room into shadows. She really needed to redecorate this room. Replacing the comforter and drapes hadn't been enough to overcome the intense, baby-girl pink she'd begged her mom for when she turned thirteen. Little did she know it would be around to haunt her twenty-five years later.

After flipping back the comforter, she double-stacked the pillows and rested on the bed. The envelope of letters lay on the opposite pillow. She reached for it. *First things first*, she thought, putting them aside. She needed all the help she could get with this job.

Turning to 2 Thessalonians 1:11, Cathy read, "With this in mind, we constantly pray for you, that our God may count you worthy of his calling, and that by his power he may fulfill every good purpose of yours and act prompted by your faith."

Before accepting the job, Cathy had gone to her Bible and prayed, all the while considering the magnitude of the task she considered taking on. The advice she wrote in the "Dear Miss Lonely Heart" column could strengthen or harm, and she determined to build, not destroy.

Even after making her decision, she asked the pastor and her friends at church to continue praying for her. Cathy knew

God would provide all the guidance she needed to complete the task.

Lord, help me understand these letters and respond with the words You would have me say. Help me to give significance to these problems that weigh upon Your children. Bless and keep them all. And if the reason they don't have true peace is because they don't know You as their Savior, take control of their hearts and give them the answers they need so desperately. Amen.

As she read, Cathy sorted the letters into stacks. The letters that struck her as pranks were immediately put aside, leaving those of a more serious nature for her to study carefully. Shelby specified three letters with responses. As she read, Cathy fell into the habit of whispering up specific prayers for the letter writers.

Dear Miss Lonely Heart,

I'm a twenty-year-old female with an eating disorder. My boyfriend of five years tells me I'm fat and even says he's going to break up with me if I don't lose weight. I can't understand why he has to be so cruel. I try to make excuses for him because he's not a Christian, but now I can't help myself and I'm afraid. I love him and don't want to lose him, either.

Overweight in D.C.

This sort of thing made Cathy see red. When someone loved you, they didn't ask you to become something you weren't. It made no sense. She grabbed her pen and began scribbling:

D.C.,

Do you realize how wonderfully and fearfully you were made by God? When He created you in the womb, He wanted only the best for you. This young man who wants to change you obviously doesn't feel the same way. Blink those love-clouded eyes and examine your relationship closely. If your weight is a reason for him to demand this change, what next? Does he find fault in other ways? Look at your relationship and remember that God directs us not to be unequally yoked. Confide in your parents or someone you trust, and get help for your eating disorder. Then focus your attention on God. He loves you as you are.

Remembering how the previous columnist had signed her letters, Cathy decided to be a little different and signed hers, "Heart."

Rereading the response, Cathy felt confident that she had advised the young woman properly. Hopefully, this young woman would realize that her boyfriend had problems of his own and would not make herself even more miserable trying to please him.

Cathy continued reading and found her eyes growing heavier with each sentence. She found it strange when another letter addressed change.

Dear Miss Lonely Heart,

Years ago, I made a major mistake that resulted in losing the woman I cared about. How do I convince her that I've changed from the person she remembers?

New Man in Washington

Even as she read the brief missive, Cathy felt something about this man. The idea that he'd changed intrigued her and she wondered why.

She wanted to answer, but laid the letter aside to give it more thought. It seemed God was guiding this column toward change. Gathering the letters and pen and pad, Cathy slipped them into the nightstand drawer. This didn't have to be finished tonight. Tomorrow she could look at everything with a clearer head.

The phone rang, and Cathy hit the mute button on the remote as she reached for the receiver.

"Hi, Cathy. How are you feeling?"

"I'm okay," she said, surprised to hear from Austin so soon.

"Will says your dad has a meeting and you need a ride."

"I thought. . . Never mind." Will had said he'd pick her up around six-thirty. Something must have come up.

"I hate not being able to drive," she grumbled.

"Austin's taxi at your service."

"If you drop me at church, I can get a ride home."

"I thought I might stick around. Will says you work with the kids."

"I work with Trey and Bella's age group."

"Bet they love having Aunt Cathy around."

"Probably not as much as I love being with them."

"Don't fool yourself. Will says you're great with kids. You always were. See you around six-thirty."

After hanging up the phone, Cathy stared at the silent television and wondered what Will and Austin were up to. Since when did her brother feel the need to fill his best friend in on her activities? And what was up with the compliments? She definitely would keep an eye on them.

Austin replaced the receiver and grinned broadly. "Thanks,

Buddy," he said out loud. When Will requested the favor, he'd jumped at the opportunity to spend more time with Cathy.

He'd always liked Will's sister, but back in high school, he hadn't wanted to rock the boat. Now he didn't care. He wanted to get to know Cathy. In fact, he planned to invite her to dinner Friday night.

Years before, when Will told him about Cathy's crush, he hadn't known what to do. Maybe his mistake had been to do nothing. At the time, he'd recognized neither of them was ready for a relationship. Intent on having fun and enjoying his youth, Austin couldn't be the person Cathy needed. They wouldn't have lasted back then.

Now, he knew what he wanted out of life, and they stood a better chance. At least, he hoped so. He wanted to become significant in Cathy's life. She was becoming pretty significant in his.

Austin arrived right on time, so they parked at the church with minutes to spare.

"The children's program meets in the activity center." Cathy indicated the rear building. "You can attend service in the sanctuary if you'd rather."

"I'm not much of a teacher, but I can be your legs."

She opened the car door and pushed her way out. "I think there's a conspiracy to keep me seated."

Austin grinned broadly. "Ah, you've found us out. We'll have to tie you to the chair now."

"No, not at all," she countered. "I'll be glad to accept your legs, all of you, in fact."

Austin stopped and looked her in the eye for a long second before throwing his arms wide. "I'm yours for the taking. Lead the way, Miss Cathy."

His humor relieved her embarrassment, but his presence inspired curiosity not only with the kids, but with the other helpers as well.

"How did you get Austin to help in children's church?" Merry asked when she brought in the kids.

Cathy glanced over to where he helped to gather items for the craft project. "You wouldn't believe me if I told you."

"Try me."

"Austin said Will told him I needed a ride to church. And then he volunteered to stick around and help me."

Merry looked surprised. "Interesting."

"Don't you start."

"Start what?" she asked a bit too innocently.

"You know perfectly well what I'm talking about, Meredith Burris."

Her sister-in-law grinned. "I think Austin's sweet."

"He is," Cathy agreed, glancing his way again.

"Oh, are we experiencing some unresolved emotions?"

"Advice-giving is *my* job," Cathy countered. "And I'm advising me to run the other way."

"Good thing you've got a bum leg," Merry teased. "You'll run slow enough to get caught, if that's what you want."

"Go away, Merry."

"Bye, Cathy." She waved at Austin as she headed out the door.

Already Trey and Bella had found their way to Austin's side and laughed at his funny faces. Cathy felt a bit envious. He'd been in their lives for such a short time and captured their attention with hardly any effort.

Other kids joined the circle, and Cathy acknowledged

Austin was good with kids. Too bad he didn't have a couple of his own.

One of the other workers called the group to order and began a lesson on Noah's Ark. After coloring a lesson sheet and playing a couple of games, they served the snack.

"That was fun," Austin said, tossing the last paper cup into the garbage can after the kids left.

Cathy continued stacking the pictures they'd colored. She'd hang them around the room before next week's session. "It really is. They're pretty receptive at this age."

"I like the innocent way they speak of Jesus' love. That little guy who tried to teach everyone to sing 'Jesus Loves Me' brought tears to my eyes."

She nodded. "Jake is a real character."

Austin reached for his jacket. "You ready to head for home?"

Grabbing her purse, she began the slow trek to the car. His older model compact had been a bit of a surprise. She expected Austin to drive a status car like Will's. So far, he'd done everything completely opposite of what she expected. Perhaps she needed to take a closer look at her expectations. Lately, she had the feeling she'd prejudged him.

Once they settled in the car, Austin turned to her. "You go in for surgery next week?"

She nodded. "I told everyone that I'll be out for a while."

"Maybe we can get a wheelchair so you can come."

"The doctor mentioned a walker, but these kids are pretty active. I'd be terrified."

"True. You'll do well to take it as it comes. No sense worrying about what you can and can't do. It's good that you don't have to worry about the job."

"My editor didn't seem bothered about my injuries. Won't

be long before the magazine with my first column comes out."

"I'm glad." He smiled and reached to squeeze her hand.

Cathy wondered at the feeling of pleasure that rushed through her at his response.

"I wouldn't worry about the column. You'll do fine." They drove along in silence for a few minutes. "Do you have plans for Friday night?"

Startled, she glanced at him. "No."

"Would you like to go out to dinner?"

"You mean as friends?"

Austin hit the signal light and quickly changed lanes. "No, I mean as a date."

Chapter 7

What on earth prompted me to say yes to a date with Austin Collins? Cathy asked herself as she sorted through her closet, searching for something to wear. Settling for a sleeveless summer dress, she slipped her other foot into a sandal. At least the dress hid most of the boot. Austin's insistence that they celebrate her first column touched a spot deep inside Cathy's heart. His heartfelt good wishes pleased her a great deal.

All the old feelings had rushed back at her with his request for a date. She felt sixteen again, and the idea scared her. It took years to get Austin Collins out of her head, but now he had returned with a vengeance. She sat on the edge of the bed and bowed her head.

Please, God, help me behave normally with Austin tonight. Help me put aside my judging of him and see him as he is, not as I want him to be. Amen.

The brief prayer offered some respite to her nervousness, and Cathy reached for the ringing phone.

"Hi, Cathy, Shelby Tate here. How are you doing?"

She sat up a bit straighter, wondering why the editor was calling her so late on a Friday. "I'm fine. I go in for repair surgery next week."

"I'll keep you in my prayers. Sorry to call so late, but I've been busy all day. I wanted to touch base with you again and let you know how pleased we are with the column. You did a fantastic job. I received an E-mail from Mr. Maitland this afternoon, saying he thinks I've picked a winner."

Cathy's heart swelled with joy. "Thank you, Lord," she whispered. Seeing the column in print had been the highlight of her week—*well, next to having Austin ask me out on a date.*

"I'm so glad," she said. "Choosing the letters wasn't difficult."

Cathy reached for the magazine and studied the column. "New Man" had been quite a challenge. While she advised the young woman not to change for a man, he claimed to have changed for a woman.

New Man,

Are you sure this woman wants you to change? I feel the first mistake couples make is trying to change one another. There's a reason for your attraction. Celebrate the differences and learn to love each other for the people you are—not for the people you might one day become.

Heart

"You did an excellent job. I think you're a natural in advice giving. We like the theme idea too. Having the reader letters connect like that gave different viewpoints to be considered."

"I don't know about being a natural. Sometimes I give more advice than most people want."

Shelby's laughter reached through the phone.

The doorbell rang and Cathy laid the magazine aside. Hopefully her dad would answer the door. She could hardly hang up on Shelby Tate.

"I won't keep you. I just wanted to thank you for a job well done and let you know I'm looking forward to your next column."

"I have been meaning to contact you about my surgery. I don't feel it's going to affect the column in any way, but you never know."

"Keep us informed. If you require assistance, we'll be glad to step in. Otherwise, we'll look forward to reading more of your delightful advice in the very near future. I can't wait to see the reader response. I think it's going to be really good."

"I hope so."

"Cathy," her dad shouted up the stairs. "Austin's here."

Placing her hand over the receiver, she called, "I'll be right down. Sorry," she murmured. "That's my dad letting me know my date is waiting downstairs."

"Date?" Shelby repeated. "Don't go falling in love on us. We just found you. We wouldn't want to lose you."

She didn't tell the woman she'd loved Austin Collins since she was sixteen. "I don't think it'll be a problem."

"Have fun. Talk with you soon."

"Bye." Cathy replaced the receiver and picked up a light jacket and her purse. She took the steps one at a time, feeling closer to eighty than forty.

Austin smiled up at her from the bottom of the stairs. "I thought we might go to one of those restaurants in the commons area near the Potomac River."

"Sounds nice."

Cathy kissed her father's cheek. Austin held the door for her, and when she started to open the car door, he called, "Let me."

She stepped back and waited, finding she felt a little strange at his gentlemanly gesture. In the past, she jumped into the car before Will and Austin drove off and left her standing there. In a way, she still expected Austin to pull such a stunt.

He'd chosen a busy restaurant, but they were soon seated and perusing menus as they waited for iced tea.

"Do you like calamari?"

"It's okay."

Austin glanced up from his menu. "I usually order it when I come here. Would you like something else?"

"No, that's fine," Cathy said quickly.

After the waitress left with their order, Austin lifted his glass toward her. "Congratulations on your first column. I got my magazine today."

She was shocked. "You subscribed?"

He grinned. "Of course I did. I couldn't wait to read the advice you offer. You did a great job."

Cathy flushed with pleasure. Hearing anyone say she'd done well would be a plus, but Austin's compliments went straight to her head. "I worried that I'd made the wrong choices."

"Not at all," Austin said. "I'm in total agreement with what you said. I have changed too. I'm not the jock you remember."

Doubt surged deep inside her. "Have you really?"

Austin's forehead wrinkled. "What do you mean?"

"Well in high school, you and Will never had much of a social conscience."

He appeared disturbed by her comment. "Is that the way you saw me?"

"Can you deny you enjoyed being a star athlete and the benefits that came with the role?"

Austin lifted his shoulders in a shrug. "Oh, come on, Cathy, I was a teenager. The most important person in my world was me. What makes that so wrong?"

Was she jealous of his popularity? No, she'd never wanted

to be popular. She'd only wanted Austin to acknowledge her existence—something he'd never done.

"Absolutely nothing," she admitted. "You have changed. The Austin I knew never would have spent time helping underprivileged people."

The waitress returned with their appetizer and plates, and they sat nibbling the fried squid.

"Tell me about your career," he said, obviously intent on taking the conversation into a different direction.

"Nothing much to tell. I joined the air force, saw the world, and now I've come home."

"How much of the world? Did you regret retiring?"

Regret wasn't the emotion she'd experienced. She'd been more than ready to move on to a new phase in her life. Coming home to be with Pop and spend time with Will and his family had been a great motivator.

"Not at all," she said. "I missed a lot while I was away."

"So did I," Austin agreed, his gaze focused on her face. "Now tell me about your time in the air force. And not the condensed version."

Cathy spoke of her E-7 Master Sergeant rank, the jobs she'd done, the places she'd been, and the people she'd met along the way. Serving her country hadn't been a bad career choice. The air force offered a wealth of opportunities. "And the plus is, I'm still young enough to do other things," she pointed out.

"Rub it in, why don't you?" Austin teased. "I'll be an old man by retirement age, and you're still a beautiful young woman."

The boy she knew would have never made a statement like that. Maybe he had changed.

"I always was impatient to finish things far in advance of everyone else."

"I remember how you always rushed around everywhere you went," Austin said.

"And look where rushing got me this time."

"Are you nervous about your surgery?"

"Yes." Cathy had prayed about the apprehension she felt. "I know God will take care of me, but that doesn't mean I can put what's about to happen totally out of my head."

"Would you like for me to be there with you?"

Cathy felt truly taken aback. "No, but thanks. Pop and Will plan to be there. There's no reason for you to waste a day, sitting around the hospital. You already do enough of that, I'm sure."

"I don't mind. Really."

"I know you don't. And I appreciate the offer. Actually, I'm pretty sure I'll require assistance afterwards. I won't be able to drive for weeks, so I'll be looking for transportation to lots of places, including therapy."

"Just call on me. I'll come running."

Their entrees arrived, and they discussed the food and a variety of other topics. Once she settled down, Cathy felt comfortable with Austin and glad that he'd asked her out. She wouldn't mind trying the experience again now that she suspected that boy she kept looking for might have grown up.

Chapter 8

The nightmare surgery was over. Cathy grimaced as she thought about the experience. Lying on her stomach, she'd felt a burning sensation up the back of her leg and then drifted off. She'd awakened to the news that her tendon had been shredded and the surgeon had made the best repair possible, given the injury.

After she spent time in recovery, they wheeled her out to Will's car for the trip home. Getting into the house had been a challenge all of its own. Walking was excruciating, and Cathy dreaded the thought of returning to the doctor's office the next day.

They debated what to do for a couple of minutes before Will swung her into his arms and carried her up to her room. She didn't bother to change out of the clothing she'd worn home.

Will returned a few minutes later with her pain pills and water. "Take these and get some rest. I'll come back later to check on you."

"Thanks, Will."

"Any time, Pest."

She knew he meant the nickname in love, but it took her back many years to the time when he really meant the word.

Leaning back into the pillows, she tried to focus on anything but the pain in her leg. The ridiculousness of the accident taunted her, reminding Cathy of how one misstep had affected her life so totally. Finally, she fell asleep and the pain had lessened considerably by the time she awoke.

Her dad tapped on the door and entered, setting a tray with a sandwich and glass of iced tea on the table.

"Mail's here," he announced, pulling the bundle from underneath his arm. "Looks like you received another batch of letters."

Already? she thought, immediately realizing the turnaround time for a monthly magazine would come rather quickly.

Her father visited for a bit before telling her he was going down to the garage. "Merry brought this by this morning," he said, placing the baby monitor on the nightstand. "She thought I might not hear if you called for something."

Cathy grinned. Practical Merry. There was no doubt her dad would return to his woodworking and forget her existence. At least this way, she could call for help if she needed him.

She picked up the sandwich and took a bite, washing it down with a sip of tea. "I'll probably fall asleep again after I eat."

"Yell if you need anything. I've nearly finished that toy box I'm making for the kids."

Her father had crafted some beautiful furniture and other pieces since buying a garage full of woodworking equipment. Cathy was glad he'd found an outlet for his creativity.

After he left, she opened the envelope and dumped the letters out on the bed. It looked like the number had doubled since last month. She quickly read the get-well card from Shelby, who reiterated what she'd told her on the phone and said she looked forward to receiving the next column.

Cathy read a couple of the letters and found her eyes

growing heavier by the minute. She was nearly asleep when Will walked into the room with Austin on his heels.

"Hey, Cath, how's the leg?"

She jerked awake, pushed up on the pillows, and smiled at the guys. "Better. Hi, Austin. You guys playing hooky again?"

"Will is. I'm off until midnight tomorrow."

"Oh." She started shuffling the letters together.

"What's this?" Will asked, reaching for one that lay on the edge of the bed. "More letters? Hey, let us read some."

She snatched the envelope from his hand. "Get a subscription. These letters are confidential."

"Spoilsport."

Cathy shook her head in disbelief. "Why are you even interested? So you can make fun?"

"It must be hard being you."

"What do you mean by that?" she demanded.

"Figure it out for yourself."

Cathy sat up on the bed, her demeanor changing with the burst of anger her brother's comment generated. "I don't need to figure anything out, William Burris. I don't claim to be perfect. I respect these people's concerns. You can't begin to understand what it feels like to be them."

"Thank you, Dr. Burris, for that invective on my character. My life hasn't been as comfortable as you seem to think. I fight the same battles your letter writers fight. The difference is, I believe I deserve the good things in life. You're obviously back up to fighting standards. I'm going to visit with Pop."

Realizing she'd gone too far as he stomped out of the room, she called, "Will, I'm sorry."

He waved good-bye, not saying a word.

"I'm sorry you had to witness that, Austin."

"Will's jerking your chain, Cathy. If you handed him a bundle of the letters, he'd give them back in a heartbeat."

"I suppose you're right. Why does he do it?"

"Because you respond so beautifully?" Austin suggested, a teasing glint in his eyes.

"I just want him to know others aren't as blessed as we are. Every day, I pray I'm worthy of this task. I feel God sent this job my way, and I want to give it my best."

"You give good advice, Cathy. And you're right about the letters—they are confidential. Will might not see them as being the same as his client files, but they are."

Unconsciously, Cathy rested one hand on the packet. "It's so sad, Austin. I read these cries for help and wish I could make a difference. I try to answer every letter even though I don't choose it for the column. These people are real to me. I pray for them."

"You're a good person, Cathy Burris. Don't let anyone, including yourself, tell you any different."

"No, I'm not," she denied. "Look how I just attacked Will. I'm no saint. I just want to make a difference in this world."

"Why?"

"Because it's what God expects of me. I'm here as His disciple, showing His light to others. At times I'm a pretty dim bulb."

"I wouldn't say that. You know. . . Well, I never really went to church much," Austin said. "I don't know what it means to be a Christian."

"It's as simple as believing, Austin. Believing with all your heart and soul that Jesus Christ died on the cross to save you of your sins."

"I believe that."

"Have you ever offered up the sinner's prayer?" When he shook his head, she said, "All you have to do is tell the Lord you're sorry for all your wrongdoings and promise to serve Him in the future. You told me you'd changed. Becoming a Christian means you make another change—a major one. You put aside your past life and live to glorify the Lord. There's no going back—only forward. It's as easy as that."

"Sounds complicated. What if I'm not ready to let go of the past?"

"You're not ready to become a Christian."

"What if I'm never ready?"

"I don't think that's a possibility."

"Why not?"

"You appreciate the children's innocent way of loving God. I know in my heart God has a plan for you."

"Hey, Aus," Will shouted up the stairs. "You about ready to roll? Those greens are calling my name."

He grinned at Cathy. "Guess I'll show him who's the better golfer. Is there anything I can do for you?"

"Tell Will I'm sorry about what I said. I didn't mean to sound sanctimonious."

"He knows. Do you need a ride to the doctor's appointment tomorrow?"

Cathy shrugged. "Now that I've run Will off, I don't know."

"What time should I be here?"

"You don't want to spend your day off sitting around a doctor's office."

Austin frowned. "It was a sincere offer, Cathy—one that doesn't have anything to do with how I'd rather spend my day. It has to do with helping you."

"And I'm a needy person. My appointment is at 9:00 A.M."

"I'll be here at eight." He leaned to place a kiss on her forehead. "Take care."

"You too, Austin."

He stopped at the door long enough to glance back and wink at her. "See you tomorrow."

After he left, Cathy lay thinking about what Austin had said. What if he never became a Christian? For the first time, she understood why God had never answered her prayers for Austin to love her. It would never work.

Chapter 9

Cathy turned on the computer and read her E-mail, noting the reminder that Wednesday was Will's birthday. It had been a month since Austin took her to the doctor's office for her cast. It seemed impossible that time could have passed so quickly and miserably.

Without question, a cast was the most sadistic thing ever invented. Glancing down at her third cast, this one done in glorious purple, Cathy considered the down sides. It was difficult to maneuver, she couldn't get her foot to sit right on the heel, and the thing was a plaster prison for her swollen leg. It wasn't like the doctor hadn't tried to remedy the situation.

She'd spent the four weeks doing little of her usual activities. Unable to drive, Cathy hadn't seen Trey and Bella other than the times their parents or Melanie brought them over. Her dad tried to entertain her but generally gravitated to his workshop the moment he ran out of stuff to talk about. She could sleep only so much and watch television even less. Therapy looked good to her. Just getting away from the house on a regular basis would be great.

At least the column hadn't been a problem, and Shelby Tate had e-mailed her to say what wonderful feedback they were getting. Cathy praised God. Knowing people benefited from the advice she'd offered felt so wonderful.

A second letter arrived from New Man in D.C. She'd answered his letter in her first column, and a glow of pride filled her at the thought of him writing again the following month. Just as quickly, it dissipated as Cathy reminded herself the success was not of herself, but of God.

Dear Miss Lonely Heart,

This woman, who recently returned to my life, is beautiful through and through, but she has a blind spot where I'm concerned. She pretends I'm only a friend. How can I make her see me for a man who loves her?

New Man

What could she say to him? She knew she couldn't run his letter in the column again. It wasn't fair to the others, but that didn't mean she couldn't respond with more than a form letter. She wrote,

Dear New Man,

My first suggestion is for you to pray about the situation. So often, we let our hearts guide us into thinking this is what God wants for us. If it is, you can rest assured He will open this woman's eyes to your feelings for her. If she's the one He intends for you, you'll be together.

Heart

The newest batch of letters had arrived the day before, and she'd been surprised to find yet another letter from him.

Dear Heart,

Thanks so much for responding to my letters. I've never been much of a churchgoer—just Easter and Christmas. And I've never prayed to God to help choose my mate.

Distracted, Cathy glanced out the window at the bird that sang from the branches of her tree as she enjoyed the crisp autumn air. *Why was he writing to a Christian magazine?* she wondered, her eyes returning to the letter.

You've made me think it's time I address this issue in my life. The woman I care for is a Christian—a dedicated one.

A true light, Cathy thought as she noted the way he'd double-underlined the words "a dedicated one."

She's the perfect disciple. She cares about people, and everyone who enters her life knows it. Family, friends, even strangers benefit from her caring. Please share with me the steps to ask Christ into my life.

Picking up her pen, Cathy jotted her response.

Dear New Man,

Don't idolize this woman. She certainly sounds admirable, but she's only human. Setting her up to be some superwoman will only make you unhappy when she falls from the pedestal.

To paraphrase Acts 16:31, "Believe on the Lord Jesus Christ, and thou shalt be saved." Asking Christ into your life is as simple as saying the words. Repent. Ask His forgiveness and move away from your past to a future with Him in control. Study your Bible. Join a church where your new family will help you grow. And when times get hard, remember you've got the Best Friend on your side. Christ is always there, loving you every step of the way.

Heart

As she closed the letter, Cathy had a good feeling. She concluded by offering a prayer for this new soldier in God's army.

After submitting the column and answering the letters, Cathy had nothing else to do—at least nothing that appealed to her. She was almost desperate enough to go downstairs and watch her father do his woodwork. What a way to spend a Saturday night.

The phone rang and she grabbed it. "Hello."

"Hi, Cath. How's the patient?"

"Impatient." Austin's laughter sounded wonderful to her.

"Sounds like you need to get out of the house. How about I take you to church in the morning?"

"You don't really want to go to church."

"Are we back to that?"

Cathy didn't argue the point. She would go anywhere with him. The advice from that very first column haunted her. Even though she'd advised others not to change, she knew she couldn't have Austin in her life until he did.

But that knowledge didn't stop her heart from racing every time he came over to check on her, her thoughts from centering on him, or the hopes that one day the dream might be fulfilled.

"Okay. Which service?"

"What if we go to the early service, then plan something afterwards?"

"What did you have in mind?"

"Lunch. I'll show you this little place I've fallen in love with."

"Where is it?"

"I'm not telling."

"Okay." Even as she agreed, Cathy knew she shouldn't put herself in temptation's way. She couldn't spend time with Austin and not grow to love him even more.

What would you have me do, Lord? He's a good friend and I don't want to hurt him, but I can't help my feelings for him, either. Is he my intended? Will You make things right for us?

"Cathy? You still there?"

His voice brought her back. "Yes. So tell me, what's the plan?"

"Whatever you feel like doing. You up to running around the Mall?"

She'd jogged the area in front of the Capitol many times in the past. "Only if you carry me."

"Ouch."

"I'm light as a feather," she protested.

"Yeah, right."

They chatted a bit longer before hanging up.

As she dressed for church the next morning, Cathy couldn't help but hope Austin accompanying her to church was a good thing. Even if they remained nothing more than friends forever, she wanted him to know God's loving grace. Maybe he only attended church today for her, but she knew God had a way of working on folks when He got them inside His doors. She finished up and went downstairs.

Austin eyed her in the dressy suit. "You've come a long way from that little girl who used to trail after us."

"Hopefully there's some improvement?"

"Not really. You're all grown up, but you're as cute as ever."

"And you're looking particularly grown up yourself."

"Touché," he said, grinning at her pointed remark. "Did your dad want to ride with us?"

"He went earlier. The deacons have a breakfast meeting once a month to pray for the community."

Cathy enjoys church, Austin thought, glancing her way when they began to sing.

Several people stopped by to say hello and how glad they were to see her. Some even offered to help out in any way they could. Austin was struck by the caring—these people really were like an extended family.

They settled in the pew as the offering plates were passed, then the pastor stepped into the pulpit. For the first minute or so, Austin focused on the man himself, then the words he spoke.

Cathy opened her Bible to what the pastor called the Beatitudes, and Austin leaned over to read them along with her. The pastor spoke of how each one affected the person living a Christian life. Austin could only agree with what he heard.

All his life, he'd aimed for the top, but there was always something missing. No goal, however great the achievement, helped ease the lack of joy in his life.

"Is something wrong?"

He looked at Cathy, seeing his behavior puzzled her. He shook his head and smiled, taking her hand in his. "No. Everything is very right. I'm glad I came."

After church, the pastor invited Austin to return. Austin knew he would.

"So where are you taking me?" she demanded as they exited the church.

"Patience, Cath."

She sighed heavily. "Oh, okay."

"You sound like Bella."

She stuck her tongue out at him, and he grinned. "Now you look like her."

"She's a cute kid."

"And you're a beautiful woman," he said, grasping her hand tighter as they walked toward the car.

When he drove into the residential area, Austin wondered if she was curious about where they were headed. She seemed surprised when he turned into the driveway.

"Who lives here?"

"Come see."

Austin opened her door and helped her up the walkway and onto the porch. He unlocked the front door and stood back for her to enter.

"Evidently the owner is a minimalist."

He agreed. Except for a couple of chairs and a sofa, the room was empty. "He's looking for a decorator. Let me show you around."

"Should we be wandering through someone's home?"

He looked her in the eye and said, "It's my house, Cathy. I moved in last week."

"Has Will seen it yet?"

"You're my first guest."

Cathy couldn't believe she was Austin's first guest. Perhaps he thought Will wouldn't appreciate it as much as she would. His actions only made her wonder what Austin planned. Buying a house was an indicator of permanency. Did he plan to stay in Washington?

"It's wonderful. Perhaps one day, I can get a place of my own."

"Your dad's place is nice."

"But it's Pop's. I'm still sleeping in that pink bedroom I wanted when I was thirteen. I'm so sick of it. Just as soon as I'm able, I'm repainting."

"What color?"

"A warm beige."

"No more pink?"

Cathy grimaced and shook her head. "Twenty-five years is more than long enough."

"Come look at the backyard. It's my favorite place."

They moved onto the spacious deck area with the in-ground pool.

"I figure having the pool will save me a fortune in spa membership fees."

"It's wonderful, Austin," Cathy repeated, finding each spot extremely appealing. "I'm impressed."

"It's a good investment. I'm tired of apartments. You would not believe the plans I have for this place, and it'll make a good family home."

What family? Cathy felt a twinge of regret. At thirty-eight, she'd allowed love, marriage, and a family to pass her by. To hear Austin anticipating those things made her wish she could push back the years.

"I thought we'd eat in the sunroom."

"Sounds wonderful. Can I freshen up first?"

"First door on the left. Meet me in the sunroom."

Cathy found the glass room overlooking the decks and backyard without difficulty. Yet another surprise awaited her as she viewed the table. The settings included matched dinnerware, flatware, crystal glasses, and linen napkins. An arrangement of fall flowers sat in the center. He hadn't forgotten a thing.

"You set an impressive table, Mister."

Austin dipped his head slightly and said thank you. "It's my mom's stuff."

It warmed her heart to know he used the things he'd inherited from his parents. He seated her and brought in their first course. She was also pleasantly surprised to learn Austin had prepared the meal. "My compliments to the chef," she said, laying her napkin on the table after finishing her chicken parmigiana. "That was delicious."

He moved to pull her chair back from the table. "Let's move to the deck. It's not too cold right now."

They spent a nice afternoon talking. Austin surprised her when he brought up the sermon.

"It was a good message."

"You're a positive influence in my life. You even made going to church a fulfilling experience."

"Not me," she denied quickly. "God. Serving the Lord is the most fulfilling experience of my life. Knowing He loves me despite myself gives me joy beyond compare."

"I want that joy, Cathy."

"Oh, Austin, it's yours for the taking," she said, thrilled by his words. "All you have to do is ask. You sound like you're close to making a decision."

"The decision's made. All that's left is the carry-through."

"Why not this morning in church when the pastor issued the invitation?"

He shrugged. "I wanted to."

Cathy understood. Fear often held new converts in the pews. What they failed to realize was, the same Christians they feared were eager to welcome them into God's family.

"That first move is the hardest," she pointed out. "Once

you step out on faith, you'll find it gets easier."

"I'm praying. Hoping to be ready to serve the Lord. To one day be the witness for Him you are."

His words reminded Cathy of "New Man," who felt the woman he loved was a perfect witness. "Don't fool yourself, Austin. I try, but I've got a long way to go before I get there. There's this guy who writes the column who feels the woman he loves is a perfect witness. I warned him not to put her on a pedestal."

Austin seemed to pale at her words. "Cathy, there's something I need to tell you. I never meant. . . I just wanted to communicate my feelings. . . ."

"What are you trying to say?"

"I've been writing letters to the column."

"What?" she demanded. She remembered how supportive he'd been. "Why, Austin," she repeated. "Did Will put you up to it?"

"Because I'm in love with you. I didn't know how to tell you, so I asked your advice."

"You're 'New Man in D.C.,' aren't you?" Even before she asked the question and watched his head nod, Cathy knew the answer. There had been a connection—some reason she felt she had to answer his letters. And now she knew why. "I'd like to go home."

"Cathy, please. I didn't mean to hurt you."

"All my life, I've tolerated you and Will teasing me. At least Will mocked me to my face. You had to sneak around and do it undercover. Did the two of you get a big laugh from my responses?"

"No one has ever read them but me. They're in my bedroom. In my nightstand."

He seemed sincere, but who knew? He had broken her heart before. Why had she given him another opportunity to do the same? Cathy found her purse and pulled out her cell phone.

"What are you doing?"

"Calling a cab."

"You don't have to do that. I'll take you home."

Cathy waited by the car while Austin locked up the house. No words passed as they traveled to her house. She refused to look at him. Once he parked, she threw open the door and started to get out.

"I love you, Cathy."

Those were the words she'd waited to hear for what seemed an entire lifetime. "You have a strange way of showing it."

"That's the problem. I didn't know how."

"I've known you too long to believe that. Will always envied you your glib tongue. He said you could sell ice cubes to Eskimos."

"This was different."

"I don't think so. You're an eloquent man, quite capable of relaying what needs to be said. There had to be another reason."

"You weren't like the others. You were my best friend's sister."

"Go home, Austin."

Chapter 10

Three days passed and Austin made no effort to contact her. He probably figured she needed to cool off first. And if that was the case, he'd be right. Cathy felt so confused. Why had he written the letters? If he had something to say, why couldn't he just say it without trickery?

The idea that Austin allowed them to waste years of love because he felt at a loss for words didn't set well with her.

Cathy opened the file containing the copies of New Man's letters. She had no idea why she'd kept copies of them. She hadn't made copies of any of the others—just his.

The phone rang and she picked it up.

"Hi. How are you feeling?" her sister-in-law inquired.

Part of her was disappointed to find Merry on the other end. "Don't ask."

"That bad?"

"Bored out of my skull. I start therapy next week."

"That's good. When do they remove the cast?"

"Friday. I'll probably have to go back to the boot."

"Hang in there. Hopefully, you'll be back to normal before long."

"Hopefully."

Merry hesitated for a couple of seconds before she said, "Austin came over last night. He told us what he did."

"I bet Will got a big laugh over that."

"He told Austin he couldn't believe he was that lovesick. I think it's romantic."

"You don't know how they were, Merry. The two of them tormented me mercilessly."

"Years ago," her sister-in-law reminded. "Will isn't involved, Cathy."

"How can you be sure?"

"I made him promise not to tease you about your job. I saw how hurt you were the night of the dinner party, and then he told me how upset you became when he asked to read some of the letters. I told him I didn't blame you and it's time he acts like an adult."

"Oh, Merry. I'm sorry. I didn't mean to cause trouble between you and Will."

"You haven't. I love my husband, but that doesn't mean I'm blind to his shortcomings. Will could be more sensitive."

"I suppose we all could."

"What are you going to do about Austin?"

"I don't know. He finally said the words I waited forever to hear, but now I don't know what to do."

"He loves you. What are you afraid of?"

It was the same question she had asked herself over and over. "That he'll realize I'm still Will's little sister."

"You haven't forgiven him for the past?"

"I can't believe he's in love with me now. All those years ago, I would have welcomed his love. Now I'm not sure what to do."

"I wouldn't have minded Will writing a few secret love notes to me."

"I'll tell him."

Merry chuckled. "Don't you dare. You know Will—he wouldn't stop with letters."

"Austin says he loves me, but why did he write the letters? It doesn't make sense. He's never lacked self-confidence for anything he set his mind to do."

"Hasn't he? I suspect he's feeling insecure about you and how you feel about him."

"I've tried to tell myself I don't love him, but no other man ever measured up to my expectations because of him."

"Then I'd say he's the one God has in mind for you. I've got to get to court. Take care, Cath. I'm praying for you."

"Thanks, Merry."

She replaced the phone and went into the kitchen. After pouring herself a glass of soda, Cathy sat at the table, debating the pros and cons of a relationship with Austin.

Deep down inside, his declaration of love thrilled her. She wanted him to love her. That desire hadn't changed over the years. She couldn't fool herself into believing Mr. Right had never come along because it wasn't time. She knew the real reason was that, in her heart, she knew her Mr. Right was Austin Collins.

The morning dragged on. Finally out of desperation, she picked up the phone.

"Hi, Melanie. Would you and the kids like to play tourist this afternoon? I'm going stir crazy. I thought maybe the Smithsonian."

"Bella loves the bug collection."

"Yuck."

Melanie laughed. "That girl will probably become a scientist. Want me to pack some snacks?"

"Let's splurge. I got my check from the magazine today. I can afford hot dogs and sodas."

"That could be pretty expensive."

"Then I'll dip into my government pension," Cathy teased.

"Is your dad coming?"

"Just us. He's out in the garage, working with his wood."

"Sounds good to me. I'll get the kids ready." Though Will and Merry provided Melanie with a car, parking would be bothersome. Melanie suggested the metro.

"Why don't you call a cab and come by to pick me up? I'll pay for the cab."

"See you soon."

Cathy went upstairs to gather her things. The phone rang again. Thinking it might be Melanie, she picked it up.

"I thought I'd call and see how you are."

"I'm still upset."

"Don't be like this, Cathy. You know I only did it because I care about you."

"Good-bye, Austin. Melanie and the kids are waiting on me."

"Cathy?"

Austin calling her name stayed with her as she replaced the receiver and went outside. She couldn't deal with him right now.

"I'm glad you thought of this," Melanie told her as they climbed into the cab.

"Me too."

They chatted, listening as the kids talked about what they would see at the Smithsonian. Wandering around inside, the two adults talked as the children ran from display to display. Cathy and Melanie followed at a slower pace.

"So how's life been treating you?" Cathy asked Melanie.

"Perhaps I should write you a letter." She glanced over to

make sure the kids were within eyesight.

"Tell me," Cathy invited.

"I talked to my mom just before we left. I miss her."

"So why not go home?"

"It's a long story, but let's just say some advice I gave my best friend resulted in her losing her boyfriend to another girl. I lost my friend."

"Did you? Or did you run away before you knew for sure?"

"I ran."

Cathy smiled grimly and admitted, "I did too."

Melanie looked surprised. "From whom?"

"Austin. I had a crush on him. Will told him how I felt, and he never said a word. I was so relieved when they went off to college, but then he kept coming to visit, so when I turned eighteen, I joined the air force. I thought I'd earn some tuition money, but before I realized it, the military turned into a career."

"Austin never said anything?"

Cathy shook her head. "I kept waiting for him to do something—laugh, make fun, but he didn't. He just kept on treating me like Will's little sister. I was devastated when he didn't acknowledge my feelings for him. Now, I find he's been writing letters to me asking for advice."

"He's been writing the column?"

Cathy nodded, grimacing at the thought.

"Oh, that's so romantic."

"You sound like Merry. Exactly what makes it romantic? I think it's devious and underhanded."

Melanie shrugged. "Most men don't care enough to ask a woman's opinion. Austin might have done it in secret, but he did ask you."

That much was true. He had asked her how to handle the

problems he felt separated them. "Oh, enough about me. Let's talk about your problem. Even if your friend never accepts your apology, why should you deprive yourself of your family and friends? Who knows? Maybe she wants to contact you but is too scared. Have you asked yourself what's the worst that can happen?"

"Only a million times a day. I know Jasmine met someone else. My family keeps me informed."

"Sounds like she moved on. Maybe it's a case of unanswered prayers. What if she'd married the guy and then lost him to another woman?"

"I never should have said anything."

"We all have regrets, Melanie—things we wish unsaid the moment they leave our lips. You can't unsay the words, but there's no reason you can't say you're sorry and move on too."

"I think maybe I'll call her the next time I'm home."

"Don't wait. Do it before you change your mind."

"I've been thinking about home a lot lately."

"I'm sure Merry and Will would hate to lose you, but they want you to be happy."

"I know."

Cathy could see Melanie was struggling with her decision. "If I were you, I'd give it to the Lord. Let Him make the decision."

"Good idea. You should do the same with Austin."

"Thanks for listening. I needed to talk to someone who isn't family. Merry thinks it's sweet and romantic. Will thinks it's hilarious that his old buddy wrote me love letters. I'm pretty angry at Austin."

"Well, he did use the column for the purpose intended," Melanie pointed out. "He wanted advice. I've been meaning to tell you I subscribed to *Agape Today* after you started doing the column. I like the magazine, and your advice is right on target. I'd love to try something like that, but then again, that's what got me into this situation in the first place."

"Thanks. This is just so un-Austin."

"Maybe he's changed."

"He's close to accepting Christ," Cathy said softly. She knew it was the reason he'd told her the truth in the first place. His conscience would no longer allow him to keep the secret.

"Aunt Cathy. Melanie. Come see," Bella yelled to them.

The two women moved to where the children examined one of the biggest cockroaches Cathy had ever seen.

Chapter 11

Cathy started her therapy, and the days turned into weeks. On Tuesdays and Thursdays, she did the activities the therapists showed her at the office, then did her "homework" the other days. Exercises that seemed simple when they demonstrated them seemed difficult when she was home trying to do them on her own. At least she wore the boot again. Getting rid of the cast was the one blessing in the entire situation.

Austin called a couple of times, but she refused to talk to him. She answered the door on Thursday to find him on the other side. "What are you doing here?"

He whipped a paint-spattered cap from his pocket and pulled it on. "I've come to paint your room."

"No way."

"Ah, don't be like this, Cathy. You wanted it repainted, and I'm willing to do it for you. Please let me."

"Why, Austin? Do you think this is going to make up for you making a fool of me?"

"I told you, no one knew about the letters but you and me. And they were legit. I really do want to know how to win your heart."

Cathy swallowed hard. Little did he know he'd had her heart for years.

"The room isn't ready to be painted."

"I'll take care of everything."

She shrugged. "Fine. It's your day off. If you want to waste it painting my bedroom, who am I to stop you?"

"Will you talk to me while I paint?"

"So that's your ruse. You think you can coerce me into listening to your explanation since you're doing me a favor."

"Actually I don't care if we don't talk about our argument. I'd like to tell you about turning my life over to Jesus last Sunday."

Tears of joy welled in Cathy's eyes. Some sort of leg spasms had kept her home from church that morning. Her mom had always told her she wouldn't feel any better at home than at church when she said she felt bad. Now she wished she'd listened to her mother's advice and gone.

"Oh, Austin, I'm so happy for you."

"You were right."

"About what?"

"It got easier when I stepped out into that aisle on faith. I'm going to attend a new Christian class for a while, then I'm going to be baptized. Will you be there for me?"

"You know I will." No matter how angry he made her, Cathy knew she couldn't miss this aspect of his life. Next to her own life-changing experience, seeing him baptized would be a highlight.

"I'm going to get my brushes and tarps from the car."

"I'll be upstairs."

Cathy began removing the pictures from the wall. She'd have to buy some real artwork to replace the unframed posters of her childhood. She tucked knickknacks she planned to keep into the dresser drawers with her clothing and started a throwaway and giveaway pile.

"If we move the furniture away from the walls, we can cover it with the tarps and we won't have to take it out of the room," Austin said.

"Sounds good to me."

"Where's your paint?"

"Down in the workshop. I'll get it."

"I'll go. You shouldn't be carrying paint cans."

"Pop will show you where it is."

After he returned, Austin found Cathy a chair and footstool and insisted she prop up her foot.

"How long did the doctor say you had to wear this boot?"

"He won't say. It all depends on how therapy goes. The therapist won't tell me anything, either."

Austin trimmed out the room and then assembled a strange-looking stick device and filled it with paint.

"Does that thing really work?"

"You bet. I can paint a room in a fraction of the time."

Cathy had to admit Austin made it look simple.

"I like the color," he said, standing back to view the completed wall.

"Me too. I was so sick of pink."

"You've spent more time in this room lately than usual."

"I'd have redecorated sooner if I'd known I was going to become a prisoner."

"How's the column going?"

Austin would bring that up. "Fine."

"Good. I'm looking forward to my next magazine. Even more, now that I know the Lord. I went back and read the others cover to cover."

"You didn't read them before?"

"Just your column."

"Looking for advice?"

"Yes."

Cathy stared at him. "Austin, why did you write those letters? Was it a joke?"

"No," he said firmly. "I didn't know how to tell you what I felt. I think I've loved you for a very long time."

She stared into his eyes. He was telling the truth. "Probably not as long as I've loved you."

"I cared about you even then. I wanted to ask you out, but you were Will's sister. He made it perfectly clear to all the guys that you were off-limits. Threatened to bust our heads in if we so much as looked at you in that way."

A wry smile touched her lips. "No wonder I didn't date much in high school. Why didn't you ever say anything?"

"Because you never did. All I had to go on was hearsay from Will. You never brought it up, and I tried to be sensitive."

"You thought ignoring what Will told you was sensitive?"

He rested the roller on the paint can and came over to sit by her feet. "You were a first for me, Cathy. Other girls flirted, but at times, you acted like I was scum of the earth. And like I said, Will warned me off. It was okay for you to have a crush but not for me to reciprocate."

"This has nothing to do with Will."

"Yes, it did. He's my friend. You were his baby sister. He was responsible for protecting you."

"That's ridiculous."

"Not if you really think about it. Friendship has a code of its own. You don't steal your friend's girl and you don't play around with his sister."

"What makes you think I would have played around with you?" Cathy demanded.

"I knew you wouldn't. You were a good girl. And though it shames me to say it now, I wasn't into good girls then."

"I know. I saw how the girls ran after you jocks. You rarely turned one away. Until me."

"I did you a favor by not involving you in the life I lived then. I cared about you that much. When you turned eighteen, I came back to tell you and learned you'd joined the military. Then I figured that by the time I got out of college, you'd be home and we could work things out. You stayed away, and I never found anyone else like you."

"Oh, Austin, I'm so confused. I'm afraid it's all a joke—that you and Will plan to get together and laugh over these letters and what we've just talked about."

"We're adults now, Cathy. Will's not involved in the letters I wrote. He doesn't know what they said, and I don't plan to tell him. I love you."

And she loved him.

A horn blew. "That is Merry. She has come to take me to therapy."

He looked disappointed. "I'll continue painting, if it's okay?"

She nodded. "Thanks for this, Austin."

"Cathy?" he called as she started out the door. "Will you at least think about what I said?"

She knew she would think of little else. "Sure."

Chapter 12

Austin was gone when she returned home. Cathy knew she owed him a huge favor. It would have been weeks before she could have done it herself. Except for the new paint smell, her room would be a more pleasant place to spend time in.

The days passed with no further contact from him. Cathy continued praying over the situation, knowing the Lord would help her make the right decision.

A surprise batch of letters arrived early with a note saying there were so many, they decided to mail what they had already. Cathy welcomed the diversion. She read through the letters, praying as she read of troubled relationships and confused hearts.

> *I really care about my boyfriend, but lately this other guy has been talking to me, and I'm really attracted to him. The temptation to go out with him is very strong, but I don't want to give up my boyfriend. If I did this, I'd have to tell him and I know he'd break off the relationship. Should I give in to the temptation?*
>
> *Confused in Virginia*

Dear Confused,

Do you really love your boyfriend? If you do, you'd never hurt him. Matthew 26:41 advises us to watch and pray that we do not enter into temptation. The flesh is weak and attraction is fleeting. You can't fight this alone. You need God's guidance—not mine. In your heart, you know what's right and wrong, so you must decide which path you will take.

Heart

Cathy reread the response she wrote, asking herself the same question. Did she really love Austin? She knew the answer was unequivocally yes. Then why was she hurting him like this? She couldn't fight it alone, either.

"Dear Lord," she prayed, "I feel certain that You intend Austin Collins to be the man in my life, and I've committed a grievous wrong by treating him badly. Please help me put aside my anger and frustration, and please help him to forgive me for my behavior. Thank You for bringing him home to You, and give him the strength to withstand the battles he will come up against. Amen."

She smiled as she opened her eyes and started to reach for the next letter on the stack, stopping when Will walked into the room.

They visited for a few minutes before he shared the purpose for his visit. "Merry asked me to stop by and pick up something you were going to loan her."

"The old issues of the magazine. They are upstairs, in my room."

"Where? I'll get them."

Cathy shook her head. "You'd never find them. I will be right back."

Upstairs, she removed a few items from the top of her closet and pulled down the half dozen or so issues of *Agape Today* Merry had asked to borrow. Back downstairs, Will drummed his fingers on the end table, looking anywhere but at the letters she'd left there. Gut instinct told her that he was up to something. "You didn't mess with those, did you?"

He stood quickly and reached for the magazines. "Give me a break. I gotta run."

Cathy felt guilty. "Sorry. Give everyone a kiss for me."

"You bet. I'll let you get back to work." Will indicated the letters with a nod of his head. "You're really enjoying this, aren't you?"

"A lot. It's been exactly what I needed."

Will smiled. "I'm glad, Pest. I want you to be happy. What about you and Aus? Are you going to be able to work things out?"

"What did he say?" Cathy asked.

"That he'd loved you for years but never acted on his feelings because we were best friends. Guess my stupid teasing is the reason you two never got together."

Cathy shook her head regretfully. "No, Will. If Austin had known what he wanted, he wouldn't have let you or anyone else stand in the way."

Her brother gave her a one-armed hug. "It'll work out for the best. Always does."

After he left, Cathy devoted a few minutes to thinking about Austin telling Will he loved her. Obviously, he hoped to show her he wasn't afraid to share his feelings anymore.

She shrugged and turned her attention back to the letters. Cathy read a couple before she picked up the white business envelope. Strange. It was sealed and there was no postage. Surely someone hadn't dropped it off at the magazine office.

She reached for the letter opener and tugged out the sheet of paper from a legal pad.

Her heart began to pound as she realized the letter she held was from "New Man in D.C." Austin had written her again.

Dear Miss Lonely Heart,

That's what you are and what you'll always be—my heart. When I started writing these letters, I had one hope: that you would show me the way to your affection. Cathy, I've always cared for you. All those years we spent apart, I hoped you were happy. I wasn't a believer, but I did ask God to keep you safe.

When you came back into my life, I realized you'd never forgiven the brash young man who dared not acknowledge his feelings for you. You're a special part of my life, and I love you dearly. If you can't see your way to becoming my wife, I pray you'll keep the friendship we've shared over the years. I don't want to lose you. I'm sorry if you believe these letters were written in jest. That was never my intent.

Love always,
Austin

His wife? Those words jumped out at her. Austin wanted to marry her?

She refused to wait another moment to speak to him. Reaching for the phone, she dialed the hospital emergency room. "This is Cathy Burris. It's urgent that I talk to Austin Collins immediately. I'm a patient of his." Well, she had been.

"He's with a patient. If you'll give me a number, I'll see that he calls you as soon as he's free."

Cathy recited the phone number and thanked the woman before hanging up. On pins and needles, she prepared to wait for Austin's call. The phone rang a few minutes later. She grabbed it. "Austin?"

"Cathy, what's wrong?"

"Nothing. Everything's perfectly right. I needed to tell you yes. I'll marry you whenever you want."

"You got my letter?"

"Yes. I love you, Austin. I always have. No one ever measured up to you for me, either. Now I know God kept us single for each other."

"I feel that way too. I'll be over as soon as I get off work tonight. I have something I want to give you, and I'd like to set the date as soon as possible. I think we've waited long enough."

"I agree." She heard them paging him in the background.

"I've got to get back to work. I love you, Cathy."

"I love you too."

Epilogue

As it had done for the past several days, the pear-shaped diamond demanded her admiration. Cathy held out her hand, watching it sparkle in the light as she waited for the phone call to connect. "Hi, Shelby. It's Cathy."

The editor returned the greeting. "I just read through the column. It's great."

"Thanks. Um, Shelby, when you hired me, you mentioned that the columnist had to be single. Does that still apply?"

"I'm afraid so. It's one of Oz's, er, I mean Mr. Maitland's stipulations that a single person advise single people."

"I see. I need to let you know I'm getting married."

"Not soon, I hope."

Cathy heard the dismay in the woman's tone. "Austin and I have decided not to wait. We're getting married the Sunday before Christmas."

Shelby's audible groan spoke of her disappointment. "I'm truly happy for you, Cathy."

"Thanks. I know it puts you in a bad situation, but I do have a suggestion for my replacement, if you're interested."

"By all means."

She sounded almost excited by the prospect. "My brother's

nanny is going back home to St. Louis, but if you can work long distance, she'd be great. Her name's Melanie Taylor. She's young and single and gives good advice."

"I don't know. Let me think about it. Oh, why not. Sure. I'll be glad to interview her for the position."

Cathy hoped Melanie would be interested. "I'll give Melanie your number. I think you'll be impressed."

"Thanks, Cathy. Where did you meet your future husband?"

"I've known Austin all my life. He's my brother's best friend. I used to tag after them demanding that they wait for me."

"And he did."

"God kept us both waiting for years. There have been some ups and downs, but I'm confident this is what God intends for us."

"I'm going to hate to see you go. You've been a wonderful columnist. Are you having a large wedding?"

"Small, informal wedding at our church. Austin is being baptized that morning."

"How wonderful. Congratulations, Cathy."

"Thanks, Shelby. I hope you can attend. I'll send you an invitation."

"I'd love to."

"And I hope Melanie works out for you."

"If she's anything like you, I'm sure she will."

Cathy said good-bye and replaced the receiver. It saddened her a bit to leave the job she'd enjoyed, but God had a bigger, better plan in mind for her—one that included Austin Collins—and Cathy wasn't about to be sad about that.

TERRY FOWLER

Terry makes her home in North Carolina, where she works for the city of Wilmington. The second oldest of five children, she shares a home with her best friend, who is also her sister. Besides writing, her interests include serving her small church in various ways, home decorating, gardening, and tracing her family roots using the Internet. She is the author of two **Heartsong Presents** inspirational romances. Terry invites you to visit her website at http://members.aol.com/terrysfowler.

Mission: Marriage

by Aisha Ford

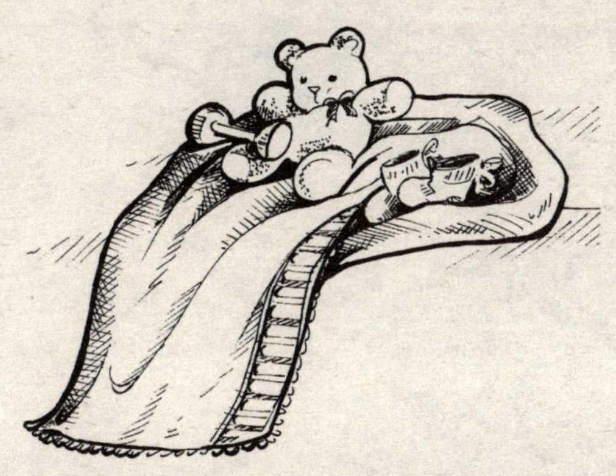

Chapter 1

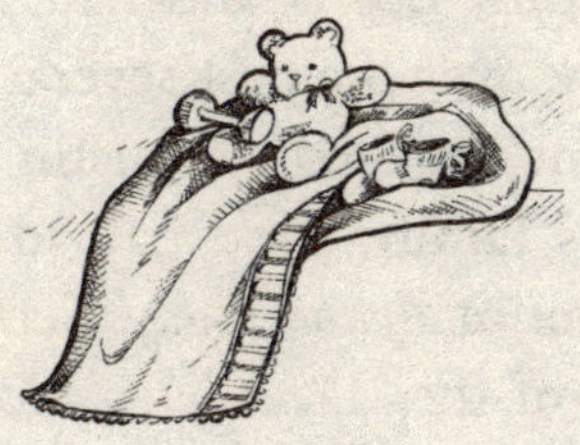

Beep. . .beep. . .beep. Click. The transmission ended. Then came the steady *whirr* of the printer doing its job. Melanie watched the paper emerge from the fax machine with the expectation of a child waiting for Christmas. As soon as the last page inched through the feeder, Melanie pulled them from the tray. Flipping past the cover sheet, she perused the letters. *Dear Miss Lonely Heart,* they began.

Melanie Taylor rubbed the side of her neck, kneading the muscles to relieve the tension she was starting to feel. In actuality, she was supposed to be getting ready for the Wednesday evening service at church, but she preferred to think about something else for the moment. These letters were a nice distraction. This new job opportunity had practically landed in her lap, and she wanted to do it right.

As the new provisional columnist for the "Dear Miss Lonely Heart" advice column for *Agape Today* magazine, she wanted to make a good impression on her editor, Shelby Tate. She could do so by responding well with the three letters she'd been faxed as a trial run at having the columnist position.

As it was, Melanie had gotten the job almost by chance, after moving from Washington, D.C., back to her hometown in St. Louis, Missouri, just over a month ago. The previous columnist, Cathy Burris, was a casual friend of Melanie's.

For the past two years, while finishing her degree at the University of D.C., Melanie had worked as a part-time nanny for Will and Meredith Burris and had gotten to know Mr. Burris's sister, Cathy, over the past several months.

When Cathy got engaged to Austin Collins, a longtime friend of the Burris family, she'd had to quit her job at the magazine. The owner of *Agape Today,* Sebastian Maitland, required the position of the "Dear Miss Lonely Heart" columnist to be filled by a single person.

Cathy's resignation left the magazine in a pinch, since the previous columnist had quit nearly seven months earlier for the same reason. Hoping to be of assistance, Cathy suggested Melanie for the job.

Although Melanie already left D.C. to return home, after a brief telephone interview, Ms. Tate agreed to give Melanie a chance at the job. She had faxed three letters for Melanie to answer; and if Shelby was satisfied with Melanie's work, she would be allowed to continue as "Dear Miss Lonely Heart."

Sighing, Melanie glanced at the final letter again. The first two would be relatively easy to answer, but this one proved to be more of a problem.

Dear Miss Lonely Heart,

I need your advice. I'm twenty-seven years old and I still get nervous around women my age. Not only can this be embarrassing, but I wonder if I will ever get past being shy. I want to get married and have a family, but by the time I've worked up my courage to talk to someone, she's already interested in someone else. What can I do?

Always the Last Guy in Line

Melanie stared at the letter, rereading it once again. Her heart went out to this man, whoever and wherever he was.

She personally was outgoing and extroverted. Her mother always said that Melanie was born with a microphone in one hand and a sign that read "Look at me" in the other.

"That child has never met a stranger," her mother told people. But Melanie's best friend from childhood, Jasmine, struggled with shyness—especially in high school—so Melanie knew how those feelings could affect a person.

As she glanced at the page again, Melanie experienced fresh doubts over whether or not she could actually do this job. Hadn't her advice to Jasmine ruined their friendship years ago? Who was she to offer advice to this man? What if she made the same mistake again?

Feeling restless, Melanie paced the room, hoping to find a distraction from her thoughts. A fleeting glimpse of herself in the mirror caused Melanie to stop and carefully examine her appearance. She looked okay, but a little cosmetic artwork wouldn't hurt.

After a few minutes of digging through her makeup bag, Melanie located her favorite foundation. The sepia liquid was a perfect match, accentuating the red and blue undertones of her dark skin. It was also the most expensive foundation she'd ever owned, so she only wore it on special occasions. While brushing on deep brown and golden eye shadows, Melanie decided that although this might not be a special occasion, she could use the boost.

A swab of jet black mascara and a dab of raisin-hued lipstick over her full lips completed the look. For an extra special touch, she misted her shoulder-length, dark brown curly twists with a bit of moisturizer and pulled the sides back with combs.

Satisfied with her work, Melanie crossed her arms and stared into the mirror. Now that she had nothing to do, the thoughts of inadequacy she had been hoping to forget returned in a rush. Maybe she should call Ms. Tate and politely inform her that she was the wrong woman for this job.

After all, I spent the last four years studying to be a teacher. I need to find a job at a school—in a classroom, not as an advice columnist.

Melanie reached for the phone to place her call, but a glance at the clock told her that the *Agape Today* offices would already be closed.

She didn't feel comfortable leaving this message on the editor's voicemail, so she decided she would place the call first thing in the morning.

"Melanie?" her mother called from downstairs. "I've got dinner waiting."

"Coming," Melanie called back. She collected the papers Ms. Tate had sent and placed them neatly on one corner of the desk. The content of that last letter had pulled open an old wound she'd been trying to forget. After four years, the hour of reckoning was fast approaching, and Melanie didn't feel ready to face what might be coming.

Melanie glanced around the foyer of the church. It had been quite some time since she'd even been inside the building. While in college, she'd spent her summer breaks in D.C., using her job as a nanny as a reason to stay away from home. During holiday vacations, she'd found some excuse to miss services or made plans to attend Sunday worship with a friend who attended another church. On the few occasions her mother insisted she come, she'd made an effort to get in and out as quickly as possible.

Now, she realized she'd just been making things harder on

herself. Obviously, she'd have to return sometime, and now was that time.

Her parents walked ahead of her and disappeared inside the sanctuary, but Melanie stood outside the doors, waiting. Jasmine had called earlier in the afternoon and asked if Melanie could meet her for lunch, but Melanie had declined and made an excuse about having to stay home and work on her new job.

Jasmine sounded disappointed and suggested that she and Melanie meet right before church, "just to talk for a bit."

Melanie couldn't very well refuse such a simple request. Besides, having gone four years without speaking was torture, and it was time they got this first conversation out of the way.

The two of them would probably never be as close as they had been, but Melanie needed a way to ease her conscience.

A young man exited from the sanctuary and nearly ran into her. He paused long enough to say, "Sorry," then headed straight to the drinking fountain.

He was dressed simply, in a striped polo shirt and jeans with tennis shoes. Well-muscled arms suggested he did more than sit behind a desk all day, and his deep almond-colored skin revealed hints of a sunglasses tan around his eyes. His jet black hair was cropped short and brushed against his head in smooth black waves. Abundant eyebrows and a broad nose were the focal points of his face, accentuated by full lips and eyes so dark, they nearly matched the color of his stubbly goatee and sideburns.

Melanie didn't recognize him, so he must have joined the church after she'd gone away. She decided it wouldn't hurt to introduce herself before he went back inside the sanctuary. If she planned to get involved in church activities again, she might as well start making new friendships and strengthening old ones. When he straightened and stepped away from the fountain, Melanie smiled brightly.

"Hi. I'm Melanie. I don't think we've met before, but I haven't been here in a while." As an afterthought, she added, "I just got back from college a few days ago."

He looked around as if to determine whether she was speaking to him or someone else. Since no one else was in the foyer at the moment, Melanie waited for him to respond.

He cleared his throat and opened his mouth, but didn't answer immediately. Instead, he abruptly bent over to take another drink of water. When he finished his second drink, he smiled. "Hi," he said. "My name's Rand. Nice to meet you." As he spoke, he walked to the far sanctuary entrance and, before Melanie could say another word, he opened the door and went back inside.

Melanie frowned. Apparently, he didn't really think it had been nice to meet her. She peered inside the small window in the door and noted that Rand had to cross to the opposite side of the sanctuary to get back to his seat. He'd obviously come out on the same side where she'd been standing, but for some reason, he had crossed the entire foyer to get to the other door—only to walk back to the other side once he entered. What was the deal with him?

Maybe it had been something she said. But after racking her brain for several moments, Melanie couldn't recall having done anything offensive. "And it's not like I bite."

Her attention was diverted when a throng of people entered, bringing a puff of crisp October air along with them. Melanie spotted Jasmine first. She looked remarkably unchanged, skinny as a rail with the same brown skin, and a short, spunky haircut. Yet, there was something *different* about her.

Melanie put up her hand and gave a tentative wave, hoping Jasmine would notice. She did, and moments later, she was pushing through the crowd to reach Melanie.

After a hug, the two friends stepped back and looked each other over. "You look good, Girl," Jasmine said.

Melanie laughed. She'd been through several different looks, from long hair to short, and she now wore about ten more pounds than she had during high school. She wasn't wearing a speck of makeup, and a gigantic pimple had appeared out of nowhere right in the middle of her forehead. Melanie felt Jasmine's statement had been overly generous. Shaking her head, she said, "Thanks for the compliment, but you really do shine. You seem different. . . . It's like you're sparkling or something."

Jasmine threw her head back and laughed. Melanie blinked. Something had changed here. The old Jasmine was quiet and took great pains not to draw extra attention to herself.

"It has been way too long since we've seen each other," said Jasmine. "We need to get together and talk." She playfully poked Melanie in the arm. "I missed you."

Melanie took a deep breath. "I missed you too."

Jasmine grinned. "Good. So, let's make up for lost time. For starters, let's put that whole argument behind us. We were both young, and pretty. . ." She shrugged and trailed off.

"I think I can say 'immature' for my part," said Melanie.

"Me too. But look, let's not dwell on it." She held out her left hand to reveal a glittering solitaire diamond ring. "I guess your mom told you I'm engaged."

Melanie nodded. "Yes, she did. Congratulations, Girlfriend." She reached out and gave her friend another hug, breathing an internal sigh of relief.

"Does your being engaged mean that you're not still upset

about Keith breaking up with you?" Melanie ventured.

Jasmine nodded. "Absolutely no hard feelings. I mean, I was really upset when Keith dumped me, and I blamed it on you because of your advice, but it wasn't your fault."

Melanie bit her lip. "I'm really sorry about all of that. I guess I wasn't as good at helping people as I thought I was. I never meant for you two to break up."

Jasmine looked her in the eye. "Listen, nobody's perfect, and I know you weren't trying to hurt me. But if all of that hadn't happened, I might not have met Jeff, so it's all worked out better than I could have hoped."

"Do you really mean that?" asked Melanie. It was hard to believe after all that had happened, Jasmine could really just forgive her.

Jasmine nodded. "I do. And I've felt like this for a while. I only wish I had been brave enough to just call you and tell you."

"And I wish I hadn't stayed away for so long," Melanie added. "I wonder how things would have been different if I hadn't run away for four years."

Jasmine shrugged. "And I wonder what would have happened if I'd told you I wasn't upset anymore. To be honest, after a few months, I was relieved Keith and I weren't together. We'll never know what would have happened, so the best we can do is pick up now. I think God wanted Keith and me to go different ways for a reason."

Melanie considered this. Her situation helped to put an end to her amateur advice columnist attitude, giving her a chance to really listen to people. A dose of reality now tempered her advice instincts, and she knew better than to rattle off the first thing that came to mind when someone asked her opinion.

She'd also met many nice people, including the Burris

family, and that relationship had resulted in her new job. Maybe Jasmine was right about God having a part in all of this.

"Hey, Jeff's late getting off from work, so I'm going to wait out here for him. I'll introduce you two afterwards, okay?" said Jasmine.

Melanie nodded and opened the sanctuary door. "I'll look for you out here."

Melanie located her parents and slid into the pew next to her mother. Coincidentally, Rand was sitting in the row directly in front of them. As she sat down, he turned around and glanced at her.

Melanie gave him a tolerant smile. Given his peculiar behavior in the foyer, she didn't expect him to even acknowledge her presence; but to her surprise, he smiled and said, "Hi, Melanie."

Of course, in keeping with what was quickly becoming a tradition, he looked away before she could answer. Her mother gave her a curious glance, and Melanie shrugged. "We met in the hallway," she whispered in answer to her mother's unspoken question.

The short message for the service was about forgiveness, a topic that Melanie considered highly pertinent, given her encounter with Jasmine. The burden that weighed on her shoulders for the past four years lifted after their talk, and Melanie just wished that she hadn't let so much time escape.

After the service, the pastor asked if anyone had prayer requests. Several people got up and mentioned needs, and after they were finished, he prayed.

Before he dismissed the service, he made an announcement. "Many of you know Alex and Karin Hill." He paused, then added, "If you don't know them by name, you've probably seen one or both of them holding one of their triplets now and then." The congregation chuckled knowingly.

"I'd like for you all to keep them in prayer over the next few weeks. Karin works here in the church nursery, and Sunday morning, she tripped over some toys and fell. She's been in a great deal of pain ever since, and this morning the doctors confirmed that she broke her ankle and will need to stay off her feet for a few weeks.

"Alex has been able to stay at home for the past couple of days, but he's got to get back to work soon, which will make things difficult for Karin. If any of you have ever spent a few hours with one baby, you can picture how challenging three can be.

"We'd like to help out as much as we can. My wife has already started a meal list for those of you willing to make meals for the family. We'd also like for any of you who feel led to volunteer to spend time during the day helping Karin with the kids, since she's supposed to be off her feet. If you think you can help out, please see Betsy or me after the service, or give us a call at home."

Melanie vaguely remembered the Hills from before she'd gone away to school. She did recall on one of her recent visits back to church, having seen a couple with three little ones all the same age, and her heart went out to Karin. Melanie remembered spraining her ankle badly during college, and she'd experienced great difficulty watching the Burris children, even though they were older and there were only two of them.

She couldn't imagine how Karin was going to keep up with her children, but Melanie determined right then to help.

As soon as the service ended, she made a beeline for Betsy Colton, the minister's wife.

"Melanie Taylor, it's so good to see you again. Your mom told me you graduated and you're home for good now," she beamed, drawing Melanie into a perfume-scented hug.

"I am, and it feels good to be here," said Melanie.

"I hope you're going to rejoin the choir. We miss your voice," said Betsy. "Why don't you come to rehearsal Thursday?"

Melanie chuckled. She was certain that after a four-year hiatus, her voice was more than just a little rusty. "I'm not sure about that, but I wanted to offer my help to the Hills. I've worked as a nanny for a family for the past three years, so I have experience with kids. My schedule is flexible and I'm able to help during the daytime hours."

Betsy practically squealed with delight. "Oh, Honey, praise the Lord. This is just perfect. When can you start?"

Melanie shrugged. "What's the next available shift?"

Betsy bit her lip. "Well. . .to tell you the truth, you can pick any shift you want right now. I've had a multitude of volunteers for meals, but I'm having some difficulty with helpers for the children. I think people are a little intimidated by the thought of keeping up with *three* little ones." Betsy got a notebook and turned to a sheet with graph markings on it. All of the spaces were blank, and Melanie felt her heart sink.

"Well, now, we have an eight-to-noon shift and a noon-to-four shift. Alex doesn't get home until six, but Karin says her brother will be able to help from four 'til six," said Betsy.

Melanie took a look at the blank sheet again. She had a feeling she was going to be the only volunteer, and she wondered if her four-hour shift would even make a dent in what needed to be done. All of a sudden, Melanie felt overwhelmed and voiced her doubts to Betsy.

"I think the morning shift will be the most hectic, so that's when she probably needs the most help. What if no one else volunteers? I don't think I have the heart to just waltz out the door at noon, knowing she won't have any more help for four more hours. My conscience would feel better if I did the noon to four."

Betsy murmured her agreement. "You're probably right about the morning shift being the one she needs filled the most. What if I take the afternoon shift this week until we get more volunteers and you take the morning? I'd do it myself, but I help with the shut-in program in the mornings."

Relaxing somewhat, Melanie said, "That works for me. I'll try to get lunch out of the way before you come, so that's not the first thing you have to do when you get in the door."

Betsy breathed what appeared to be a sigh of relief. "Thanks, Melanie. You're a real sweetie pie."

Someone behind Melanie cleared his throat, and she had a feeling the throat in question belonged to Rand. He took a look at Betsy's list, and Melanie suppressed a giggle. Surely he wasn't planning to take a shift. She could just imagine this man trying to watch three babies.

Betsy spoke up first. "Rand, can you hang on for a second while we schedule baby care? Melanie and I will cover both shifts for this week, and hopefully some other brave souls will offer their help." She grinned and winked at Melanie.

"I heard what you said about lunch," Rand said with a glance toward Melanie. "If you tell me what time you'll feed them, I can leave work for a while and come help." He shrugged and added, "They can get pretty rowdy at mealtimes."

Melanie blinked. What did he know about babies?

As if understanding Melanie's confusion, Betsy spoke up. "Oh, Melanie, this is Rand Anthony, Karin's brother."

"You're the *uncle*?" Melanie questioned. Somehow, when

Betsy had mentioned that Karin's brother would help, she hadn't pictured a man so. . .young. . .and attractive.

He smiled politely and nodded. Melanie noticed that he seemed much more at ease than he had earlier.

"Oh, he's wonderful with the kids, Melanie. Thanks so much, Rand." Betsy put a hand on Melanie's shoulder. "I've got to run and catch the women's fellowship director before she leaves. I'll let you two work out any further details of the schedule."

After Betsy's departure, the two of them stood silently, and Melanie racked her brain for something to say. She hated awkward moments, but she really didn't know what to say, given Rand's unusual behavior earlier. "I'm really thankful that you'll be able to help out with lunch."

Fortunately, her attempt to get the conversation going again proved successful, and she breathed a sigh of relief when Rand answered. "No problem. I wish I could help more, but I can't take off from work."

"Where do you work?"

"I do construction, mostly building houses. I moved here six months ago from Chicago, and I'm still getting settled in, but I like my job and being closer to my family."

"I just got back in town too. I've been working as a nanny, so hopefully, that will help me out with your sister's children."

He nodded and glanced around the rapidly emptying sanctuary. From the look on his face, Melanie decided that he was either bored with the conversation or needed to talk with someone else. She gracefully ended the conversation, and predictably, Rand made his escape.

Melanie watched him retreat, feeling mildly disappointed. He seemed like a nice guy—someone she'd like to know better, but apparently, he didn't feel the same way about her.

With a small sigh, Melanie headed out to the foyer to locate Jasmine. She refused to let Rand's disinterest get to her, but she couldn't shake the growing anticipation she felt at the prospect of seeing him again.

Chapter 2

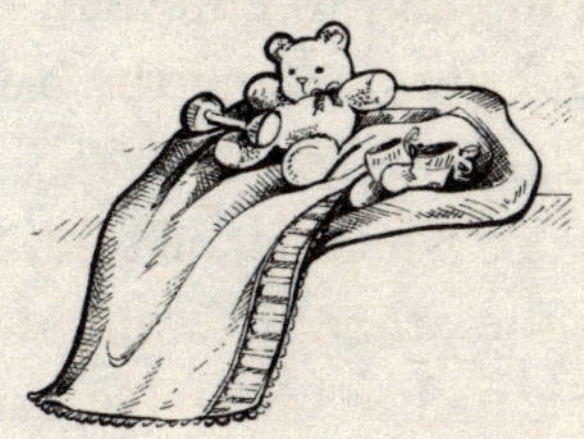

Gilbert, no! Put that back!" Melanie set Gwen down in the playpen and rushed over just in time to prevent a hungry little Gilbert from ingesting a fistful of soil from a potted plant. As she wiped the remaining clumps of dirt from his hands, a loud wail erupted from one of the other babies.

Melanie carried the now-whimpering boy to the playpen and picked up little Grace. Moments later, Gwen, disturbed by her brother and sister's cries, joined in the chorus.

Melanie looked at the clock and suppressed a groan. Alex had taken Karin to a doctor's appointment, and they weren't due home for another hour. Melanie hoped to put off lunchtime until at least eleven-thirty, but it seemed the kids were hungry *now*. Betsy wouldn't be able to help out for two more hours, and Rand wasn't due to come until noon. That left Melanie on her own for this go-round.

The only problem was, she couldn't very well run to the kitchen and leave three wailing babies in their playpen. Judging from their escalating state of fussiness, they wouldn't be consoled until they had lunch.

What have I gotten myself into?

Melanie leaned over the edge of the playpen and spoke in

a soothing tone. "Hey, kiddos, let's work together here. You calm down and then we'll do lunch. How does that sound?" She gave them her brightest smile, but they only cried louder.

As she searched for toys to entertain them, the back door swung open, momentarily startling the babies into silence.

Rand came over and picked up Grace. "It's okay, Sweetie. Uncle Rand is here." To Melanie, he said, "You have to get her quiet first, and then the other two calm down easier."

"Thanks." Melanie rocked Gwen back and forth in her arms. "You're here early," she said, both curious and grateful that he was now here to help.

Rand gave her a quizzical look. "Would you rather I came back in an hour?"

Melanie shook her head, wondering if he was serious. "No, no. I'm glad you made it. I think they're hungry, but I couldn't let them cry like this while I got lunch ready."

"My shift ended a little early, so I thought I'd check and see how you were doing since Karin's not here."

Had he come an hour or two earlier, Melanie would have had the distinct impression he had come to check up on her, but his current timing couldn't have been better.

"How about I finish calming them and you get lunch started?" Rand suggested. "When they're hungry, I can't console them for long."

"Are you sure?" The idea made sense, but Melanie wondered if he could handle the task.

"Positive. You go ahead." Rand placed a now-quiet Grace back in the playpen, took Gwen from Melanie's arms, and shooed her into the kitchen.

Melanie quickly prepared finger food and finished slicing bananas. She doubted that Rand would appreciate such a small lunch, but considering the circumstances, a couple of sandwiches were the best she could do.

Ten minutes later, she headed back to the family room to announce that lunch was ready. Rand and the triplets were sitting on the floor, playing with building blocks. Or rather, Rand was playing with building blocks while the triplets watched.

"Kudos to you for getting them quiet. You'll have to teach me your secret sometime."

Rand shrugged, looking slightly embarrassed. "I don't have a secret. Maybe they're just used to me."

"Then let's hope they get used to me soon. Lunch is ready."

"Good." Rand scooped up the girls, and Melanie took Gilbert into the kitchen. Melanie got them situated in their highchairs. She let Rand eat his two sandwiches while she helped the babies eat. For all of the fuss they had put up, now that lunch had ensued, they seemed far more interested in throwing food on the floor than putting it in their mouths.

I'm out of my league here, Melanie thought with a sigh. It had been a few years since she had worked with babies, and never had she faced the task of working with three infants all the same age. There was drool to wipe, hands to clean, and diapers to change —usually in triplicate.

Melanie closed her eyes for a moment to reflect on the enormity of this job. She couldn't back out now, but to say she felt inadequate was an understatement. As Melanie fought to keep her resolve strong and remain positive, Gwen hurled a banana slice at Melanie's forehead and giggled when it stuck there. Melanie wiped the sticky, drool-covered banana away and blinked to hold back the tears forming in the corners of her eyes.

"You okay?" asked Rand, setting down his glass of milk.

Melanie turned away and nodded, embarrassed to be caught

crying like one of the babies.

She heard Rand dragging his chair away from the table, and she wondered if he was going to head back to work. She knew he had only promised to help during lunch, but she could use his "uncle" expertise for a bit longer.

"Hey." Melanie was startled at the touch of Rand's hand on her shoulder, and he pulled it away as quickly as he placed it there.

"Sorry. I'm just a little jumpy," she apologized.

Rand nodded silently. "I just want you to know I think you're doing a good job. I know this is pretty intimidating at first, but once you get to know them and they get to know you, things will go smoother. And I promise to get here as often as I can to help."

Melanie laughed nervously. Having a man tell her how to watch babies seemed almost comical. Still, he had a point, since she was the one who had been reduced to tears after only three hours with the triplets.

Grace began whimpering softly, and Melanie took a deep breath, anticipating more cries from Gwen and Gilbert.

Rand held out a hand. "I'll take care of them. Why don't you eat your lunch?"

Melanie didn't have much of an appetite, but she was too tired to protest. Besides, he had to head back to work soon, and she had at least another hour or so until Betsy came for the afternoon shift.

Minutes later, Rand announced the babies needed a diaper change. "But I'll do it before I have to leave."

Melanie shook her head and swallowed the last of her sandwich. "I'm finished eating, so I'll help." No use in sitting around watching him change diapers. She didn't want Rand to think she was a complete ninny.

Working together, they got the diapers done in record time.

"You need anything else before I leave?"

Melanie shook her head. "I think we're set. I'm going to attempt to get them down for a nap."

"Good idea. It'll go quicker if you turn down the lights a little and play that CD Karin got for them."

"Thanks for the tip. Where is this CD?"

"I think it's on top of the stereo. It's a collection of lullabies she found at the Christian bookstore a few weeks ago. The babies really seem to like it."

"I'll definitely use it. And thanks again for coming. I'm sorry if I seemed a little overwhelmed earlier, but I think I've got a handle on things now."

"Good. See you later." With that, he was gone. Melanie noted he seemed quite a bit more personable than he had at their initial meetings. Maybe he was just one of those people who needed time to warm up.

Melanie found the music and took Rand's advice. Within minutes the three wee ones dozed their way to dreamland, and Melanie found time to read the first couple of chapters of a new inspirational romance Jasmine loaned her.

The story had a promising beginning, but Melanie's thoughts kept returning to Rand. What was it about him that intrigued her? He was full of surprises. One day, he barely managed to say hello, and the next, he was working side by side with her, diapering babies, and giving tips on how to put them down for a nap.

Melanie smiled, remembering the image of Rand, tall and muscled, gently cradling little Grace. *How adorable.*

Melanie always had a soft spot for men who loved babies

and little kids, and Rand fit the description exactly. He'd make a great dad someday.

If I don't watch out, I'll find myself falling for him, she realized. Her job helping Karin made for a precarious situation with Rand. Suppose he had a girlfriend or fiancée—then what? She needed to think of him as no more than a friend so her feelings for him wouldn't interfere with her work with the babies.

A message from Shelby Tate awaited Melanie when she got home from the Hills' that afternoon. Her answers to the trial run of questions had proven satisfactory, and the job of answering the "Dear Miss Lonely Heart" column was now hers.

"I got the job!" Melanie did a little dance around the couch before she composed herself.

Melanie replayed the answering machine message to get the rest of the details. Within a day or so, someone from the magazine would mail the rest of the letters to Melanie, and she could choose the ones to answer for the next issue.

The questions she'd sent in for her trial would be used in the very next issue.

"Wow. I didn't imagine I'd see my work in print so soon." The news about the job was so exciting, Melanie had to tell someone. No one else was at home, so she decided to give Jasmine a call.

After they talked about Melanie's new job, their conversation changed from topic to topic until they realized they had been on the phone for over an hour. "I should get off the phone. I think I'll surprise my mom and start dinner. I'll call you later this week."

"Okay. You have a good time with those babies and try not to get stressed again," Jasmine reminded. "They're just babies, so things are bound to get a little harried sometimes. But not every baby-sitter gets bailed out by her charges' handsome uncle."

"Oh, please," Melanie laughed. "But you do have a point."

"About the handsome uncle?"

Melanie sidestepped the question, not yet willing to concede that she did indeed find Rand quite attractive. "No—I'm referring to what you said about things getting harried. I guess I'll learn as I go along. Even though Karin has to stay off her feet, things seem to go much better when she's around. I'm looking forward to her being there during my entire shift tomorrow morning."

"That'll definitely be easier," Jasmine agreed.

Moments later, after the conversation ended, Melanie returned the phone to its cradle—only to have it ring again.

"Melanie? It's Betsy Colton."

"Hi, Betsy. I thought you were helping out at the Hills' today."

"I was and had to leave early. My youngest daughter, Joan, got sick at school and they called me to come pick her up. Fortunately, I got my mother-in-law to take my spot at Karin's. But now I think my other children are coming down with whatever Joan's got."

"Oh, no, that's terrible. Is it serious?"

"Probably just a bug, and hopefully they'll be over it in a week or so. But I just don't think it's a good idea for me to work with those babies right now. I'm not feeling up to par myself, but I can't tell if I'm sick or just plain tired. If I have caught this germ, the last thing I want to do is get those babies sick when their mother has to be off her feet."

Melanie agreed. "But what about the afternoon shift? Have we got someone to cover that for us?"

"No, we don't. I was hoping that you might be able to take over for this week. Next week, I should have a clear picture of what's going on here in my family. Then I can work that shift, unless some benevolent soul decides to volunteer."

Melanie thought for a few moments. She'd already turned in the "Dear Miss Lonely Heart" column for the next issue of the magazine, and a new set of letters wouldn't arrive for several days.

Her schedule wasn't exactly brimming over. In fact, she'd already decided to look for another job to keep her busy when she didn't have to work on the letters.

She supposed she could put off her job search until Karin Hill's ankle healed. She might as well put in full-time hours while she was at it.

"You know what, Betsy? I think that's a good idea. In fact, I'll take the morning and afternoon shift until Karin's ankle is better." As soon as the words left her mouth, Melanie wondered how far in over her head she'd gotten herself. Oh, well. No turning back now. This job would only last for a few more weeks, and then she could find a paying job.

Betsy thanked her profusely, and Melanie headed off to the kitchen to start dinner. As she worked, Melanie realized Rand was right: Caring for the babies would get easier once they all got used to one another.

All that evening, she wondered, *So why am I still nervous?*

Chapter 3

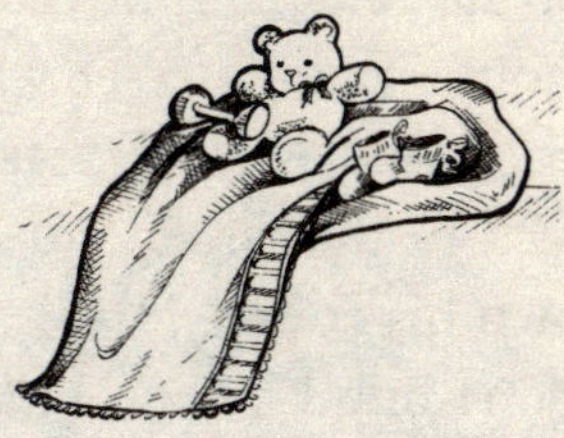

The question that plagued Melanie all evening didn't occur to her until the next morning. Melanie was in the kitchen, helping Karin feed the triplets baby cereal, when the Answer opened the basement door and said, "Good morning."

Blinking in surprise, Melanie barely managed to squeak out a hello.

"Hi, Rand," Karin said to her brother.

Melanie couldn't contain her curiosity. "I didn't realize anyone was in the house besides us and the babies," she said to Karin. Karin's husband, Alex, had been rushing out the door when Melanie arrived twenty minutes earlier, and she felt certain she would remember seeing Rand come in and head downstairs.

Karin laughed. "Oh, Melanie, I was so out of it yesterday. I forgot to tell you that Rand is living downstairs right now. When I got back from the doctor and you told me that he had come home to help with lunch, I just assumed that he'd told you that."

Melanie shook her head slowly. "No, we didn't really talk about anything except the babies."

Rand laughed. "We didn't have time to talk about anything *but* the babies. If I recall, they were pretty fussy when I got here, so you went to the kitchen to make lunch."

"He moved here because of work six months ago, and he's living with us until he has time to look for a place of his own. He's at work most of the time, and he didn't want to rush out and buy a house without a chance to see what's on the market."

"That makes sense," said Melanie, ready to let the matter drop. Rand had moved to the far side of the kitchen and was hurriedly gulping down his coffee.

"Of course, we don't mind having him around. He's wonderful with the babies, and they love him. When he moves out, we'll be sad to see him go."

"Well, I'm heading out to work now. I'll see you all later." Rand put his mug in the sink and gave Karin a hug, then gave each of the babies a kiss. They cooed happily, and Gwen even rewarded him with a return kiss, smearing a trail of cereal on the back of his neck with her little hand.

Apparently, Rand didn't feel it, because he put on his jacket and headed toward the garage. Melanie wondered if she should say something. Karin, busy checking Grace's diaper, didn't seem to have noticed, either.

Knowing Rand, it might make him uncomfortable if she pointed out the smear to him, but she couldn't let him walk out of the house like that.

After a split second of hesitation, Melanie grabbed up one of the damp washcloths Karin kept handy for the babies and ran after him.

He was just about to step into his pickup when she stopped him. "Wait a minute," she said.

Rand's eyebrows lifted in surprise, and for a moment, that trapped look he'd had in the church foyer returned to his face.

"You have something on your neck," she explained, holding

the washcloth out to him.

Rand put his hand to the back of his neck and yanked it away, grimacing. Melanie gave him the cloth, and he wiped the cereal away. "Thanks," he said, looking grateful. "I didn't realize that was there. I mean, I've gotten pretty used to their sticky little fingers, but most of the time, they don't leave much behind except drool."

He handed the cloth back to Melanie. "Thanks again. I wouldn't want the guys at work teasing me about that all day. They already think it's pretty funny that I baby-sit on weekends instead of going out."

"Why don't you go out?"

He shrugged. "I guess I wouldn't know what to do or where to go. I've been too busy to do much besides work, baby-sit, and go to church since I got here." He gave her a wry smile. "That's not quite true. I generally get out on Sundays after church to go to open houses, but that's about it, and I wouldn't call that recreation."

Melanie laughed. Rand reminded her of a turtle. He took a while to come out of his shell, and sometimes he poked his head out and ducked right back inside. Still, there were scattered moments like this, when he seemed comfortable and at ease.

"What's so funny?" he asked.

This time it was Melanie's turn to shrug. "I was actually thinking you'd make a cute turtle."

Snap! Her flippant sentence sent the turtle back into his shell.

As soon as she finished speaking, Melanie knew she'd made a mistake. *Why didn't I realize how silly and even insulting that would sound before I said it?* "Um, I think that came out wrong," she began.

Rand turned around so that his back was to Melanie. "Did I get it all?"

"Almost," she said, grateful for a change of subject. "There's still a little smudge." Rand reached for the cloth and unsuccessfully tried to locate the elusive remainder.

"Here." Melanie took the cloth and wiped the last of the cereal away. "There you go. It's all gone now."

"Thanks again."

"No problem." Melanie wished she could take back her turtle sentence and put Rand at ease. *What can I say to fix this?*

"I'll see you later," he said, interrupting her thoughts. "At lunch."

"Thanks," she said. "I appreciate every bit of help I can get."

"No problem. Just make sure Karin takes it easy on her ankle."

"I will," she said. The garage door opened, and Melanie waved good-bye as Rand drove away.

Rand returned as expected during lunch and convinced Karin to sit down for more than two minutes. She'd spent the entire morning moving around, assuring Melanie that her ankle didn't hurt so much, but by eleven-thirty, Karin's slow pace and the set of her jaw convinced Melanie that the ankle wasn't doing as well as Karin had led her to believe.

With Karin seated and making sure that most of the food went into the triplets' mouths, the three of them managed to carry off lunch without a hitch.

Just after Rand went back to work, Lena Milton, a woman from church, stopped by, bearing three large casseroles.

"It looks like you're set for dinner for the next few days," Melanie remarked as she arranged the pans in the freezer.

"No kidding." Karin watched from her chair, where she balanced Grace and Gwen on her lap. "Even with three babies, we'll be able to reheat those for several days. I really appreciate all of the help."

Melanie grinned. "You should be glad I volunteered to help with the babies instead of cook. I might be good with kids, but I'm not much of a whiz in the kitchen. Last night, I made dinner to give my mom a break, but we ended up reheating dinner from the night before."

Karin laughed. "That was me before I got married. After a couple of weeks of my pitiful attempts in the kitchen, Alex kept finding ways for us to stop by his parents' house around dinnertime. I took the hint and got serious about cooking."

"Was it hard?"

"Not really. I just had to focus on what I was doing. The cookbook his mother gave me on our one-month anniversary spelled things out pretty well." Karin winked. "Alex says the look on my face when I opened that package was so funny. He was relieved, but he didn't know how I would take it."

"So what did you do?"

"I debated between getting really offended and stalking out of the house or hugging her. I was hurt and embarrassed, but the hug won out in the end. She did the right thing as tactfully as she could."

Melanie sighed. "I guess I should take your advice before I get married. My parents have a dinner party to attend tonight, so I'll get a chance to dig out some cookbooks and see what I can do with a recipe."

"When are you getting married?" Karin's eyes lit up with curiosity.

Melanie felt her cheeks grow warm. "Oh, no, I'm not engaged. Not even seeing anyone at the moment. I've been too. . . busy, I guess."

"Why don't you put off your cooking experiment for another day and have dinner with us tonight?"

Melanie briefly considered the idea. She enjoyed spending time with Karin, and she wouldn't mind getting in a few more moments of conversation with Rand. She had a feeling he would not be so thrilled to come home and find her still there. He'd seemed nervous enough at lunch. "I don't think so. . .maybe another time."

Karin laughed, mistaking Melanie's reticence for exhaustion. "I promise you won't get asked to change any diapers. Once Alex and Rand get home, they pitch in and help. You'll be officially off duty."

"Oh, no, that's not it. I just wouldn't. . ." Melanie searched for a way to be honest and not drag Rand into the conversation. "I don't want to intrude on your family time together."

"Trust me, you're not intruding. As much as I hate being off my feet, I love having you around. I spend my days with three babies and get in adult conversation when the men get home, but I still don't have much time to spend with girlfriends. It's nice to have another woman around."

Melanie hesitated and Karin shook her head. "I won't take no for an answer. You're staying and that's final."

The two women shared a laugh before Gwen interrupted with a whimper. "My nose is telling me it's diaper time for her," Karin announced.

Melanie nodded. If Gwen needed changing, then the others did as well. But at least she wasn't on her own as had been the case for most of yesterday.

Chapter 4

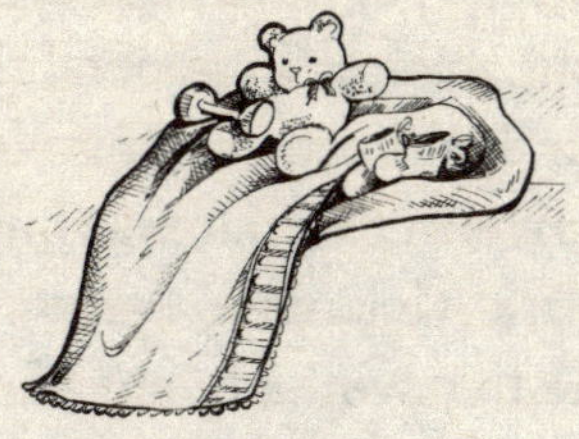

Dear Always the Last Guy in Line,

Don't be so hard on yourself. Women get nervous too, and it's not easy to put your emotions on the line not knowing if the other person feels the same way. Relax. Don't put too much emphasis on developing a romantic relationship.

Take a deep breath and say hello. Make small talk. Find out her interests, her likes, and her dislikes. People often say that the best marriages stem from friendships. If the friendship goes well, then you might consider taking the relationship further by asking her out. It may take a while to get to this point, but if it gives you peace of mind to take this route, then I think it will work out better in the long run.

Miss Lonely Heart

Rand silently scanned the article twice more, then closed the magazine. He hadn't really expected to find an answer to his question in the "Dear Miss Lonely Heart" column, but he'd thought it was worth trying. She always seemed to give good advice; and while he wanted a woman's perspective on his problem, he hadn't been able to muster up the courage to ask for Karin's opinion.

This advice from "Dear Miss Lonely Heart" seemed somewhat universal—almost a pat answer. It didn't give any specific tips about overcoming shyness in general, but it arrived in the nick of time. Melanie had been helping Karin with the babies for nearly a month. His sister's ankle was improving, but she and Alex had decided to ask Melanie to continue helping.

They weren't able to pay much, but Melanie accepted. She had interviewed for a job at a private school, but she wouldn't start teaching at the academy until summer school began. Since she had her heart set on teaching at the Christian Academy, she was willing to wait, rather than take a job elsewhere and quit once an opening came at the private school.

Rand, however, was happy that Melanie's current schedule allowed her to spend more time helping Karin, because it provided more of an opportunity for him to see Melanie.

She usually arrived for work after he left for his job, but occasionally he stopped in to help with lunch. Although she left for the day before he got home, she and Karin had gotten to be good friends, and Melanie often stayed for dinner.

During these meals, Rand remained mostly silent—not wanting to get all tongue-tied, but having a difficult time finding something clever to say. They eventually managed to have a few one-on-one conversations, but Melanie did most of the talking.

Rand could rattle off a string of adjectives to describe her: funny, pretty, charming, smart, inquisitive, tenderhearted. . . and fearless. He'd watched her at church, mingling with others. Where he felt inclined to hang back until someone spoke to him, Melanie did the opposite.

He wished he could be just as bold as she, but he had a hard enough time trying to come up with things to say when people started a conversation with him.

To this day, he still felt embarrassed to remember the first time he'd encountered Melanie at church. First, he'd exited the sanctuary so suddenly that he almost ran into her. Then, after she introduced herself, he stood for several moments wondering if she was speaking to him or someone else. By the time he realized that she was indeed talking to him, his throat went dry and he had to take another drink of water just to blurt out a simple sentence.

Making matters even worse, he'd crossed the foyer just to avoid walking past her again. At the time, he'd thought it the only solution to keep him from appearing so nervous; but the more he thought about his actions, the more he knew he had only succeeded in acting aloof.

Rand clapped his hand to his forehead and groaned as he replayed the scene in his memory. How in the world could he possibly change Melanie's view of him?

One thing was in his favor. Even after that forgettable scene, Melanie was still kind enough to speak to him when Mrs. Colton introduced them after the service. And lately, she continued to be polite—even friendly. Surely that meant she didn't dislike him completely.

But if Melanie is ever going to take me seriously, I have to get brave and stop letting the slightest thing make me uncomfortable, he decided. Dear Miss Lonely Heart was right. He had to start somewhere, and friendship was the perfect place to begin.

Lord, give me courage. . .and lots of it, please, he prayed.

Melanie opened yet another jar of strained peas. Taking a sniff, she wondered how the babies could happily gulp down spoonful after spoonful of the stuff.

Today, it appeared that lunchtime would be a solo expedition. Karin had gone grocery shopping, and Rand had mentioned that he might not make it home to help. It didn't matter, now that she was used to the routine. She would have liked the adult company, but she had gotten rather experienced at feeding three babies at once.

Karin had taught her a handy trick involving the rolling office chair from the computer desk in the living room. During mealtimes, Melanie moved the chair to the kitchen and positioned it in front of the three high chairs. This allowed her to roll back and forth between the hungry triplets and quickly feed whichever baby happened to be crying for more food. In the early days, she had done this job by standing and bending over to dole out spoonfuls of baby food. Not only had that process been slower, but she'd also had a major backache after a few days of bending at that angle for half an hour.

Several minutes into lunch, after the triplets had finished the peas and were now happily eating sliced bananas, the phone rang. Melanie grabbed the cordless extension that lived on the kitchen table. A cordless phone was another valuable tool for anyone who had to keep an eye on more than one baby.

While the phone didn't ring constantly at the Hill residence, people did have a knack for calling either just when the babies nodded off to sleep, during feedings, or when they were in that cranky stage after they woke up from a nap. Having a phone that didn't anchor her to one area was a big help.

"Hello?"

"Hi, it's Rand."

"Hi, Rand. Karin's not here. She went grocery shopping, and I don't expect her back for at least another hour."

A long pause ensued from the other end. "Rand? You still there?"

He cleared his throat. "Yes. Actually, I'm not calling for Karin. I wanted to ask you something. Are you free this afternoon, around three?"

"Three? I guess I am. Karin said I could leave after she got home from the store. But don't you work until six?"

"I'm getting off early. Can you go?"

Melanie paused. "I guess so. . .but where are we going?"

"Oh. I forgot. The Butterfly House. Unless you prefer somewhere else?"

Melanie grinned. "No, that sounds fun. I've only been there a couple of times. Will you pick me up, or should I meet you there?"

Rand was quiet for several moments. Finally, he said, "I'll pick you up at your house at three."

"Sounds fun. I can't wait." Melanie noticed that Gilbert was tossing his banana slices on the floor instead of eating them. "I'd better let you go; we're in the middle of lunch and most of it is going to end up on the floor if I don't get off the phone."

"Sorry. Oh, and one more thing," he said.

"Yes?"

"Just so you know, this trip to the Butterfly House is just a friendly outing. Not a date or anything. Just. . . ," he trailed off.

Melanie could sense his discomfort, and she felt compelled to say something to ease the tension. "Just two friends going to the Butterfly House. A fun, friendly. . .thing to do." Melanie closed her eyes for a second, imagining how inane that must have sounded. But she'd made it this far. She could surely come up with something intelligent to salvage the rest of the conversation. "That's fine. I'm looking forward to it."

"Good."

She could hear a sigh of relief from his end. "I'll see you at three." She hung up the phone before either one of them could say something to drag things out any longer.

After she returned the phone to the kitchen table, she went to work, wiping up the sticky banana from the formerly clean floor. What had Rand's call been about?

The invitation itself had been a surprise, coming from a man who could barely utter a single sentence to her. While Melanie had puzzled over whether or not he was asking her out on an "official" date, Rand had answered the question himself, informing her that this would merely be a friendly outing.

Okay. I can deal with that. But a part of her wished Rand hadn't added the disclaimer to the trip.

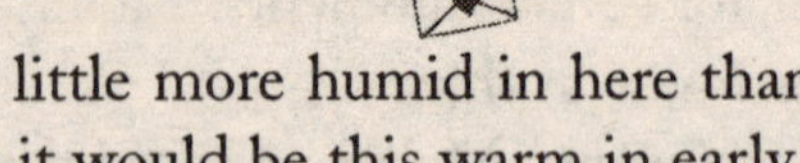

"Wow. It's a little more humid in here than I remembered. I didn't realize it would be this warm in early November—even in a greenhouse." Melanie fanned herself with the laminated paper featuring pictures of the various butterflies from around the world that were housed in the conservatory.

Rand tugged at his collar. "We are having unseasonably warm weather, but yes, it is a little hot in here." He pointed to a tree branch on the side of the path. "Look at the bright blue on the wings."

"So pretty," Melanie agreed. "It reminds me of a fluorescent light with a metallic glint. And look how big it is." As they watched, the large butterfly fluttered its wings and flew away.

"It's so graceful, it almost looks like slow motion." They walked a few more steps to round the corner and stopped as they came upon a small pool of water.

The large conservatory looked and felt like a tropical rainforest. Lush, exotic plants lined both sides of the main path. Colorful flowers and blooms decorated the vines and other plants. Sunlight streamed in from above, shooting rays through the fine mist that hovered in the air. There were hundreds of butterflies flitting here and there. In the background, voices of visitors exclaiming over the sights mingled with the noise of water splashing down the small fall into the pond.

The atmosphere was wonderfully pleasant; it would make a great backdrop for a romantic date. Only this wasn't a date, according to Rand.

"There are seats around the next corner, if you want to sit down," he suggested.

Melanie nodded, unable to think of anything to say. Her stomach felt like a mirror image of the swarm of butterflies that danced through the air around them.

They found the alcove Rand had mentioned and sat down on one of the small benches to soak in the scenery. Rand seemed content to just sit quietly, pointing out things here and there; sometimes a butterfly, sometimes a flower.

"They say if you sit really still, a butterfly might land on you," he told her.

"Really? Let's see."

For the next few minutes, she and Rand sat as still as they possibly could. A few of the flying creatures came near and some hovered, but none actually decided to rest on either of them. Melanie shrugged. "I guess they're not interested in us. Maybe if we had some fruit or some of that nectar they keep drinking out of those feeders. . ."

Rand laughed and stood up. "Let's see the rest of this place." He held out his hand for a fraction of a second, then pulled it back and briskly walked toward the main path again. Melanie followed behind, pretending to be absorbed in examining the plant life but feeling puzzled. After a few minutes of silence passed, Melanie decided to restart the conversation, but Rand beat her to it.

"So what else do you do when you're not helping Karin with the kids?"

Melanie smiled with relief. Small talk was definitely her forte. "Not much, actually," she admitted. "Read, clean house, run errands for my parents." She almost mentioned her new job at *Agape Today* but decided not to. She didn't want to publicize her position right now—at least not until she was more settled and certain she could do the job well. Besides, what if friends she knew had written in and asked for advice? How would they, and she, for that matter, feel about having her privy to such personal concerns?

Melanie chuckled. Such a situation could have a happy ending. Cathy, the previous columnist, had unknowingly communicated with the man she loved for months before he admitted to writing the letters. Now, they were engaged and would be married in less than two months, on Christmas Eve.

Glancing at Rand, who was still several steps ahead of her on the path, Melanie tried to imagine she and Rand unwittingly developing a relationship through the column.

She chuckled quietly at the idea. Rand just didn't seem the type to ask anyone for advice. He might be quiet, but he seemed to know what he wanted, and she couldn't imagine him sharing his concerns with anyone who wasn't very close to him—not even through the anonymity of an advice column.

"What's so funny?"

Melanie didn't dare mention her true thoughts. With a shrug, she quickened her pace and caught up to him. "A private thought, that's all." Feeling brave, she added, "Does this friendly outing include ice cream?"

Rand raised his eyebrows. "In November?"

"It's not that cold outside. But my personal feeling is that it's never too cold for ice cream—even if you have to sit by the fire to stay warm while you're eating it. Come on, it'll be my treat."

He laughed. "Okay. We'll stop for ice cream afterwards."

Chapter 5

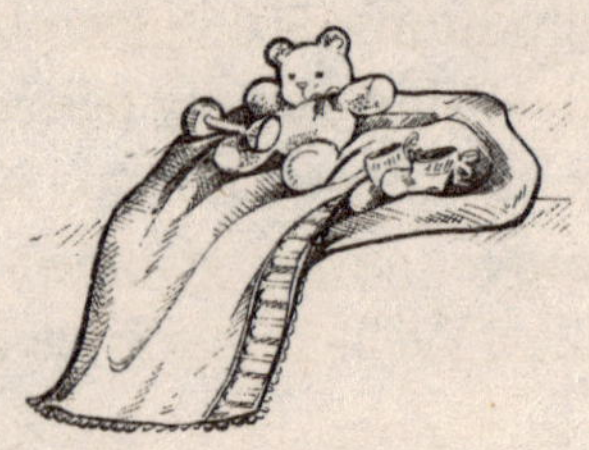

The next few weeks passed quickly with the flurry of preparations for the triplets' upcoming first birthday. Their actual birthday fell on Thanksgiving Day this year, so Karin opted to hold a party for the trio a full week before the official date.

Melanie was surprised but pleased that Rand found more opportunities to arrange additional "friendly" activities for the two of them. On Thanksgiving Eve, he proposed a trip to bike at Forest Park. Melanie tried to change his mind at first. "We've got a houseful of company coming tomorrow and we've just started cooking."

Her mom, standing nearby, waved at Melanie to let her know she didn't mind if Melanie went out for a while.

"Okay, I'll come, but I haven't ridden a bike since I was twelve. I'm not sure I won't fall off," she'd said and laughed. "I don't even know if my old bike is still around here. Why don't we just walk?"

But Rand insisted. "I've got two bikes. If after a few minutes, you still can't get your balance, I'll put the bikes in the truck and we'll walk."

His prediction proved true. After a few minutes of wobbling

around the parking lot, Melanie decided she trusted herself enough to continue with the biking plan. Ten minutes later, she was confident enough to challenge Rand to a race. She pedaled at top speed; and as the wind fanned her face and ruffled its fingers through her hair, she felt like a carefree twelve year old again.

After the race, they pedaled at a more sedate pace, until Rand mentioned he wanted to take a break. "Let's stop when we get up there," he said, pointing ahead to the left of the road.

When they reached their destination, Melanie was surprised to find a small waterfall tucked next to the main road. Carved into the hill and flanked by trees on either side, the picturesque fall was surprisingly strong. The water didn't trickle but actually rushed over the rock, and it foamed white and bubbly in some places.

"Wow, this looks like something in a picture," she said as she climbed off the bicycle.

"It's nice and quiet. I saw it this past summer, and I like to come here every once in a while."

Melanie shook her head, and they neared the smallish pond where the water collected at the bottom. "I've lived in St. Louis my entire life and I don't remember ever seeing this. You've been here for less than a year, and you've found such a pretty spot."

"Really?"

"Really. My mom took me to Forest Park all the time when I was little, but I don't remember this."

"Maybe you've forgotten it."

"Maybe," Melanie agreed. Walking to one side of the flat, grassy area surrounding the pond, Melanie noticed a path that led to the top of the falls. "Let's go exploring and walk to the top," she said, feeling adventurous.

Rand looked uncertain. "We can see it just as well from down here. The path doesn't look all that safe."

Melanie gave him a pleading look. Of course, Rand's proclamation made sense. The path hadn't actually been paved, but it was clearly there to allow access to the top. "Come on. We'll just have to be careful."

With a resigned sigh, Rand nodded and followed as Melanie took to the path.

The top was no more than fifty feet ahead, but the path did have its difficulties. Some parts were grassy; other sections were bare, dusty ground. In a few places, the rocks served as stairs of sorts, but in other areas much bigger rocks and exposed tree roots made the terrain more arduous. Obviously, this path had been forged over time by other eager explorers like them.

When they reached the halfway point, they stopped at a flat area and turned around to look back down the hill. "We're a lot higher up than I thought," Melanie said.

"Yeah, it looks a lot smaller from the bottom." Rand glanced at Melanie, then back to the bottom of the hill. "Do you still want to keep going?"

Melanie nodded, determined to continue the trek, even though her legs had begun to feel a tad wobbly from the bike riding. *I need to get to the gym more often.*

For the remainder of the hike to the top, Melanie moved cautiously. Twice, she nearly tripped, but Rand caught her before she could take a tumble. After the near misses, he kept his hand close to her back but not quite touching her unless they were on uncertain footing.

Melanie couldn't suppress a smile. He was always a perfect gentleman. When they made it to the top, Melanie had to sit down on one of the large rocks on the path, and Rand took a seat next to her.

"Nice view," he said. "I should have come up here before now."

Melanie was surprised. "You mean you've been here all these times and you never walked to the top?"

"No, I guess it never occurred to me that there was more to see from this angle."

"Then, I'm glad we came today. You got me to ride a bike again, and I got you to be adventurous and climb this hill."

Melanie stood up, hoping to explore a bit more before they made their way back down. The waterfall appeared to be man-made, beginning in a small pool of water at the very top of the hill. It then flowed down over a wide ledge of stone that dropped off, creating some of the force that caused the foam as it flowed down the hillside.

Melanie wondered if she could stand on the wide ledge where the falls began their journey. She edged as close as she could to one of the bordering rocks and gingerly stepped on it.

"Where are you going?" Rand asked, standing up and moving toward her.

"That ledge." Melanie pointed in the direction of her destination. Two more flat rocks to cross, and she would be there.

"I don't know if that's safe."

"I'm here now." Melanie stood proudly on her chosen rock. Not only had she made it to the top, she now stood at the center of the beginning of the fall. A thin sheet of water flowed over the ledge, so she was, in fact, standing in the waterfall.

"You should see the view down there from here," she said, gesturing for Rand to join her.

"Wet rocks are slippery, and these tennis shoes don't have enough traction," he pointed out.

Melanie looked down at her own tennis shoes. *Oops.* "I didn't do too badly, don't you think?" she said, laughing.

Rand laughed too. As she teased Rand for being too chicken to join her, Melanie felt the beginnings of a twinge in her hamstrings. Yikes. She knew what that meant. If she didn't get home and apply some liniment to her legs, she'd pay for the impromptu bike ride with sore legs for the next two days. The twinge must have registered in her face.

"Are you okay?" Rand sounded concerned.

Melanie grimaced. "I think I overdid the bike ride. All that exercise mixed with this chilly air. . . ," she trailed off and lifted one leg up a couple of inches off the ground. "In movies, people always look so happy and cheerful after vigorous exercise. No one ever gets muscle spasms."

"I think you're always happy," Rand said quietly. "And the cold air makes your cheeks a little rosy. It looks. . .you look. . . pretty."

If Melanie had been anywhere else, she might have been able to take the compliment in a more dignified fashion—maybe even had the presence of mind to flirt back or bat her eyelashes or something.

She was standing on one foot on a slippery rock, wearing the wrong shoes, and battling a cramp in her leg.

The pain of another leg cramp combined with the shock of Rand complimenting her looks in such a serious way was too much. Before she realized what was happening, she landed on her backside on the center of the ledge, her left arm submerged in water up to her elbow. She heard herself shout and wondered if people nearby could hear.

As she regained her wits, Melanie took note of her situation. One more foot to the right, and she would have fallen over the dropoff. One more foot in the other direction, and her whole body, rather than just her arm, would have been in that several inches of cloudy, cold water in the pool.

Within seconds, Rand was at her side, pulling her to her feet, but something slippery threw him off balance. He didn't completely lose his footing, but he did end up standing in the pool, calf-deep in cold water.

Rand gasped loudly, and Melanie could imagine how he felt. Her arm was still numb from the frigid water. "I'm sorry," she said, as Rand carefully climbed to the ledge and ushered her safely back to the path.

After they reached dry ground again, Rand sat down to squeeze some of the excess water from the bottom of his jeans. It didn't do much, but Melanie imagined that every little bit helped. Then he took off his shoes to wring them out the best he could.

"I'm sorry," she said again. "I should have listened when you warned me about the shoes."

Rand shrugged. "It didn't make any difference then. You were already out there."

Melanie rubbed her hands together. Why hadn't she brought her gloves? "I should have been content to see the view from here. If I hadn't gone out there, I wouldn't have fallen, and you wouldn't have tried to rescue me."

Rand put his shoes back on and stood up, removing his jacket. "Here, put this on," he said, handing it to Melanie.

Shaking her head, she refused. "No, you need it more than I do."

Rand looked down at his feet. "I can't exactly put this around my legs, can I?"

Melanie smiled. "I guess not, but I already have a jacket,"

she protested. "We just have a short ride to the parking lot. Keep your jacket."

Rand frowned. "I can't let you ride; it's too windy, and the back of your jeans is soaked. Your legs will cramp worse. When we get to the bottom of the hill, I'll ride back and bring the truck here."

Melanie understood his concern, but she figured she could make it to the lot. "I'm coming with you," she said firmly. She'd put him through enough already.

Rand opened his mouth in protest, but Melanie shook her head and moved ahead of him to pick her way back down the hill. "I'm coming with you," she repeated.

Rand groaned. "Fine, but at least take my jacket and wrap it around your waist. It may help shield your legs from the wind a little."

Realizing he meant business from the tone of his voice, Melanie took the jacket and did as he instructed.

Then, before she could get away, he grabbed hold of her hand with a firm grasp. "I'm not taking a chance on any more accidents."

He was silent for the next few moments, while Melanie wondered how in the world she would ever apologize for this fiasco. Unexpectedly, Rand broke out laughing.

"What?"

He shook his head. "You amaze me sometimes. Never in a million years could I have dreamed this up." He chuckled quietly and then added, "At least the water wasn't partially frozen."

Melanie giggled and silently prayed to thank God that Rand wasn't upset. "Hey, can I ask you something?"

"Yeah."

"Remember, a minute ago when I insisted on riding back

to the car with you, and you didn't want me to?"

He nodded.

"You said, 'Fine. But take this jacket.' "

Rand gave her a puzzled look. "And?"

"But you didn't agree."

"No."

"So why did you say, 'fine'? Why do people say that when they obviously don't agree with something? I mean, you can tell by their tone of voice that it's not okay with them."

Rand sighed. "I don't know. Everyone does it, though."

Melanie giggled again. "Maybe people should quit saying fine when they don't like something."

"And say what?" Rand gripped her hand even tighter as she jumped down from a large rock.

She shrugged. "I don't know. Maybe they should keep the same tone of voice and just say, 'not fine.' Wouldn't that be more honest?"

Rand stopped and put his hand to her forehead. "Are you sure you're not coming down with something? You're talking strangely."

Melanie didn't push his hand away, but she did laugh. "I'm just teasing you, Rand. But it is something to think about. Saying things are fine when we don't mean it is an obvious lie."

Rand nodded. "I guess you're right. I'll keep that in mind." He smiled and shook his head again. "Melanie. . .where do you come up with these things?"

"I don't know."

Still laughing, he said, "You are really something, you know that?"

She laughed at his comment, but her brain insisted on analyzing his statement. *Really something? Something good. . .*

bad. . .special? What does he mean?

Rand Anthony was hard to figure out. Melanie rather liked the challenge.

Chapter 6

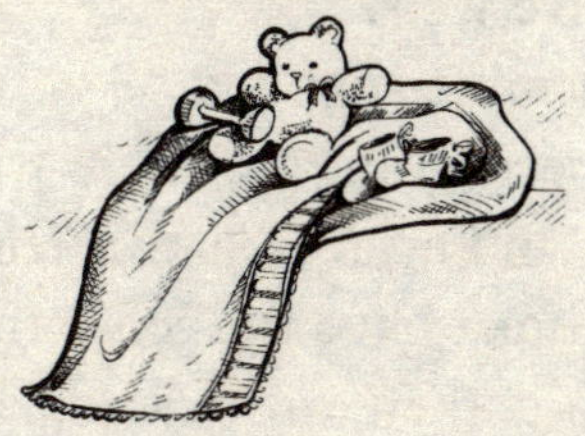

During the weeks leading up to Christmas, Melanie and Rand spent even more time together. Their friendship was now close and comfortable. They had passed the initial phase of awkwardness while they got better acquainted, but their friendship still remained just that—friendly.

When Rand asked Melanie out to dinner two days after Christmas, she felt certain their relationship was on the verge of change; but she was troubled, not knowing which direction Rand wanted to take.

"So where's he taking you tonight?" Jasmine asked.

Melanie held the receiver with one hand and used her free hand to apply lipstick as she spoke on the phone. "A Mexican restaurant."

"Really? Is it the one that always has the long waiting list?"

"I think so." Placing the cap on the tube of lipstick, Melanie opened her eyes wider and brushed on a coat of mascara.

"Let me guess. This is a friendly outing as well."

Melanie shrugged, even though Jasmine couldn't see her. "Yes." She hesitated, then asked, "Do you think that's a bad thing?"

Jasmine sighed. "Shouldn't you figure that out for yourself?

I mean, you're the one who writes the advice column."

"I know, but I'm too close to this particular case. We've been going on these friendly. . ." Melanie stopped to think of the perfect descriptive word.

"Excursions," Jasmine supplied.

"Right. We've been going on these friendly *excursions* for nearly two months, and even though I feel like I'm getting to know him better, I don't have the sense that he's interested in being anything more than my friend. There are moments where I feel he might have a romantic interest, but then he always jumps right back into buddy mode, and that's confusing."

"But you care for him."

"Yes." Melanie didn't attempt to deny her feelings. "And I'm nervous every time we go anywhere together. Sometimes, he gets this really serious look on his face, and he opens his mouth to tell me something, and then, nothing. He just flat-out jumps to another subject.

"At first, I thought he was going to tell me something like, 'Melanie, I really care for you. Let's be more than friends.' But now. . ." Melanie sat down at her desk and sighed.

"Now, I feel like he might be planning to say the opposite. Something more along the lines of, 'Melanie, I think you're a good friend, but I have the feeling that you care more for me than I do for you. Maybe we should stop these friendly. . .excursions.' "

Jasmine laughed, and Melanie felt a little upset that her best friend didn't seem to empathize with her. "Can you please tell me what's so funny?"

Jasmine laughed for several more seconds, then finally answered. "I seriously doubt you have to worry about Rand saying that."

"Why not?" A surge of hope welled up inside Melanie.

"Because I have never heard Rand say that much at one time. If he's planning to let you down easy, it'll probably take him two or three visits to get the whole thing out. You know how quiet he is. He just doesn't talk in long, rambling sentences like that."

Melanie wished Jasmine were in the same room with her so she could toss a pillow at her. "You know what I mean. So he might not say it like that. Every time I see him, I'm on pins and needles that he's going to break things off with me. I don't want that to happen."

"Then talk to him about it."

"I can't do that."

"Why not?"

"Because. . .I know him. And he would get really flustered if he felt like I was pressing him to make a decision."

"Okay, then don't. Just wait."

"I can't do that, either."

A long pause came from Jasmine's end until she finally said, "You can't ask him, and you can't *not* ask him. But you're a nervous wreck because of it. Hmm. . .why don't you write a letter to 'Dear Miss Lonely Heart'?"

"I already told you, I can't give myself advice about this. I'm asking you because I can't see the forest for the trees when it's about me."

"Then pretend it's me. I'm seeing this guy and falling in love with him—you are falling in love with him, right?"

"Yes."

"So, I'm falling in love with him, but he's given me no real indication of where our relationship is going." Jasmine took on a melodramatic tone of voice and sighed. "Please help me,

Melanie. I just don't know what to do."

Melanie laughed. "That Southern accent was terrible. Please don't quit your day job to become an actress."

"I won't. Now give me some advice, and quick, because he's picking you up in twenty minutes."

Melanie shook her head. "I can't do it. I want something more to develop between me and Rand, so I'm willing to stick around and even risk getting hurt in the process. It sounds strange to say that because if a woman wrote me and asked the same question for the column, I'd tell her to confront him about it or move on and protect her emotions."

"Like with me and Keith," Jasmine said quietly.

Melanie nodded silently. The circumstances had been slightly different, but she had given Jasmine that exact advice in high school. Keith Watters, a popular guy in their school, had dated Jasmine for nearly seven months, but he refused to use the term "going steady" to define their relationship. To make matters worse, Melanie had witnessed him flirting with other girls on several occasions.

The sound of Jasmine's voice broke into her thoughts. "I know we said we would put this behind us and not dredge it up anymore, but I feel like we need to talk about it, if only just this once.

"When you told me to ask Keith if he was serious about me, I trusted you as my friend and I did it. I'd heard rumors about him seeing other girls behind my back, and I ignored his flirting for as long as I could. Like you are now with Rand, I was willing to stick around and wait things out to see how Keith felt—until you told me I had to do something.

"You want advice, and I'm giving it to you: Find out how he feels. Preferably *before* the senior prom, Melanie. I would not wish that experience on anyone. Finding that Keith was just stringing me along because his parents wanted him to date someone nice was heartbreaking. Him turning eighteen the night of prom and declaring his independence from me and his parents will never be a happy memory."

Melanie's heart still hurt as they recalled. Finally, Jasmine had given in to Melanie's urging to find out how Keith really felt. Only she opted to ask him right in the middle of the dance floor, in front of everyone. He had shrugged, given her the facts, then announced that since he was eighteen, he no longer felt the need to abide by his parents' wishes. He unceremoniously dumped Jasmine and spent the rest of the evening with the real love of his life, Daphne Jenkins—whom he'd been secretly dating all along.

"Look, Melanie. I know I was upset with you—I even blamed your advice as the reason Keith dumped me. But we both know that's not true. Our relationship wouldn't have lasted much longer. I wish I had taken your advice sooner, before letting myself get so attached to him. So don't blame yourself. I was silly to let you run off to Washington, D.C. for all those years, letting you think I was angry with you.

"If, for some reason, Keith and I had lasted longer, I might not have met my fantabulous fiancé, Jeff."

"So you're really not angry with me?"

"No, I'm not. But I am giving you a dose of your own advice. I know Rand isn't exactly a mirror image of Keith, but that doesn't mean quiet men are unable to hurt people. You should watch your emotions; and if you can't, you need to find out where he's coming from, and soon."

Melanie took a deep breath. "You're right. Maybe you should write the 'Dear Miss Lonely Heart' column instead of me."

Jasmine laughed. "No, thanks. Besides, I'm engaged, so I'd have to quit soon anyway. Now that I have given you some advice, I think I shall retire from the business altogether. Having been on both sides of the same piece of advice, I can state, for the record, it's a lot easier to dish out advice than take it."

"Amen to that, Girlfriend. Don't worry about me. I'll take it—no matter how bad it tastes on the way down."

Rand couldn't help feeling pleased with himself. Dear Miss Lonely Heart's advice was working like a charm. For nearly two months, he'd managed to take Melanie out once or twice a week, giving himself the opportunity to become better acquainted with her—without feeling any pressure or nervousness. They were good friends—he was confident of that fact.

The only problem was, he still couldn't work up the nerve to ask Melanie out on a real date. He'd tried several times, and a few times, the words had almost made it out of his mouth.

But his nerves got in the way, and he always managed to change the subject at the last minute. He wished he could know what Melanie would think of being more than friends before he asked her about it. The last few times he'd been about to ask her, he'd watched an almost imperceptible veil of dread creep into her eyes. For all he knew, Melanie knew where he was heading with these "friendship dates," and she simply hated the idea of being anything more than friends with him.

Rand couldn't help feeling a little discouraged. He had poured his heart and soul into getting to know her. They talked, laughed, and shared ideas and funny stories with each other. She knew his dream of starting his own construction company, and he knew that she entertained the idea of opening a children's bookstore.

But there was something unspoken between them, and it grew every time they saw one another. Where was the relationship going? Rand promised himself that he would address the topic before the evening ended.

As he and Melanie rode to the restaurant, they talked mostly about the antics of the babies. Grace, Gwen, and Gilbert were learning to walk and, in the process, always found a way to get into everything in their reach.

"I feel like I'm running an obstacle course," Melanie laughed. "Every morning, Karin and I try to figure out what we need to move so they won't be tempted to disturb it, and every day they manage to amaze us by discovering something totally unexpected that amuses them."

"Tell me about it. I can't find anything nowadays, and Karin is forever telling me, 'Oh, we moved this here because the babies got into it.' I told Alex that one of these days, we'll come home and find everything in the house on a shelf four feet off of the floor."

"That's a good idea," Melanie joked.

When they reached the restaurant, there was a long line of customers hoping to get inside. Rand was grateful that he had thought to make reservations in advance. Feeling bold, he carefully placed his arm around Melanie's shoulders and led her toward the reservation desk.

The hostess informed him that there had been a slight mix-up with his reservation. The person he'd spoken to on the phone had put him down to arrive at eight, instead of seven.

Rand's heart sunk. This was a no-win situation. According to the current estimates, they wouldn't get him in until 8:15. And if he waited for his reservation time, he and Melanie still wouldn't get in for at least another hour.

"You're welcome to have a seat in the atrium," the hostess suggested. "If a table opens up before eight, I'll slide you in."

Rand did not relish the idea of waiting around for an hour. He had planned a quiet evening for the two of them, and this change of plans had already interrupted the focus he would need to have that talk with Melanie.

But, he couldn't make the decision for both of them without asking her opinion. It would be rude. He turned to Melanie to ask if she wanted to wait for their reservation or find a different restaurant. But, before he could say anything, a man emerged from the main dining area and shouted Melanie's name.

The man strode toward them. Before he reached the halfway point, recognition registered on Melanie's face. "Danny Andrews! Is that you?"

"Melanie Taylor. It is you. I was sitting at our table and thought you looked familiar." The man smiled and gave her a friendly hug. "It's good to see you again."

"How's your sister?"

"Robin? She's good. In fact, she's here with me. Why don't you come and say hello?"

Melanie nodded and moved to follow Danny into the dining room, then stopped. "Oh, I'm sorry." She reached for Rand's hand. "This is Rand Anthony, a friend of mine. Rand, this is Danny Andrews. We were good friends back in high school."

The way she'd phrased her sentence gave Rand a bad feeling. She introduced him as merely a friend, but she made the distinction that this Danny was a *good* friend. He wondered if that was any indication of the way Melanie felt about him personally.

Rand smiled and said hello.

"We can't stay long," Melanie said. "They confused our reservation, and I think we're going to try a different restaurant."

"Hey, I've got an idea. We've got room for two more at our table. Why don't you come back and share ours?"

Melanie looked at Rand before answering, but he could clearly see the expectation in her eyes. What reason did he have to keep her away from old friends? He shrugged, "I guess that's okay with me."

Melanie squeezed his hand. "Thanks." As they followed Danny back to his table, Melanie spoke in a low tone. "I know they are complete strangers to you, but Danny and his sister are so sweet. I think you'll like them."

Now that Melanie had used the word *sweet* to describe Danny, Rand doubted very much that he would like this man at all. But, to spare Melanie from feeling uncomfortable, he smiled and nodded, trying to look casual. His hopes for that serious conversation had all but vanished into thin air.

Back at the table, he was introduced to not only Robin, Danny's sister, but he also met Keith Watters, another classmate of Melanie's, and Keith's girlfriend, Valerie.

"Melanie!" Keith jumped up and enveloped Melanie in a hug—one that definitely seemed more aggressive than the light embrace Danny had given her. "You look gorgeous, as always," said Keith.

Rand didn't miss the look of distrust that Melanie gave Keith. While Danny asked the waiter to bring more chairs, the table occupants shuffled their seats to make room for Rand and Melanie.

To Rand's displeasure, the two seats were placed in between Keith and Danny, and Robin and Valerie sat next to one another.

That left Rand with two choices. He could either let Melanie sit next to Danny, the "sweet, good friend" or he could sit next to

Danny and let Melanie sit next to Keith. The latter sounded even worse, so he pulled out the seat next to Danny and let Melanie sit there. He didn't fully trust either man, but keeping her away from Keith seemed the most sensible thing to do.

That man eyed Melanie as if she were his next meal, and everyone had noticed. Rand felt sorry for Valerie, who now glared angrily at Keith.

After the waiter came and took everyone's orders, Rand felt as though he and Valerie must have become invisible. The four friends laughed and talked about old times, while he and Valerie, who hadn't come on the scene until recently, had nothing to add to the reminiscing.

Rand didn't mind not talking; he was used to being quiet. He said what he needed to say, when he needed to say it. Some people pegged him as shy and introverted. Others figured he was the strong and silent type. He couldn't fully agree with either opinion; he thought himself to be a mixture of both.

What he did know was that by sitting and listening, he could learn a great deal of information without being a nuisance and asking a lot of questions, so he sat back and listened. And learned.

Keith Watters had been somewhat of the big man on campus during high school. He also came across as a ladies' man. Somehow, he had hurt Melanie or someone close to her. Rand didn't know the details, but he figured as much from her body language toward Keith. As the evening wore on, Melanie eventually warmed up to the guy, but it didn't take a rocket scientist to see that she still kept him at arm's length.

Rand had met guys like Keith in college. They boasted and bragged, partied hard, and aged early. Keith was no exception. He spent a good deal of time bragging about his spectacular job at an advertising agency in Chicago and his new house, SUV, and the lavish parties he threw.

"If you guys want to have fun, you ought to come up and visit. We'll make a weekend of it," he kept saying. Though he used the phrase "you guys," Rand had the impression that Keith's comments were directed more toward Melanie than the rest of the group.

Danny and his sister seemed nice enough. They politely tolerated Keith and his spectacular tales and always managed to direct the conversation back to more moderate ground.

Valerie acted bored and sighed frequently. Rand wondered how serious she and Keith were. She looked like a supermodel and she knew it. She and Keith looked good together, but they didn't appear to have any lasting bonds. As it turned out, they had only met two weeks ago and had come to St. Louis on a weekend getaway so Valerie could meet Keith's family.

Rand had the feeling their relationship would be short-lived—especially if Keith didn't stop eyeing every woman within a fifty-foot radius.

Finally, mercifully, Valerie sighed long and loud enough to get Keith's attention and the two decided to leave just before dessert. As they made their exit, Keith pulled a wad of bills out of his pocket, making sure everyone saw his cache, and loudly announced that he would cover the tip as well as his portion of the bill.

Keith and Valerie left in a cloud of cologne, perfume, and overly pretentious good-byes. Rand was relieved to be rid of them. By the time the dust settled after the high-maintenance pair made their exit, Rand was ready to sit back and relax for the first time that evening. Instead, he discovered he had a bigger problem on his hands: Danny.

Or rather, Danny and Melanie.

Chapter 7

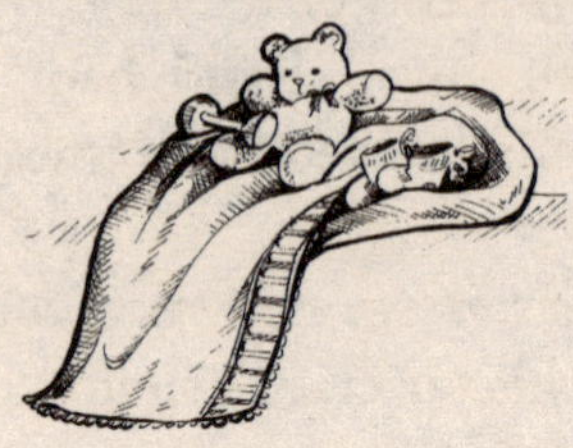

"That was an interesting evening, don't you think?" Melanie smiled, trying to sound more upbeat than she really felt.

"I guess interesting will do until I come up with a better word." Rand tapped his hands on the steering wheel, and Melanie knew he felt frustrated.

"You didn't have to split the rest of Keith's bill with Danny." Melanie shook her head. "I can't believe he flashed all that money and then left less than half of what he needed to pay for his dinner."

"I couldn't just leave it all for Danny to cover." Rand shrugged. "Besides, it was almost worth it, just to have him gone for the rest of the meal."

Melanie laughed. As nice as it had been to catch up on old times with Danny and Robin, she, too, wished the evening could have been entirely Keith-free. Danny had confided that Keith had breezed into town without any notice and practically begged them to have dinner with him. "I got the feeling that he had gone through his entire phone book, and I was the last person on the list," he told Melanie quietly while Keith recounted his latest adventure in the Caribbean.

"You know, everyone from the old days tries to dodge him when he comes to town. Robin thought we should be polite and come, so we did. And it's a good thing we did. Otherwise, I might not have seen you. . .and that would have been a terrible meeting to miss."

Later, Danny had asked about her relationship with Rand.

She'd shrugged, wishing she had a clear answer herself. "We're friends."

"Is that so? Just friends?"

"That's how he defines it, yes."

"Then he won't mind if I call you sometime?"

Melanie didn't think Rand had heard Danny's blunt question, but she twisted her napkin, feeling uncertain of what to say.

"You've never mentioned Danny before," Rand said.

Melanie shook her head. "I haven't even thought about him in years. We were friends. . . I think we once had a mutual crush on each other, but nothing ever came of it. Robin and I were cheerleaders together. Danny ran track and is a math genius. He helped me with my homework so much, I'm probably forever indebted to him."

She sighed contentedly. "It feels good to reconnect with old friends. I fell out of the loop since I've been gone for so many years."

Rand grunted in reply. If she didn't know Rand better, she could easily imagine that he might be a tad jealous.

Don't kid yourself. Melanie looked over at Rand. He stared straight ahead, not taking his eyes off the road for even a second. No, he gave her no reason to believe they were more than friends.

A few minutes earlier, when she and Rand prepared to leave the restaurant, Danny told her, "Melanie, I don't know Rand. He seems like a nice guy, but he's your friend. How about I call you in a few days? By then you can tell me for sure if you two have a more than buddy-type relationship, and if you do, I won't bother you again. But if you are truly just friends, I'd love to take you out."

"Okay," Melanie had nodded. She and Danny were alone in the lobby for a few minutes. Robin had detoured to the ladies' room, and Rand had gone to get the car. Although Melanie had no reason to distrust Danny, she wished Rand hadn't left her alone; or at least she could have walked to the car with him. The weather wasn't that cold.

Surely he realized that Danny was interested. Rand's nonchalance could only be read one way. He truly saw her as only a pal.

Remembering her promise to Jasmine that she would find out Rand's intentions and feelings bolstered by her own curiosity, Melanie decided it wouldn't hurt to ask.

"Rand?"

He hesitated for a moment, then said, "Yeah?"

"Are we still. . .friends?"

He looked sideways at her, a startled expression on his face. "What do you mean?"

"Remember when we first started spending time together and you said it wasn't an official date, but just something to do for fun? I mean. . .is our relationship still the same? Just friends and nothing else?"

Rand didn't answer for a long time. He seemed to be deliberating over what to say. Finally, he sighed. "Yes."

Melanie nodded and faced the window. So that was it. She guessed she should feel relieved. Danny was a nice guy. Handsome, successful at his job, and a devoted Christian. *So why am I not excited?*

Melanie remained quiet for the rest of the ride home. Rand didn't seem disappointed in the least, and she didn't want to risk the chance that she might choke up or, even worse, cry.

Lord, this hurts. . . . Why did I let myself fall in love with him before I knew how he really felt?

Not fine. Not fine. Not fine at all. The memory of Melanie's joke that day at the waterfalls echoed in Rand's thoughts late that night. Only now, it wasn't so funny.

He sat on the couch with the TV tuned to an old sitcom, but he paid no attention to the show. He'd watched Danny and Melanie laugh and talk the entire evening. Yes, Danny was interested in Melanie. Yes, he'd heard him hint that he should take Melanie out sometime.

Melanie had politely held Danny off, but as soon as they were in the car, she'd put her true feelings on the table. She'd asked Rand if they were "just friends." What was he supposed to say? Her question was a simple formality. She probably planned to date Danny even if he told her how he really felt.

I should have told her the truth, Rand thought, feeling miserable. But would it have made any difference? Did she already have feelings for Danny? Had she been in love with him all these years?

Once again, I'm last in line, Rand decided. But this time, it was all Dear Miss Lonely Heart's fault.

After all, she had given him the bad counsel. Rand spotted a pad of paper on the coffee table. He had one more thing to do before he put this whole ordeal behind him.

It was too late to get Melanie back, but he would not hesitate to let Dear Miss Lonely Heart know how things had turned out because of her passive advice.

Chapter 8

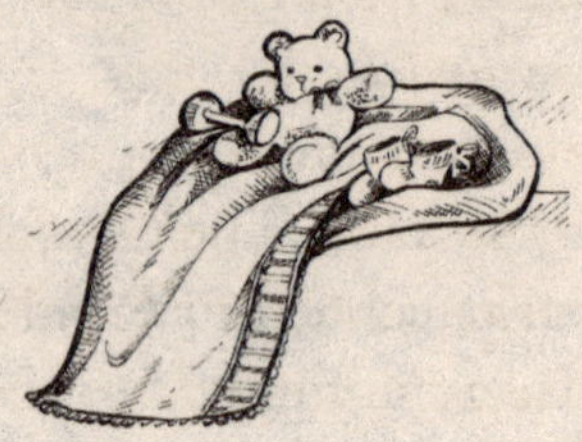

"Miss Taylor?"

Melanie turned from her lesson plan as a voice interrupted the line of students who came to turn in their book reports. "Yes, Timothy?"

Timothy shuffled from one foot to the other, an "uh-oh" look on his face. "I think I left my book report at home."

"Oh?" Melanie tried to look serious but not too stern. In the weeks since she'd begun her unexpected stint as a substitute second-grade teacher, Melanie had gotten to know her class of sixteen children quite well.

Meredith Gray experienced sneezing fits during art class. David Wells hated sweaters and fidgeted endlessly whenever his mother sent him to school dressed in one. And Tim Fraser was a darling, if forgetful, seven year old.

Not a day passed that the boy didn't forget something—his scarf, his lunch, his permission slip. . .and today, his book report.

"You'll have to try harder next time, Tim. I'll call your mother and ask her to make sure it's in your backpack tomorrow."

Tim smiled his wide, gap-toothed grin and nodded vigorously. "Thank you, Miss Taylor."

"You're welcome, Tim," she said, using the tone Jasmine

dubbed her "teacherly" voice.

As Tim returned to his seat, the bell rang, signaling the end of the school day. Melanie smiled and stood at the door as her flock filed out, telling them good-bye and listening to the various stories they wanted to tell her.

After the last student left, she returned to her desk and sighed with relief. She still had a ways to go before she settled into the academic routine as a teacher.

Looking back, Melanie viewed the New Year's Eve call from Mrs. Payton, the headmistress of the academy, as a blessing in disguise. The second-grade teacher, Mrs. Arthur, was under doctor's orders to remain off her feet for the next three months until she gave birth to her first baby. Rather than hire Melanie as a short-term substitute, the headmistress asked Melanie to take over the class for the remainder of the year. This proved fortunate for two reasons. One, she would already be acclimated to the academy's procedures and routine before the summer session. Two, she no longer needed to dodge Rand while helping Karin with the triplets.

Melanie certainly missed her time with the babies, and the two weeks at school passed painfully slow. She got the chance to see the triplets on Sunday for a brief few minutes, but seeing and holding them only made the separation more painful.

She wished she could spend more time with Karin as well, but the situation with Rand made any contact with their family an impossibility for the present.

They hadn't spoken since the night of the dinner with Danny and Keith, except to exchange "hellos" at church.

Danny called the very next morning to ask her to a movie. She accepted and felt miserable the entire evening. He treated her like a queen, but her heart ached for Rand.

With a sigh, Melanie gathered up her coat and papers and made her way to the car. She took a circuitous route home, passed by Karin's house, and debated whether or not to stop in and say hello to the people who'd come to mean so much to her in such a short time.

After several moments of hesitation, Melanie decided against stopping and went straight home. She could feel a headache coming on, and she needed to grade her student's papers—with the exception of Tim's book report.

As soon as she stepped into the house, the telephone rang.

She had long since stopped allowing herself to wonder if Rand would call, but she couldn't hide a ray of hope that crept into her voice. "Hello?"

"Melanie, I'm glad to catch you at home." It was Danny, winding up to ask her out again.

Melanie didn't say anything. She'd already managed to turn him down twice since their initial date. He was a good friend, but that was the extent of her feelings for him. "Danny, I'm. . .I've got papers to grade, and I need to start dinner."

"I know you're busy, Miss Melanie, but tomorrow's Friday, and I was wondering if you want to come to a play at my church. It'll only last about an hour or so, and it's supposed to be a comedy. You sound like you need to be cheered up."

A laugh would do her good. Afterwards, she could explain to Danny that she wanted to remain only his friend, nothing more.

"Okay, I'll come."

"Pick you up at six-thirty?"

"Sure."

Melanie hung up the phone and went straight to her room to tackle the pile of book reports. The monotony might not be so bad since she had enjoyed the book as a child.

An hour later, her mother tapped on the door.

"I forgot to start dinner," Melanie said.

Her mom shook her head. "I stopped at Grady Bakeries and brought home French onion soup and croissants."

"My favorite." Melanie grinned.

"You look tired." Her mom came into the room and sat down on the bed.

"I have a headache coming on," Melanie admitted.

"And you miss Rand," her mother added.

"I do."

"Does he miss you?"

Melanie shrugged. "I get the feeling he doesn't. He hasn't called, and we barely speak at church."

"Maybe you should call him."

"Or maybe I should leave things as they are. He's obviously not interested, and I'd only be making things harder on myself."

"Did you ever wonder if Rand felt intimidated that night when you met Danny at the restaurant? He seems like such a quiet person, maybe even shy, and I wonder if he told you he thought of you as a friend because that's what he thought you wanted him to say."

Melanie had considered this idea, but it seemed too far-fetched, even for Rand. He might be shy and quiet, but they knew each other well. He wouldn't lie to her, so he had only tried to spare her feelings before she got too attached to him. Only he'd spoken far too late.

Now she had to do the same with Danny. *Lord, please give me the right words to say when I talk to Danny tomorrow. . .and when Rand finds someone he loves. . .help me not to get jealous.*

"No, Mom. Rand meant what he said, and I have to stop being sad about it. I have plenty to keep me occupied. . .my teaching, my column—"

"Oh! Your column." Her mother jumped up and left the room. Melanie heard the sound of footsteps going down the stairs, then returning. Her mother came back bearing a large envelope. "These were in the mailbox today. I guess your editor sent you more letters to answer."

Melanie took the envelope and opened it. Some were new letters, and some were replies to the ones she had answered personally, unable to include them in the column.

She pushed the bundle aside to save for later. If her advice had backfired on any of her readers, as it had done to her, she dreaded hearing the bad news.

"It's too bad Melanie can't help with the triplets anymore. Not only do I miss her, I miss the extra pair of hands," Karin laughed.

Rand ate a bowl of cereal—no easy task with Gilbert on his lap. Rand did his best to keep the little boy's hands out of the bowl.

"Yeah, I miss her too."

Karin gave him a curious look. "I got the idea that you two. . .broke up."

Rand frowned and gently held Gilbert's hand still. "We didn't break up; we were never dating in the first place."

"Oh." Karin's wide-eyed expression gave the impression she didn't quite believe him. "Well, I've invited her over several times to visit, but she always has something else to do. I wonder why."

"She's dating someone else. Maybe they spend a lot of time together."

Karin wiped her hands on a dish towel. "I didn't know that. But I guess that could take up some of her time. Plus she has her students and that column she writes."

Rand perked up at this new bit of information. "Column?"

"Oh." Karin froze for a second. "You know, she actually didn't want that to get out. She wanted to make sure the job went smoothly before a lot of people found out. I suppose it's okay that you know, as long as you keep it under your hat."

"What column?"

"An advice column, for that *Agape Today* magazine. I think it's called Heart. . .something."

" 'Dear Miss Lonely Heart,' " Rand said, his appetite suddenly gone.

"Yes, that's it. Do you read it?"

"Yeah, I guess you could say that. At least, I used to." He stood up and carried Gilbert to the playpen, where Grace and Gwen played quietly with colorful blocks.

"I'm going to work, and I'm going to the men's basketball fellowship afterwards. I might not get home until nine or ten."

"Do you think you could stop and get ice cream on your way back? I'm in the mood for bubble gum flavor."

"No problem." Rand grabbed his hat and coat and hurried out to his car. All the way to work, he couldn't stop thinking about Melanie writing the "Dear Miss Lonely Heart" column. Did she know all along he had written the letter?

Had she befriended him because she felt sorry for him? Part of him wanted to know the answer, and part of him wanted to leave things as they were.

What should I do, Lord?

"Miss Taylor?"

"Yes, Tim?"

"Here's my book report. My mom put it in my backpack

this morning, but it fell out on the bus, and I put it in my pocket so I could 'member where it was. . .but I forgot until just now."

Melanie gave the boy a smile. His memory was better than her own today. The lunch bell would ring shortly, and she hadn't even remembered to ask Tim for his report.

"Thank you, Tim. I'll grade this for you during lunch."

"Thank you, Miss Taylor." Tim made his way back to his seat, and Melanie opened her briefcase to find her grading pen and stickers.

As she searched through the case, she saw the bundle of the *Agape Today* mail. She'd gone straight to bed after finishing her paperwork the night before and hadn't read a single letter.

Glancing around to make sure that her class was fully occupied with a silent reading assignment, Melanie decided to look through some of them.

She read the new messages first to decide which ones to answer in the next column. Then came the stack of feedback.

To her surprise and relief, page after page contained a positive response. "This was an encouraging batch of reader mail."

Feeling proud of herself, Melanie moved on to the very last page.

Dear Miss Lonely Heart,

Remember me? Always the Last Guy in Line? Guess what? I followed your advice to the letter, and I still lost the woman I truly loved. I did exactly what you said about proceeding slowly as a friend, and we became such good pals that she had no qualms about running straight into the arms of a better friend—and apparently one with more romantic potential than I have. Thanks so much for your great advice. . . . I'll be sure to use it again the next time I want to bomb in a relationship.

Always the Last Guy (of course!)

Melanie closed her eyes, feeling thoroughly reprimanded. She couldn't even begin to compose a response. Not right now. To be perfectly honest, she didn't feel much like trying to soothe the pangs of someone just as lovelorn as she.

Maybe I should try to get this guy for myself, she mused. *After what we've both been through, we'd be cautious and considerate of one another's feelings.*

With a resigned sigh, Melanie returned the stack of letters to her briefcase. Right now, she needed all of her creativity to compose a farewell speech for Danny. The "Dear Miss Lonely Heart" letters would have to wait until tomorrow.

Lord, give me the right words to say—to Danny and the magazine readers. I'm not as much of an expert as I thought I was, and I don't want to mess up anyone else's life.

Chapter 9

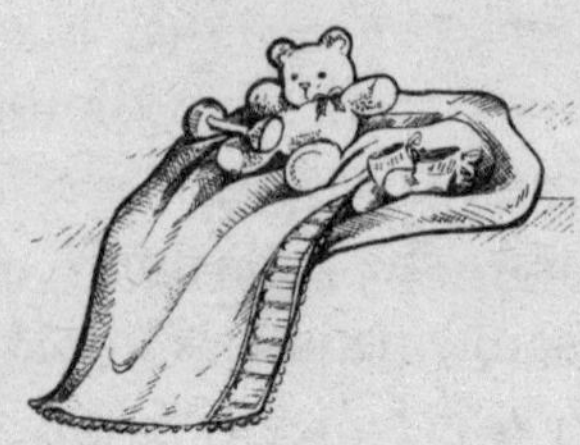

"Aren't you glad you decided to come?"

Melanie laughed. "You were right. I needed to laugh."

Danny opened the car door for her and then went to the driver's side and got inside. "Want to go for ice cream?"

Melanie laughed. "You know me, I'll eat ice cream any day of the year." Her stomach was a tangle of butterflies. "I need to talk to you about something."

"We'll talk on the way to the ice cream shop," Danny said, starting the car.

"I'm not sure you'll want to go for ice cream once I say what I need to say," she warned.

"I already know what you plan to tell me."

Melanie blinked. "You do?"

He nodded. "You can't see me again. You're in love with that friend of yours—that guy you were with that night at the restaurant."

"How did you know?"

"How could I not know? I was being optimistic when I asked you out. But ten minutes into our first date, I knew your heart wasn't in it."

Melanie chuckled. "Then why did you keep asking me out?"

He shrugged. "I hate to lose." He pulled into the parking lot of the ice cream shop. "I guess this is our last date. I don't know what happened between you two, but if I were you, I'd call Rand tomorrow and tell him how you really feel before it's too late."

He got out first and opened the passenger door for Melanie. The ice cream shop was surprisingly busy, given the fact that it was midwinter.

Danny ordered a cone with mint chocolate chip, and Melanie got a cup of strawberry cheesecake ice cream.

"Let's sit over there in that corner," Danny suggested. He led the way to the small table, and Melanie followed.

Feeling like a weight had been lifted off of her, Melanie was able to relax and laugh at his jokes. Danny was a good friend, and thankfully, he was able to accept the truth.

Thank you, Lord. What an answer to prayer. Now, if only the same could happen with her offended reader. Tomorrow morning she planned to write "Always the Last in Line" an apology. She would offer her sincere prayers that the Lord would help him to patch things up with the woman or bring him his perfect mate.

After that was done, she would take Danny's advice and call Rand. Maybe there was still a chance to make things better with him too.

Tonight, she would relax and have fun. Seconds after she plotted out her course of action, Rand himself entered the ice cream shop.

At first he didn't see her, but he happened to glance over at them while he waited on his order. He frowned and turned away.

"Well, what do you know," Danny said quietly. "You don't

have to wait until tomorrow after all. Go on over and talk to him now."

Melanie shook her head. "No, he doesn't like being the center of attention. I'll call him and meet him face to face, just the two of us."

"Then take him outside and talk to him," Danny urged.

Melanie considered the idea for a moment. Danny had a point. Rand would only be more confused if she didn't set things straight as soon as possible.

"You're right." Melanie stood up and moved to the counter, but Rand was gone.

"You're too late. He got out of here pretty quickly, and I don't blame him. I'd do the same thing if I were in his position."

Melanie slumped down in her chair, feeling defeated. "I guess you're right. I've only messed things up more by hesitating too long again. I should have marched up to him and told him that I love him."

Danny licked his cone and grinned. "Why don't you go run after him, shouting, 'I love you!' at the top of your lungs? It'll give everyone around here some entertainment."

"You are so silly," Melanie said, laughing. "I already told you that Rand is very shy. He'd melt into the ground if I did that."

"A man in love can be surprisingly bold," Danny said, suddenly serious.

Melanie shook her head. "I can't risk embarrassing him. This will have to wait until tomorrow."

Rand made it halfway back to his truck and stopped in his tracks. *I've done it again. She thinks I don't care.*

After praying about how to resolve the situation with the facetious letter he'd written, Rand felt convinced that he should apologize in person.

Regardless of whether or not he personally knew the columnist, he would never have accused someone that way in person. The anonymity of communicating through the letters had given him a chance to blow off steam, but he should have prayed rather than get angry at Dear Miss Lonely Heart.

He'd planned to visit Melanie first thing in the morning. Even if he couldn't win her heart, he needed to confess about the letter. He knew Melanie wouldn't intentionally offer bad advice to anyone. The fault lay with him.

I should have told her how I felt long before that night.

He had followed Melanie's advice but beat around the bush far too long. Because of it, she had chosen to date Danny. That couldn't be remedied, but he owed it to himself to at least open his mouth and be honest—about everything.

He marched right back into the store and over to Melanie's table.

"Melanie."

She turned around, a look of surprise on her face.

"Yes?" She stood up. "Let me explain something."

Rand shook his head. "Not fine."

"What?" A bewildered look settled on her face.

He cleared his throat. "I said, '*not fine.*' " He gestured to Danny. "I know you two have a relationship now, but for the record, I want you to know. . .that is not fine with me.

"I let you go because I thought you didn't care, and maybe you don't. But I gave you the impression that I didn't mind. I said fine, and I knew all along things weren't fine. I lied to you, and I owe it to both of us to tell the truth."

Melanie started crying, and Rand didn't know what to do. He wanted to put his arms around her, to hold her and comfort her, but that didn't seem appropriate with her boyfriend sitting two feet away.

He looked at Danny, who simply shrugged. How could the man let her hurt like that and not do anything?

Feeling frustrated, Rand sat down the sack of ice cream he still held and grabbed Melanie's hands.

"I have another confession to make. I wrote a letter to your column, only I just found out this morning that you wrote the column."

Melanie gave him a blank stare.

"Actually, I wrote you twice. The first time I asked your advice. Then a few weeks ago, I wrote back to tell you that I thought your advice was horrible."

"Always the Last Guy in Line," Melanie spoke the words slowly. "I planned to write you an apology tomorrow."

"I'm here to tell you that your advice was fine. I messed up. I wasn't honest."

Melanie nodded rapidly. "Me too. I–I'm in love with you."

Rand felt like someone had knocked the wind out of him. He looked to Danny, who sat eating his ice cream, seemingly unaffected by what Melanie just said.

"What?"

"I love you," she told him. "I was going to tell you tomorrow. . .but now seemed like a good time."

"What about. . . ," he trailed off, looking toward Danny.

"We're just friends. Really. Friends. But it's you I love."

Rand couldn't contain his happiness any longer. "Melanie. . . I love you too." He paused and cleared his throat. He needed to say what he had on his mind before he lost his nerve. "Melanie, I do love you and I want to spend the rest of my life with you. Would you. . .marry me?"

Melanie nodded, her eyes speaking with unshed tears.

Overjoyed, Rand pulled her into his arms and kissed her.

After a few moments, Melanie pulled away laughing. "Oh, Rand, I'm so happy."

"I am too," Rand said without hesitation.

"Uh, oh." A mischievous glint danced in her eyes.

A trickle of dread crept over him. "What now?"

"This afternoon, after I read your letter, I seriously considered giving up my column, but then I decided I would apologize to you and stick with it. Now I *have* to quit."

Rand shrugged. "Forget the apology. It was my fault anyway. You deserve the job, so just keep up the good work."

She shook her head. "I can't. 'Dear Miss Lonely Heart' has to be a single person—the magazine owner insists on it. That's why the last two writers had to give up the position."

"So?"

"I'm the third 'Dear Miss Lonely Heart' in less than two years. The magazine will have to replace me soon."

Rand leaned forward and kissed her again. "They'll get over it."

"I guess so," she said reluctantly.

Rand drew her into his arms again. "Thanks for the advice. You did us both a favor. Now. . ." He looked Melanie in the eye. "Is everything settled?"

"For the moment, everything is fine. And I mean that."

"Good. Because I think I need another kiss."

AISHA FORD

Aisha resides with her parents and younger sister in Missouri. Through her writing, Aisha hopes to present a message of complete trust in Jesus Christ. "The best guide for living is to follow the biblical example of Jesus—the route by which we will reap the most lasting rewards," Aisha says. "Though none of us is perfect, God is the inventor of grace—and He is patient above and beyond what we can ask or imagine." Visit Aisha's Web site at http://www.aishaford.com.

I Do Too

by Pamela Kaye Tracy

Chapter 1

Three of them were stuck in the right-hand corner of her bulletin board—each one innocent-looking, square, and with gold trim. Shelby Tate shut her left eye, took aim, and sailed a highly sharpened pencil at the latest wedding invitation. As if meeting an invisible barrier, the pencil fell short. Landing amidst a stack of magazines, an unopened twelve pack of soda, and a broken printer, it joined the last four pencils to attempt the Tate kamikaze mission.

A dart would have been more effective.

Three of them! All gifted advice columnists and now all ineligible to write the "Dear Miss Lonely Heart" column because of a simple band—as gold as the trim around their wedding invitations—proclaiming to the world not just "I DO" but for two of them already "I DID!"

Advice columnists were not a dime a dozen, no matter what the Great Oz thought, but at least Melanie agreed to one last column.

Sebastian Maitland might sit in the corner office with "Publisher" nameplated on the door, but to Shelby's mind he was simply the Owner's Son. His first day, she'd nicknamed him O.S.—for owner's son—but quickly changed it to Oz, because clearly the man lived in fantasyland.

"Ten o'clock meeting," Olive Perkins reminded as she delivered a press release and patted Shelby's cheek. "No sleep again?"

Shelby resisted the urge to run and look in a mirror. Were there black circles under her eyes? Olive could walk without making a sound. The whole office agreed she also read minds. Over sixty, with twenty years' experience, Olive displayed the manner of a highly skilled professional. Visitors to the *Agape Today* headquarters always assumed Olive controlled the office. Shelby usually felt like a youngster in dress-up trying to imitate.

Olive stood over six feet tall; Shelby placed only a shoelace over the five-foot line. Olive's penetrating brown eyes and steel gray hair never looked unruffled. Shelby's brown eyes—described by her only brother as "puppy dog"—showed every emotion, and her long black hair resisted any attempt at style.

Without a doubt, Olive was the best fact checker on either side of the Continental Divide. The woman verified facts with the speed of a Lear jet, and she rarely made a mistake. "Shelby?" Olive stared pointedly at the clock.

The daily nine o'clock meeting, another of Sebastian's ideas. He wanted all *Agape Today* writers to work as a team. While he watched, they made reports, bantered ideas, and scrutinized failures and successes. On paper, *Agape Today* looked as organized as ever. In reality. . .Shelby bit her lip and tried not to think about it.

Theodore Maitland, the owner of *Agape Today,* started the Christian magazine as a ministry, a ministry he personally had no time for. Zach Maitland, Sebastian's uncle and the former publisher, willingly put off retirement and pitched in to help start *Agape Today*. He'd brought his publishing experience straight from the bait-and-tackle-type magazine his branch of the family established over fifty years ago. In fact, Zach's own son now published the popular fishing tabloid. For three years, things went just fine at *Agape Today*. Then, Zach retired and Theodore's favored son returned home.

Sebastian's first executive decision limited features and boosted advertising. He designed a Venn diagram and a flip chart, both supporting a magazine's need to be 65 percent editorial and 35 percent advertising. Shelby, of course, believed their high sales record was a result of limited ads. As human interest stories took a backseat, the distribution chart on Shelby's wall stalled at 42,000. She'd projected 50,000 by the end of the calendar year. Sebastian's changes to the magazine's content and these daily meetings kept her from achieving her goals.

Shelby slipped into the conference room as Oz said, "Let's pray." The staff approved of Sebastian's desire to start each day with prayer. Shelby bowed her head and tried to concentrate. *Pay attention to the words,* she told herself. Up until three months ago, prayer had come easily to Shelby. She loved talking to the Father: thanking Him, asking advice, praising Him. Now Shelby struggled. Guilt about work and personal decisions made her shy away from God instead of embracing Him. The more she promised herself to return to the fold, the more she backslid. Shelby knew her errors but couldn't seem to get back on track.

"Nice you could join us." Sebastian wore a white shirt again.

The man must own a dozen. Looking at his shirt kept her from meeting his eyes, where she knew disapproval—or maybe disappointment—loomed. Was he like Olive? Could he read minds?

"Is the cover spread ready?" In an irritated voice, the one reserved only for her, Sebastian combined annoyance with courtesy.

"No." Shelby glanced at the clipboard in her hand. A yellow

sticky note spelled out their newest problem. She set it on the table, giving it a disdainful look as if it had suddenly developed a foul odor.

Oz raised an eyebrow. "No?"

"We found a great picture of a man named Max Williams pulling a young girl from a car during the Oklahoma flood."

"And?"

"Come to find out he's a thief."

With a cover headline proclaiming "Today's Heroes," the pros and cons of exalting a criminal proved too controversial for Sebastian to okay. To Shelby's mind, Max Williams's decision to risk arrest in order to save a child exemplified a potentially powerful story. Max Williams's exploits paralleled a "thief on the cross" type of tale. Shelby's fingers itched to cover the story.

"We have three more cover options, each taken from Oklahoma City press releases." Shelby passed around the clipboard with the possibilities, letting the others take a look.

October's "Disasters" theme emphasized those who overcame obstacles. The staff voted on a new cover, and the meeting quickly turned to brainstorming ideas for the white space still available in the November "Singles" issue.

Shelby, always one to try to tie stories together, wondered if she could manage a sequel to the Max Williams saga. According to Olive's research, Max Williams was single. *Single and in jail—not exactly the place to meet your mate.* The thought came unbidden to Shelby's mind. Max was good-looking in an overgrown boy kind of way.

"Shelby, you with us?" Sebastian drew twenty-seven wobbly squares—each one representing a full four-page spread in the "Singles" edition—on the white board behind him. Last month's "Disasters" squares had been drawn neatly and solidly, purposefully.

Must be a guy thing. Just the thought of commitment made Oz nervous, Shelby figured.

Only three pages were assigned. Sebastian made no secret he considered the "Singles" theme a disaster.

He, with his conservative bent, balked at promoting the computer dating trends. He cringed at the idea of anyone having a first date arranged by the staff of a cable television station and filmed in minute detail, and the man positively turned green at the thought of highlighting personal ads in his magazine.

"The perfect place to meet your future mate is church," he insisted. "We need to—"

Shelby held up her hand and stopped him. "Yes, we will emphasize meeting your mate at church, but do you have any idea of the shortage of single men who attend services?"

"I go to church."

"When did you last have a date?"

Oz blinked, his eyes becoming high-quality camera lenses zooming in on her. He drawled, "Right before I took over working here."

He didn't move, but then, he didn't have to. Shelby wondered how he managed to exude power, and all with a simple look of his dark, almost black eyes. Nothing about Oz appeared simple.

Sardonically, one corner of his mouth inched upward before he asked, "You?"

The entire staff paid rapt attention. Sebastian, an unknown entity, had spent all of the *Agape Today* lifespan in Europe. No one really knew anything about his past. During the two months he'd headed *Agape Today,* only Olive had managed to get close to him. Shelby, on the other hand, lived, breathed, and functioned completely in connection with *Agape Today*. The staff knew where to find her at almost any hour of the day or evening.

She didn't date. They all knew it. Her life centered around the magazine, her cat, and until recently her church.

She had no time to date.

And, in the three years she had lived in Washington, no one ever asked.

Olive brought up the embarrassing subject. "It's your own fault."

"What?" Shelby clicked on an advertisement and moved it to a later page before cutting and pasting it to size.

"It's your own fault you don't date."

"I don't have time to date. In case you've forgotten, once Zach left, for two months we had no acting publisher. I lived here 24/7."

Olive set proofed pages on the desk and perched on the corner. "Shelby, is something bothering you?"

"About the magazine?"

"No, I mean in your life. If you need someone to confide in, I'm available."

"What on earth are you talking about?"

"I'm talking about this recent need you have to always be the pit bull, biting holes in the pant leg of whoever threatens your territory."

"Pit bull. They're tough dogs. I should get one."

"Someday, you're going to wake up, look around, and be alone." Olive stepped smartly to the door and closed it behind her.

"I should have stayed home today," Shelby muttered.

"What?" Sebastian didn't knock.

Shelby bit back a response. Mentally, she repeated the statement, *"He's my boss"* five times before asking, "May I help you?"

"I'm assigning Alexis the television dating scam—"

"You can't assume it's a scam."

"That's why I'm not covering it. I realize I'm biased. Would you prefer to work the personal ad angle or the computer dating scene?"

Shelby hit spell-check before asking, "Which one do you want?"

"Neither."

"Fine, I'll do both of them."

"No, it's time I take on some of the day-to-day writing exercises."

"Exercises? Mr. Maitland, you can't think of assignments as exercises. Your lack of emotion will show up in your articles. The readers will notice."

"I'll be objective. I want to understand every aspect of this business."

"Then start with something small. Write advertising copy."

The Great Oz stare came again. Shelby fought against it, but squirming seemed the only response.

"No," Sebastian said, "I intend to take a more active role, starting with the November issue. I'll take the personals; you can do the computer dating." He took a small notebook out of his pocket and scribbled in it. "Now, what about 'Dear Miss Lonely Heart'?"

An opportunity! Shelby pointedly looked at the mounds of paperwork stacked on her desk. "Let me have Melanie keep it up for a few more months until I have time to find a suitable replacement."

"You interview anyone yet?"

"No, I haven't even placed an ad."

"Why not?"

"Lack of time. Priorities. It's on my to-do list, believe me."

Sebastian did the thing with his lips again. One corner inched upward. It made him look sneaky. As Shelby put her fingers on the keyboard, an unsettling feeling fluttered in her stomach. He looked much the same as he had right before he asked her—in front of everyone—if she dated. Come to think of it, a lopsided smile preceded every unwelcome utterance from Sebastian.

"What are you thinking?" Shelby refused to let him see her squirm.

"I'm thinking you should take over the 'Dear Miss Lonely Heart' column. You have all of the qualifications. You think you know everything, and you're single."

"So are you. And you're the one who wants writing exercises." She grinned. "We'll drop the 'Miss' and make it 'Dear Lonely Heart.' You're hired."

Chapter 2

Sebastian checked his watch as the elevator slid to a stop on the third floor a few seconds before 6:00 A.M. The first and second floors housed Maitland Accounting. A distant Maitland cousin rented the fourth floor as his law office. Sebastian liked getting to the office early. He enjoyed the sound of his steps echoing through the hallways. He wanted the quiet time alone to prepare for the day.

The doors swished open and the lights greeted him. Every single light.

Shelby.

Due for vacation, she seemed determined to prove she couldn't be spared. A more efficient walking, talking, breathing, *Agape Today* encyclopedia couldn't be found. Between her and Olive, they kept the magazine in top form. Leaning against the wall, Sebastian took the notebook from his pocket and flipped to the last page. He kept his prayer list handy. Patience already took up lines one, four, and twelve. He added it again, number nineteen. With a wry grin, he acknowledged he might as well cross out every patience notation and just pencil in Shelby's name.

Until he'd met her, he'd not understood the precept so

often taught in his business classes. He didn't like finding out firsthand why so many newly arrived CEOs and upper-management types were advised—and wanted—to clean house and hire all new people. Shelby Tate resented him, and she let him know it at every opportunity.

She'd make an excellent partner but instead took the role of a thorn in his side. In all honesty, he deserved her ire. She loved her job, while he merely functioned.

He tucked the notebook back in his pocket and started for his brightly lit office. There was something about the woman, if he could call her that. Sometimes, when he caught sight of her slight form from the corner of his eye, he thought a schoolgirl had snuck into the building. She was like a pebble in one's shoe. Of course, once the shoe came off, in many ways, the pebble resembled a precious gem.

Where had that thought come from? Sebastian shook his head. Pretty soon, his prose would be as flowery as hers. Precious gem? The terror of writing the "Dear Lonely Heart" column must be playing havoc with his mind. *Time to lay the assignment back on her desk.* She knew everything. Or, at least, she thought so. He certainly believed she did—when it came to the magazine.

Her door stood open. What he hoped to be an empty coffee mug perched precariously on the corner of the desk. It rested atop an open dictionary and bumped against a vase of dead flowers. Her office was too small. She needed space, windows, and lots of organization cubbies.

Black hair fanned out, covering up whatever paperwork she'd been working on when sleep finally overtook determination. Sebastian wondered if the woman knew how to sleep in the dark. He doubted it. Then, he wondered why that thought intrigued him. He'd wait before telling her "Dear Lonely Heart" belonged to her again.

He headed for the break room and started a fresh pot of coffee. After ridding the room of the burnt residue from Shelby's last Folgers effort, he cleaned up the rest of the room. A few soda stains pointed to where she'd poured her drink. Cookie crumbs lightly dusted the table. The woman possessed no domestic skills when it came to the kitchen. Fast food and potato chips probably dominated her grocery list.

Five minutes later, he headed for his own office. A fifty-pound blue marlin took up more than a fair share of shelf space behind Sebastian's desk. Interspersed among the fishing trophies were photos of Zach Maitland shaking hands with important people—all of whom loved to fish.

Sebastian needed to redecorate or at least clear out the office. He didn't want the frills and clutter his uncle did. The *Agape Today* staff wouldn't even notice his Golden Gloves welterweight trophy, nor would they give a second glance to childhood sports memorabilia. Of course, they might be impressed with his Sunday school perfect attendance awards and his church camp photos. They tended to judge success by newsworthiness. Zach, with his arm around Jimmy Carter, looked impressive, or at least the wide-mouth bass the ex-president held did.

Sebastian straightened a framed copy of one of Zach's early magazine articles. The man loved publishing. Still, according to the letters arriving weekly at the *Agape Today* office, Zach felt quite at home on the mission field and couldn't rave enough about the importance of the ministry.

Agape Today was a ministry, one entrusted to Sebastian. He'd always considered himself a more hands-on kind of man, but maybe he'd find his niche here. The pen was mightier than the sword, after all. At least, Zach and Shelby kept saying so.

Sebastian sat at his desk and opened the morning paper. Maitland Publishing took precedence in his life now and so did reading competing newspapers every morning.

Even at almost twenty-eight years old, Sebastian still enjoyed pleasing his father. Though his dream was to go into law enforcement, no police officers graced the Maitland family tree.

In the silence of the morning, Sebastian could hear Shelby's computer keys clacking. So, she no longer snoozed. Should he stop by her office, he knew he'd see a cool, collected woman. She'd be in yesterday's clothes, but she'd still be cool and collected.

On newspaper number two, at page four, just after an article about a clown who robbed banks—Shelby really influenced him, he realized, for he'd checked to see if the clown was single—he realized he no longer heard typing. Sebastian waited a moment, grabbed his portfolio, and headed down the hall to watch her through the open door. She stared at her computer. One leg crossed over the other. Her foot jiggled in agitation. She had a pencil stuck in her hair; make that two, no three.

"Everything all right?"

She whirled around. One pencil came loose and tumbled to the floor. "Yes, why?"

"Just seemed strangely quiet, that's all."

"Well, I'll admit to the quiet, but I think you're responsible for the strangely." Her eyes glinted.

"Har, har. What are you working on?"

"The Max Williams story. His father deserted the family when Max turned four."

"It happens to plenty of people, and they don't steal for a living."

"And they're boring to read about. This is an opportunity."

She was sizing him up. He knew it.

A section of her hair fell as yet another pencil worked its way loose. She didn't notice. "Do you have your sample letters for 'Dear Lonely Heart' done yet?"

He almost told her no, almost told her he'd decided to pursue other topics of interest; but it irked him, this obvious attitude that she expected him to fail. "Yes."

"Good, let me see."

"Well, I've only done one. I—" He cleared his throat. This woman exuded too much power for him. She could teach him plenty, if only he didn't get the urge to strangle her every time she peered at him with a know-it-all expression.

"Here." He thrust the article at her.

He couldn't read her expression but found himself mouthing the words as she read. He'd picked what he'd thought to be the most common of problems. Ones he'd heard some of his college peers discussing.

Dear Lonely Heart,

I'm in love with a man who, although he says he loves me, insists until we're married, he should be allowed to date other women. I've told him this makes me uncomfortable, but he says I'm neurotic and jealous. I'm not getting much sleep. Please advise me.

Wanting More in Montana

"And your advice?" Shelby carefully set the letter on top of the dictionary, next to the coffee cup, beside the dead flowers.

Sebastian noticed a card hanging limply from a now-shriveled stem. Unfortunately, he couldn't see the writing to discern the sender. He took another paper from his portfolio. Careful not to knock anything over, he circled her desk, stood behind her, and read over her shoulder:

Dear Wanting More,

Get rid of him. Get a life. Find someone new.

She went completely silent. And silence coming from a woman who always had the final word worried him. One thing about Shelby: She could talk, and she'd explain any detail to him as if he were ten years old, whether he wanted her to or not.

"Sebastian, have you read some of our past issues? I mean, especially the 'Dear Lonely Heart' column."

"You don't think this says it all?" He, for a wild moment, really wanted her opinion.

The last of the errant pencils now twirled wildly between her fingers. Her hair fell to her shoulders. "It's certainly to the point, but, well, my experience with the people who write us, especially women—hey, make that either sex—says nothing is quite as cut and dried as this response."

"The guy is clearly a jerk."

Shelby nodded. "But she thinks she's in love."

"She'll get over it."

To Sebastian, it looked like Shelby started to choke. Just when he thought maybe he'd need to pound her on the back, she regained control.

"You're right," Shelby said slowly. "Who could be in love with a guy that selfish? But," her eyes darkened as she studied the letter, "she's very much afraid, both of what she has and what she might be risking. And she might not be able to recognize what love really is. I don't know. Sounds a little bit like lust is coloring her decisions."

He looked at her, sitting so at-home behind her desk. This was her forte. He couldn't begin to fathom her comfort in the publishing environment. He envied it and her ability with words. This must be the Shelby his uncle mentioned so highly. A caring, devoted editor who took the time to think about the needs of both the magazine and its readers. He'd never expected Shelby to so easily pinpoint an emotion he'd completely missed.

Sebastian wondered if she'd spoken this openly in front of Uncle Zach. Not that lust needed to be a dirty word—just not one you bantered around a Christian magazine office. It probably wasn't a word to use in the "Singles" issue, either, although it certainly figured into the theme. Another thought entered Sebastian's mind. Clearly, the word lust didn't faze Shelby.

It shouldn't bother him, either. After all, they were in a new millennium. So, was it an age difference thing? Shelby was barely twenty-four, just a few years out of college.

Sebastian was only four years her senior, but they were worlds apart. He felt like a prude, and he didn't like it. The sound of Olive's footsteps coming in their direction saved Sebastian from saying or doing anything he'd regret.

Shelby rambled on, "It's easy to give advice, but unless you temper the advice with understanding and compassion, it will never be taken."

"What?" Great, he'd been having warm and fuzzy thoughts about Wonder Woman here, and she'd been so oblivious to his thoughts, she'd continued letting him know the exact what and ifs of his job.

Agape Today, his job. A job he seriously needed to get a handle on.

There'd been a strange look on his face.

Oh, no, she'd hurt his feelings—something she'd previously considered impossible to do. Guilt convinced Shelby to reach for his "Dear Lonely Heart" response. She closed her eyes after reading it. The passing of time—roughly twenty minutes—did not improve his prose.

She really wanted to zip home, take a shower, change her clothes, and locate Max Williams. Instead, it looked like she'd be spending time helping the man who stole her job. Her fingers tightened around the paper. She should let him flounder. She should go ahead and print the totally left-brain reply and let the letters to the editor erupt. But, no, that would hurt the magazine.

Worse, somewhere in Montana, a woman actually struggled with this problem, and she'd be hurt. Shelby bowed her head and, for the first time in weeks, talked with God. Pettiness might keep Shelby from talking to God about her own problems, but she found it easy to converse with Him about "Wanting More in Montana." She felt better a few minutes later.

Grimacing, she started to stand. She could never be "Miss Lonely Heart." The people who wrote cried for answers, and sometimes Shelby knew this tiny advice column could never be big enough to give the kind of help these people needed and deserved. Only God could do that.

At the moment, Shelby needed help; and for the first time, *Agape Today* proved more a trial than a healing. She glanced at Sebastian's answer, so straight and to the point, so male.

He hadn't been able to pen an appropriate answer. Could she? Did she dare try? What would Hope, Cathy, and Melanie advise? And if the three previous columnists knew about Shelby's personal struggles, what suggestions would they offer? She could use their help, if only she could find the courage to call.

Shelby looked from the three wedding invitations, tacked on

her bulletin board, to the certificates of achievement displayed on the wall. They'd only been in business three years, and yet *Agape Today* had already received many reputable awards. Zach Maitland had accepted the prizes, but Shelby had earned them, with Olive's help.

Except for turning on his light early in the morning, Shelby avoided Sebastian's office. As she stepped down the hall, she compared his corner to the rest of the floor.

Quiet.

It hadn't been this way when Zach worked there.

Sebastian studied a newspaper. He made notes in the margins and occasionally looked at the ceiling as if in thought.

She cleared her throat before saying, "Do you mind if I add a bit to your answer?"

He didn't say no, at least not right away. She'd expected an immediate veto. Maybe there was more to the man than she credited him for. He looked out of place in this office, but Zach's big, blue, dead fish centered above Sebastian's head actually made Oz seem a bit more human.

She'd always liked this office. Begrudgingly, she admitted she even admired Sebastian a little for leaving some traces of the prior owner intact. Maybe if Sebastian allowed his uncle Zach some influence, this younger Maitland wouldn't be so tense. He tended to look so rigid, and earlier, in her office, he'd seemed more tense than usual.

"Like what?" he finally asked.

He didn't make this easy. She blamed the slight misting of sweat on her brow from lack of sleep, rather than nerves, and continued. "Think about it. We need to deal with the issue of loneliness."

"Go on." He gave her his full attention.

He'd strayed too far from his usual personality traits of annoyance and courtesy. Seeing Sebastian look interested made her want to dash for the safety of her office. Loneliness might be a topic better left alone. And mentioning the word lust in a Christian magazine might cause repercussion. The editor in her shouted "Sensationalistic Prospect," the Christian in her whispered, "Tread Carefully."

"You're 'Dear Lonely Heart,' " she finally said, changing her mind about adding a bit. He could do it. "You need to give her some options. Try to spell out a workable solution."

"Help me."

"I'll read your response. Then we'll talk."

He grinned, leaning back in his chair and folding his arms across his chest. "Not good enough. You've let me know I fall short as a 'Dear Lonely Heart' author. I need you, Shelby."

A few hours later, Shelby left the Great Oz's office. She'd gone in there intending to become "Dear Lonely Heart." Instead, it looked like the column now belonged to "Dear Lonely Hearts." They'd hashed out an acceptable response to "Wanting More in Montana," one she felt absurdly proud of. One she'd never have managed alone. She and Sebastian were going to write the responses together.

Shelby needed an aspirin.

Chapter 3

The clang of silverware and the buzz of conversation seemed surreal to Sebastian. The League of Christian Businessmen met on the first Monday of each month. Zach had scheduled a year's worth of business commitments for Sebastian. Networking, Zach stressed, spelled the difference between ruin and riches.

During his early days at *Agape Today*, Sebastian loved going to meetings. Since he knew nothing about the publishing world, meetings took him out of the office where he felt inadequate and put him in a more comfortable social venue. He could talk shop, even if he didn't know how to put together copy, figure headline points, or verify facts. Today, Sebastian's thoughts strayed back to the office. More precisely, his thoughts focused on Shelby and her—no, *their*—column.

The "Dear Lonely Heart" column might prove the means by which Sebastian got his foothold into the *Agape Today* mindset. Teaming up with Shelby was a brilliant plan. She spoke newspeak with a native tongue. Maybe Sebastian wouldn't disappoint his father, after all.

He wished he could feel as inspired about writing copy for the "Singles" issue. Shelby inspired him, but interestingly enough, neither one of them acted like poster children for today's single.

Hmm, maybe Shelby could be the answer to more than one prayer. Truthfully, he felt no desire to pursue the personal ads alone. He didn't want Shelby investigating computer dating without some type of. . .of. . .chaperone? Bodyguard? Certainly a man who longed to be a police officer would be perfect for squiring a roving reporter around the pseudo-dating world. He might even luck into unearthing the Shelby his uncle Zach kept raving about.

Sebastian needed to stop thinking about Shelby. It was bad politics to mix business with pleasure. Even if the politics seemed a pleasure to do business with. Looking around the room at the Gates Hotel, he wondered how each of the men in attendance had met his mate. Sebastian also pondered how many, like he, were still single.

A man stepped behind the podium, quieted the auditorium, and offered a prayer of thanksgiving. Soon after, a waitress placed a breakfast of eggs, ham, and English muffins in front of Sebastian.

"So, what do you think, Sebastian?" Henry Ross, CEO of Ross Computer World, reached for Tabasco sauce to put atop his eggs.

"About what?"

Henry laughed. "I didn't think you were listening."

"I'm sorry, Henry. Taking over the magazine has been a bit tougher than I anticipated."

"I'll bet. Zach said it got so he had to budget time to sleep." Henry and Zach's friendship dated back to their high school days. Both men were now bald, and each was more interested in his grandchildren than in football scores.

The speaker, a financial advisor, started a lengthy monologue about money and the small businessman. Sebastian wondered why Henry even bothered to attend. Neither the business nor the man qualified as small. These community involvements were expected of the owner of a newly formed, locally based business. Sebastian attended all kinds of meetings, ranging from the Rotary Club, to the League of Young Republicans, and including the Coalition of Concerned Publishers. Name it, and Sebastian's name graced an invitation. Only the Shriners seemed to have misplaced his address.

Shelby attended just as many meetings. At the moment, Sebastian knew she sat ensconced with one of the ladies' groups in the area.

Funny how until this morning he'd never noticed how her exotic brown eyes complemented her midnight black hair. Of course, this morning as she rushed from his office, she hadn't looked sweet. No, she'd looked mad enough to spit.

He'd take her on in a spitting contest. She just might be a worthy opponent.

After finishing a second cup of coffee, Sebastian smiled in the speaker's direction and jotted down ideas in his pocket notebook. He usually paid attention to any speaker out of respect, but the urge to work overpowered him just now.

The *Agape Today* staff currently worked on six months' worth of content. "Disasters" and "Singles" rated as top priority at the moment. Each had impending print deadlines. After "Singles" came an "Animals" theme, followed by "Hobbies," then "Politics" and "Careers." Connecting each story with a Christian angle made their magazine stand out.

Agape Today aimed to meet the needs of Christians, ages twenty-five to forty-five. Marketing determined that the readers wanted a religious thread but not so much it overpowered the main idea of the story. Sebastian read most of his competition and knew some Christian magazines were heavy-handed with the religion, while others were too thrifty. Thanks to Shelby, *Agape Today* managed to fulfill the expectations of the readership.

At noon on Saturday, Shelby checked her watch, saved her information, and logged off her computer. Listening to the sound of a horn blaring outside her office window, she relished that Washington on the weekend felt much the same as midweek. The hustle and bustle of the city made her feel alive.

Shelby wished that, like her siblings, she considered spending time at home a cherished event. Instead, dread was a constant companion. She was the Tate child who never managed to fit in.

Enough self-pity. Time to put the magazine to bed, or more accurately, to an afternoon nap. She swept a stack of papers off the top of her desk and into her briefcase before heading out the door.

The family reunion had kicked off last night, and her father was none too pleased about his youngest child missing the huge Friday night dinner. Right now, Mom was probably putting the last bowl of gravy on the table before calling the hordes to lunch. There'd be hugging in the front room, swimming in the backyard, board games in the family room, and enough food in the kitchen to feed all the tourists at Mount Vernon.

And, Shelby knew, Dad would be put out by her missing lunch today. Her father, much like Captain von Trapp in *The Sound of Music,* expected his offspring to be lined up and accounted for in a timely manner. Only, Shelby's dad didn't need a whistle; all he needed was The Look. She'd be on the receiving end of that look within minutes of her arrival.

Thinking about her father's gift of getting the job done by simply staring reminded her of how Sebastian tended to do the same thing. She didn't want to compare the two men.

There'd be some cheek pinching and lots of questions when she got home. Shelby knew just what Aunt Edna would say: "Got a beau, Shelby? What? Well, men don't like bossy females."

A duffle bag took up the backseat of her Camaro. Shelby brushed cat hair off the front passenger seat and felt a moment's grief at leaving Freedom at the kennel.

Pulling out of the parking spot, she took one last look at the Maitland Publishing building. It seemed more like home than her family's place; her office more a testimony of the real Shelby Tate than the every-item-is-coordinated-with-the-bedspread-and-curtains room in Sage, West Virginia. Her room there had been decorated three times while she was growing up.

Luckily, she didn't remember the Winnie the Pooh years, but she could still close her eyes and remember the lavender years and white enamel matching furnishings. It was hunter green and peach now, with wallpaper border and no canopy bed. Nothing would be under the bed, and no fingerprints would smudge the walls. Outside of clothes, there'd be no evidence of the girl—now woman—who had once resided there. Her bedroom, more a guest room, would look ready to grace the cover of some home furnishings magazine.

Shelby crossed the Potomac River to West Virginia, state of her birth. It was almost like her very breathing slowed down. Eerily, the radio rock station phased out. Country took its place. Shelby sighed, squirmed, turned the radio off, and tried to find comfort in the familiar landscape rolling by with the hours.

There were more Tates than usual and no room in the

driveway. Or maybe the usual number attended, and Shelby just felt overwhelmed. She parked on the lawn and grabbed her bag. The smell of freshly cut grass made her pause. She'd missed the feeling of soft blades under her feet. D.C. had acres of sidewalks and streets. Here, Shelby took a step back in time. She still missed the games of basketball, four square, badminton, and hide-and-go-seek.

When she'd been all of seven, she'd holed up in a tool shed until she'd fallen asleep. Hours later, she'd awakened in the dark to find she'd been locked in. Thank goodness, her oldest sister never considered giving up the hunt. Shelby had avoided the shed from then on, becoming almost ill if she needed to fetch something from inside. She also became the first Tate child to need a nightlight. Her father tore the shed down and added on to the garage.

Then, there were Saturday nights huddled with Cynthia, Amber, and Shannon in front of the fireplace with Nancy Drew. Best of all were Gramma Rose Tate's visits. The tiny woman always entered the house carrying a basket of homemade muffins and, instantly, a homey feeling filled the Tate mansion. Gramma didn't care about designer clothes. She didn't mind mud on her floor or untied shoes. When Shelby turned thirteen, Gramma gave her a journal for Christmas. Shelby had been writing ever since. Rose Tate had passed away only three months ago, about the time Zach Maitland moved to Africa.

"Shelby!" Cynthia opened the front door. The big sister, and the clingy one, mothered them all.

"Hi, Cynthia. How's it going?" Shelby knew the hug would be unavoidable. It would be sincere, too, as would the quick embraces and kisses from her two other sisters, Amber and Shannon. Her brother, Daniel, was somewhere overseas now, thanks to the air force. He wouldn't join the Tate law firm for two more years.

Perfume, powerful and expensive, swirled under Shelby's nose. For a moment, she leaned into the hug, remembering a twelve-year-old Cynthia who pulled all the girls into her bedroom and instigated fashion shows with their mother's clothes. As the smallest, Shelby always managed to look ridiculous. Even then, Shelby realized the differences between herself and her siblings. The clothes belonging to her mother trailed the bedroom floor like a sleeping bag wrapped around a Chihuahua. Her sisters had been Mom's height—Amber already taller.

Cynthia, the nesting sister who made her money in family law, still didn't notice anything unusual. "Well, the twins have eaten so much that they're both sick. And little Shelby's been asking about you."

Only Cynthia would dream of naming her daughter after Shelby. The dark-eyed three year old looked like her youngest aunt. Cynthia called the child beautiful. Someday, Little Shelby would look in the mirror and notice that while everyone else reigned six feet and blond, there she stood five feet, with hair as black as tar.

"Aunt Big Shelby!" Little Shelby rushed out the front door, tripped over the step, and landed at Shelby's feet. The little girl quickly scrambled back to her feet, a slight cut on her chin the only evidence of the mishap. She grinned and held up her arms. Not a crybaby, this one.

"My, my," Shelby said, easing her bag off her shoulder and picking up her niece to swing in a high circle. "You sure are excited."

"Mom said I could sleep with you tonight and that you'd teach me how to play Concentration."

"Oh, boy." Shelby raised an eyebrow in Cynthia's direction. Cynthia's agenda was clear: Being near children will make Shelby want children.

Chapter 4

Bad news for Sebastian meant calling Olive to come to the office on a Saturday afternoon to help him find paperwork that should be at his fingertips. Worse news meant calling Shelby, at her family's house—during a reunion, no less.

"I'm sorry to bother you—" He paused. He shouldn't start a conversation with an apology, at least not from him. She was his employee.

He went through three different Tates before he got the one he wanted. Shelby sounded breathless, as if she'd been running. "Sebastian?"

He wasted no time. "I can't find the tax return papers. Do you, by any chance, know where they are?"

Silence came from the other end of the phone. She didn't sound like she was running anymore. He could almost feel her ire over the phone wires. Meeting the quarterly filing date had always been a pain, especially to Shelby, who hated spending any time balancing her budget when she could be writing. He waited a moment. "Shelby? You still there?"

"Aren't they due Monday?"

"Yes."

"I met with the accountant yesterday. And—"

"And you were supposed to pass them on to me. They're not in my in-box."

Now he could hear her breathing. "That's because they're in. . .my briefcase. Oh, no."

Anger didn't even tap him on the shoulder. Shelby Tate had made a mistake. He loved it. The woman who hated his number projection charts and called him boring since he wanted to do a bit more with advertising had taken the tax return papers to her family reunion. He'd tease her later, after the papers were postmarked and accepted.

"When are you coming back to work?" Sebastian asked.

"She's on vacation until Tuesday." Olive, standing behind him with this morning's newspaper, narrowed her eyes in a Don't-you-dare-give-her-an-excuse-to-come-back-here sort of look.

Sebastian knew as well as anyone how many vacation days Shelby was due and how seldom she took them. He also knew how reluctantly she went to this reunion.

"I can head back tomorrow."

"Not good enough. I'm heading to your place right now. Can you give me directions?" Sebastian flipped open his Rolodex. "According to Olive, your parents' address is 303 Country Club, in Sage, West Virginia. What's that? A two-hour drive?"

"About. Look, really, this reunion isn't that important. I can be back to the office bright and early tomorrow."

If it were up to her, Sebastian thought, Agape Today *would be a one-woman magazine.* "I'm on my way."

"I'll meet you somewhere." Shelby's voice sounded crisp.

She didn't want him at her parents' house. Why? Was it him, specifically, or did she really want to come back to the office that badly?

Sebastian handed the phone to Olive.

"He's out the door, Love." Olive handed Sebastian an address and motioned for him to make her words true.

He stood and hurried to the door, amused by how much he looked forward to spending time in the country with Shelby. Sage, West Virginia had a baseball museum and the best family-owned Mexican restaurant he'd ever eaten at. Even if Shelby barred him from entering her home, he'd make an evening of it. Time enough to do the tax return tonight when he returned.

Olive continued, "He didn't want to wait. You know men. Now don't worry, we'll take care of those papers just fine. You enjoy your family."

Luckily, Sebastian had driven through Sage a time or two and knew exactly where the pancake house by the freeway was. A frantic cell phone call assured him she knew he was coming. It also enabled her to call the shots. He'd meet her at seven.

At least, he would have met her if not for the flat tire. Not his, but a frightened-looking elderly woman who reminded him too much of his aunt Rena to drive by.

His aunt Rena wouldn't have known about her flat spare tire, either. And it was just bad luck that his cell phone chose that moment to blink a low battery message.

His watch read eight-thirty when he pulled into the gas station next to the pancake house. Shelby was long gone. His city map showed the Tates' house to be located on the outskirts of Sage.

He went through a quaint downtown, past lots of open land, to houses big enough to comfortably shelter the Washington Redskins—and their friends. He'd never have guessed Shelby came from a wealthy family.

Lights were on in the backyard and noise drifted over the

rose bushes. Sebastian parked on the grass next to Shelby's car, figuring if she could, so could he.

A tall blond woman opened the door. "You must be Sebastian Maitland. I'm Bridget Tate, Shelby's mother. Come on in. She's in the back, playing volleyball. Let me go get her."

Mrs. Tate led him into the living room and motioned toward the couch. He started to sit, but the lure of family portraits convinced him to walk around the room. They were a photogenic family, especially the gentleman hanging over the fireplace. Judge Sheldon Tate.

Sebastian mentally kicked himself. He should have figured out the connection. Now Shelby's drive to make a name for herself made sense. Did the judge have anything to do with Uncle Zach hiring her? Nah, Zach didn't care if you were a cousin to Billy Graham himself.

A large portrait hung atop the fireplace. A family of Vikings smiled at him, except for the daughter posed at the far right.

He went back and studied the other pictures. Shelby's sisters were ballerinas; Shelby was an equestrian and so was her brother. Shelby's sisters had obviously been in a good number of theater productions; Shelby played softball, what looked to be second base. Senior photos showed blond girls with bouncy curls in pink dresses. Shelby'd worn jeans and a T-shirt to the photo session, as had the brother.

"She's beautiful, isn't she?" Mrs. Tate crossed the room to stand by Sebastian. "Our little rebel. She's in the middle of a volleyball game. She says to step out back."

Enough Tates to fill a bus surrounded the net. Sebastian smelled hot dogs and popcorn. His mind started to consider how long ago he'd eaten lunch.

"Here!" Shelby's voice carried over the family's clamor.

She wore gray sweats and a dark blue T-shirt. Both were well worn and sported holes. Her hair, pulled back in a ponytail, swung from side to side. "We need another player." Her words challenged him to beg off and the other side to disagree with her adding a non-Tate clan member to their game.

Ten minutes later, dressed in her brother's old workout clothes—right in length, but tight just about everywhere else—Sebastian took his place next to Shelby. He could see, by the gleam of the backyard lights, that her desire to win overtook her annoyance at his presence.

The smiles he'd received from cousins, aunts, uncles, friends, all welcomed him, not as Shelby's boss but as a potential suitor. He'd seen the looks before, and usually it sent terror all the way to his knees. This time, though, he felt a bit smug, and all because he knew that Shelby felt annoyed about the assumptions her family made. As for him, he didn't have to do anything, just smile and let the family assume.

He didn't have time to antagonize her—and, oh, how he wanted to—any further once the game started. Shelby may not have looked like her family, but she had their grit. Every Tate, or variation of, was determined to win. It wasn't unlike the annual Maitland baseball game. Sebastian smiled. He'd love to have Shelby as a secret weapon at his family's next reunion.

The ball went out of bounds, and some tall blond male chased it into the bushes. Shelby sidled over and from the side of her mouth said, "We win, I'll not only teach you how to be 'Dear Lonely Heart,' but I'll also throw in a free journalism lesson on the inverted pyramid style of writing. They win, and you're on your own."

Man, she was beautiful. How had he missed it? Sebastian figured he must have been spending too much time thinking about deadlines and letterhead.

His fingers itched to touch the curve of her eyebrow. Sweat glistened on her forehead, and Sebastian wondered if she tasted of salt. He inched closer to her and from the side of his mouth whispered, "We win, and you become my 'Gal Friday,' and you go out to dinner with me next Saturday night."

Her mouth opened. Sebastian couldn't remember her ever being speechless.

"Or, I don't play." He felt better than he had in years. The fresh air and energy in Sage, West Virginia, revived him. Of course, being with Shelby helped. Boy, what a hole he'd buried himself in while trying to be the ultimate force at *Agape Today*. Three months wasted. He could have been playing cat and mouse and having the time of his life.

Sebastian decided to break one of the golden rules at Maitland Publishing. No doubt about it, he might be about to fall in love with one of his employees.

Shelby opened one eye. On the floor an air mattress had seeped air all night, but little Shelby no longer slumbered there. She'd probably crawled in bed with her mother at some point. Sebastian Maitland slept down the hall, sharing a room with two of Shelby's young cousins. Oh great, her first thought upon waking had Sebastian at the hub. Last night, after a tremendous volleyball victory, Shelby's father invited Sebastian to stay and attend church the next morning. Shelby kicked Sebastian's ankle, but he ignored her. What was wrong with him?

If he called her "Gal Friday" one more time, she'd kick him again. Shelby squeezed her eyes shut. All because she'd accidentally packed the tax return papers, Sebastian had wormed his way into the bosom of her family.

Cynthia loved him and invited him over for a Sunday lunch sometime next month. Little Shelby thought his lap the perfect size. And Father, who never asked Shelby any questions about *Agape Today*, suddenly had some insights about the state of publishing. Shelby had no illusions about her father's interest. He wanted to make sure her job was steady. After all, Shelby remained the only Tate offspring to not choose law as a career.

Listening to Sebastian glorify *Agape Today*, Shelby almost believed in her future. Except she could envision the number chart on the wall, and Sebastian kept giving over editorial space to advertising.

The alarm next to the bed sounded. Shelby squinted at the time. In D.C., lately she'd been skipping Sunday school and church. Sunday was the only guaranteed uninterrupted office time at the magazine. It had been Zach's policy that no one worked on Sunday. Since Sebastian hadn't sent out such a memo, Shelby figured the old rule null and void—or at least, that's what Shelby kept telling herself. She never managed to believe it.

Her father called her name before she could agonize fully over what to wear. Risking his wrath, she hurried into her jeans and a pullover sweater.

Sebastian waited at the bottom of the stairs. He wore a suit belonging to Cynthia's husband. Except for the shortness in the sleeves and the tightness at the shoulders, Sebastian's outfit was standard. Even the white shirt was pretty much what he wore to the office all the time. A slightly raised eyebrow demonstrated his opinion of women who wore jeans to Sunday morning worship.

They wound up in the backseat of Shelby's father's car. It smelled of aftershave and coffee—scents that always reminded her of her father. They spelled out comfort and fear at the same time. Comfort, that her every need would be taken care of. Fear that she wouldn't, couldn't, live up to his expectations.

Most everyone else had left. Shelby hugged the door until one last latecomer climbed in. Aunt Edna. Trapped in the middle, Shelby had to choose between overwhelming perfume and too much male. Shelby pressed her knees together and made a determined effort not to sit too close to Sebastian.

Man, he was big and square. And he smelled better than Aunt Edna. The same aftershave as her father, only Sebastian didn't make her feel safe at all. Oh joy, by the smirk on his face, Sebastian knew he made her uncomfortable. The sly smile he directed out the window proved that he enjoyed the whole farce, right down to Aunt Edna, who kept up a continuous commentary about Shelby's many virtues all the way to church.

Funny, Shelby sat next to Sebastian at office meetings—and he scheduled one every day—but she'd never noticed the size of his hands. Right now, one rested on top of his knee, way too close to her knee. It would only take a slight muscle spasm, and his little finger could touch her leg.

Not enough sleep, Shelby told herself and tried to sidle a bit closer to Edna.

"Are you blushing, Big Shelby?" he whispered, using her family nickname in an entirely too-familiar way.

"I don't blush." Shelby picked at a broken thread near the knee of her jeans. Hmm, the overwhelming perfume smell really wasn't that bad. Actually, it smelled quite pleasant. "What scent are you wearing, Aunt Edna? I like it."

Edna beamed. "It's Spring Bouquet. I got it from your aunt Lucille. She had gall bladder surgery two weeks ago. . . ."

Shelby stared straight ahead. Sebastian, a more considerate, compassionate human—and one who had not shared numerous rides to church with Aunt Edna—supplied timely "ohs," "reallys," and "uh-huhs" until they reached the church's parking lot.

Sebastian followed her dad's example and offered Shelby assistance out of the car. He looked completely at ease. A gentle smile, the first she'd seen from him, convinced her it was meant especially for her. The man was morphing right in front of her eyes. He turned into a young Uncle Zach and completely disarmed—make that charmed—her.

She wanted to follow Aunt Edna. But that would be rude, and Sebastian was technically her guest. His hand slid over hers, his little finger—the one she'd recently noticed for the first time—caressing her tender palm, a palm that hadn't been tender a few moments ago. Shelby froze. A slight tug reminded her that his touch shouldn't render her immobile. She allowed him to guide her across the parking lot.

Sage Valley Church never changed. To Shelby's memory, the grass was the greenest, the bricks the reddest, and the driveway managed to always have the same available spots for those regular members who didn't need to call ahead to reserve parking or pew space. It had changed in one area, though. It shrank. The walk to the front door only took a nanosecond. The foyer had lost so much space that, once inside, Shelby stood shoved against Sebastian.

During childhood, Shelby's best friend had been Michelle Greenspan, the minister's daughter. Michelle's father had a Bible full of proper behaviors for Michelle to follow. Shelby's father had his law library *and* the Bible.

Michelle turned into Suzy Homemaker after she married Roland Ketchem and now actually followed her father's rules willingly.

Shelby took a deep breath. She was leading the Great Oz into the church of her youth. These people knew everything about her. From the time she'd dropped the money plate in third grade, to the time she'd backed into Minister Greenspan's car in tenth grade, to the fight about wanting her navel pierced as her senior gift.

"Mama likes the class about Corinthians, but you young people check out the choices and go where you want." Shelby's father took his wife by the elbow, directing her into the church the way he tried to direct his brood through life.

The greeter pressed a visitor's badge on Sebastian's suit. Before the words "Welcome to Sage Valley Church" evaporated into Sunday morning mist, Shelby saw Michelle approaching with great white shark speed across the foyer.

"Shelby!" Michelle, with a two year old clutching her leg, recognized news when she saw it. Shelby Tate attending Sunday school with a man was front page.

Shelby took a moment to offer a quick thanks to God for not allowing her to wear the dress. Shelby Tate attending Sunday school with a man *and* wearing a dress might disrupt services too much. As if playing the part, Sebastian gripped her elbow in a possessive movement. He stayed there too, like a piece of lint that no matter how often brushed away seemed statically connected forever.

Shelby forgave Sebastian his blatant invasion of space.

On Michelle's coattail was Regina Gentry. Both Michelle and Shelby had labeled Regina "The girl most likely to have a perfect life." To Regina, perfect life meant married life. Her life wasn't perfect yet.

"Michelle, Regina, hi." It had been months, and to her surprise, Shelby felt glad to see them.

Regina stared at Sebastian.

Shelby did too. There was nothing wrong with Regina ogling Sebastian. It shouldn't bother Shelby at all. Not one bit. Not even half a bit.

But it did.

"This is Sebastian Maitland," Shelby introduced offhandedly. What was this sudden attraction to her boss? She'd wanted him to drop off the face of the earth since she'd met him. Why change directions now?

Regina's eyes lit up.

Shelby looked toward the ceiling. She tried to close her mouth, but the words came out anyway. "Sebastian, I'm going to check the bulletin board for our choice of classes. Regina, Sebastian's been researching the personal ads. You've gone that route. Give him some advice."

Regina gasped and turned to Michelle. "You told!"

As Shelby hightailed it to the bulletin board, she snuck a furtive look at Sebastian. He met her eyes and grinned. He knew exactly why she'd turned him over to Regina. Shelby forced her gaze away. What had just happened? She had the gut feeling, if she didn't, she'd either laugh or fall in love.

Neither was the proper action to take with one's boss.

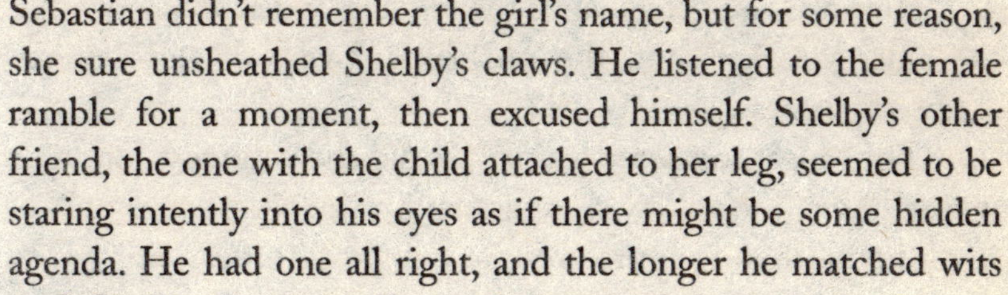

Sebastian didn't remember the girl's name, but for some reason, she sure unsheathed Shelby's claws. He listened to the female ramble for a moment, then excused himself. Shelby's other friend, the one with the child attached to her leg, seemed to be staring intently into his eyes as if there might be some hidden agenda. He had one all right, and the longer he matched wits with Shelby, the more advanced the agenda became.

Right now, Shelby looked to be memorizing the schedule

of classes, no doubt delaying her return to him. Obviously, by how many people stopped to greet her, she was loved. Also, she wasn't comfortable in church, at least not the church of her childhood. Uncle Zach had mentioned that she didn't seem comfortable in their home congregation, either. She'd changed churches just a few months ago, Sebastian remembered. He wondered if she was happy.

"Have you been here before?" The personal ad lady leaned over his shoulder.

He'd always been able to attract single females on a mission. He preferred Shelby, the fish who needed to be lured.

"No, but I'm enjoying myself," he answered politely before following Shelby to a Sunday school class.

The topic was the Prodigal Son. The teacher, a man who looked very much like Shelby's father only with less hair, gave them time to discuss the flaws and redemption of the younger son. Sebastian could actually feel Shelby growing tense next to him. The urge to reach over, touch her hand, soothe her, almost became realized. Any female but Shelby, and he would. In the middle of Sunday school was not the place to experiment with action/reaction.

"I've always identified with the older son." Shelby finally spoke up, interrupting in an uncompromising voice.

"How can you," challenged the teacher, "when you know that the older son represents those Christians who do not demonstrate forgiveness?"

"The oldest son acted human, as did the youngest son. Isn't it true, if we don't show compassion on the oldest son for acting human, then we ourselves are guilty of his very sin?"

From the front, a gentleman turned around and offered his opinion. A woman agreed, while another professed doubt.

Soon a lively discussion ensued. Sebastian walked out of the class with more understanding of the parable than he'd achieved in all his years of Sunday school combined.

He touched Shelby's shoulder. "You know, I can remember identifying with the older son. Eventually I just accepted the principle behind the parable, but until today, I never understood it." Sebastian quickened his steps to keep up with Shelby. Though she measured a good foot—and then some—shorter than he, he still needed to make an effort to keep pace with her.

This could be the way he spent the rest of his life, matching wits with a woman who not only knew Sebastian's world, but also God's.

Sebastian hoped.

Chapter 5

Monday never rated as his favorite day, until now. Sebastian studied the office so recently vacated by his uncle. Too small, at least for what Sebastian wanted; but take Olive's office, right next door, by tearing down the wall, and he could share space with Shelby.

"Where do you want this box?" Olive peeked over a pile of what could only be called debris.

Zach Maitland apparently threw nothing away. Sebastian found restaurant receipts in the corner behind the file cabinet. On the top shelf of a bookcase, Zach stored napkins from last Thanksgiving.

Sebastian pulled ancient Valentine cards out from under the computer table. The card Shelby had sent his uncle was the funniest. Sebastian kept it. He didn't want anything else, and eyeing the benevolent gaze of the once-proud blue marlin, Sebastian knew he'd refrain from decorating their office with a taxidermied motif. The marlin looked a bit insulted to be residing in a box.

Their office—his and Shelby's. . . Sebastian liked the sound of it. *Now to take care of the marlin.* "Can we throw it away?"

Olive turned a little pale. "Will you take the blame when Zach returns?"

"Zach won't be returning to work here."

"Trust me," Olive said. "He'll stop by, he'll remember the dead fish, and he'll ask."

It took them all day to clean the office. Zach's belongings now called a hall closet home. The carpenters—Olive's nephews—arrived at five. By the next morning, Sebastian's office now included what used to be Olive's. Knocking the wall down took hours. Sebastian figured it would take a while longer to remove the wall from around Shelby's heart.

He wondered who'd built the wall and how strong it stood.

How would Shelby react when she came back and discovered he'd changed the office around? According to Olive, Shelby hated change. He believed that. She still wanted Uncle Zach back.

A new desk, in a new much larger office, waited for Shelby to transfer her belongings. Bookcases, twice the size of her old ones, stood ready for more books. He felt a twinge of guilt as he unplugged her computer and carried it down the hall, so he ordered fresh flowers to be delivered the day Shelby returned. Guilt still lingered, but he'd applied a small bandage. Maybe the purchase of new office supplies would counteract the misdemeanor of flip-flopping her office with Olive's without permission. Not that he needed permission, since he was the boss. And he wanted her time. He wanted her knowledge. He wanted her.

"Promise me that I'll get to be here when she arrives for work tomorrow morning," Olive said wryly as she wheeled her overhead projector into Shelby's old office.

Sebastian knew his staff figured Shelby would throw a fit. He expected it too. But surely after a few days, weeks, months, she'd see that working together benefited everyone involved. He'd give her a budget to decorate her office. She deserved it after all the time and energy she'd invested in the magazine.

Unlike Olive and Alexis—the other assistant editor—Shelby didn't appear to collect anything, unless *Agape Today* paraphernalia counted. Olive had bears everywhere. Alexis was into frogs.

Sebastian grinned. Uncle Zach had been a great fish collector. A fish stapler still swam around the office. The staff claimed Zach used it to keep an eye on them. Every time Sebastian packed it, Olive took it out and put it back on his desk.

He moved the stapler to Shelby's desk. She deserved it. Uncle Zach, Olive, and Shelby had been a team. Hopefully, being Gal Friday would inspire Shelby to include Sebastian in her high esteem. He doubted it would happen at first, but time often overcame obstacles.

Sebastian retrieved Zach's blue marlin. It looked right at home above the rack where Shelby hung her coat. Shelby could use it as a corkboard. While he thought of it, he should get her a dartboard. Three wedding invitations fairly glowed with lead residue. They deserved a break from Shelby's target practice.

"Phone," Olive called.

It took about two minutes of negotiating with the printers for Sebastian to remember why he hated Mondays and, since coming to *Agape Today,* Tuesdays. Deadlines. He'd gotten a good price, but now the layout needed to be finished in time for a Monday/Tuesday printing.

This month, Sebastian was actually on time. Taking out his notebook, he let out a sigh of relief that he'd managed to stay on schedule during the two days he'd spent rearranging Shelby's office. From Olive's careful innuendoes, he knew his actions weren't unacknowledged by the staff. They recognized the signs of Cupid's arrow when they saw it.

He'd gotten a little carried away. Maybe. If anything, he wanted to prove to Shelby that he was starting to get a handle on things—but how? The "Dear Lonely Heart" column! He'd start that for the next edition. A mailbag full of letters rested against the wall, enough to sort through, and the only problem he wanted to solve was his own.

He sat at his desk and brushed a bit of ceiling dust off his jacket. The carpenters had done a good job, but at his insistence, they'd rushed.

No matter what, he'd answer the first letter he drew. Nope, not another woman complaining about her boyfriend wanting to date around. The next letter dealt with a girlfriend possessing a ketchup addiction. Not *Agape Today* material. It took hours, but Sebastian continued on until he found three letters he thought suitable.

Giving advice actually came quite easily. Shelby often scolded about length, so Sebastian made sure to add extra sentences. She'd also grumbled about his tone. Well, no doubt men would have a different tone than women. This time, since he'd written more advice, his tone would make sense.

Sebastian didn't want to admit that he didn't understand the concept of tone. Didn't tone come naturally? Shouldn't Shelby be glad the tone of their magazine articles varied?

According to his daytimer, he needed to devote this afternoon to investigating the personal ads. Signing on to the Internet, he plugged in the keywords: Christian, personal, looking, date. The ads he found online were not on any site he'd trust. Some needed to be censored. Still, he jotted down a few notes to himself. The abbreviations alone were worth copy. A James Bond look-alike wanted a Mae West younger woman. A sports fanatic wanted someone to watch Friday night baseball with. A woman claiming to be a relative of Joan of Arc looked for a male willing to change the world.

Sebastian signed off the computer and took last Sunday's paper from the break room. Locally, two full pages of personals garnished space, yet only three ads mentioned wanting potential suitors with religious affiliations.

Sebastian wrote down their post office box numbers and called for Olive. She actually looked enthused about writing a form letter asking for interviews. Next, Sebastian called the university. By sheer dumb luck, he got in touch with a sociologist, Dr. Mason Huff, who'd written a book about dating via the personal ads.

According to the expert, the personals remained a vaguely unresearched area. People did meet and marry via the written word, but no survey or study could determine the percentage who stayed together. In today's busy society, men and women—who a mere decade ago would have met their mate during a social venture—now claimed to have no time to leisurely look for a significant other.

Relationships established by those meeting via the personal ads were not decades old. Researchers seemed to have no opinion about the longevity of modern "mail order" brides. Would they be called "personal ads ordered" brides? Shelby most likely could come up with something catchy, like "Newspaper Nuptials."

"And most of them lie," Huff said.

"About what?" Sebastian put down his pencil. He'd been doodling a personal ad for Shelby.

"About the way they look, their age, what they do for a living."

"But they'll get found out. Why do they bother to lie?"

Huff chuckled. "Because even if it takes them a hundred dates, they might get lucky and find someone who doesn't care."

Interesting. Sebastian made a note to compare the ages, looks, and professions of all ads he found specifying a believer as a potential suitor. Would he also find that these advertisers lied? Would the percentage of liars be the same?

Huff rambled on. "Women are looking for someone older to help take care of them. Men are looking for someone younger. Studies say that men are always on the lookout for women of childbearing age."

The biggest hindrance, Huff said, was that most advertisers came from prior relationships and had children.

Shelby would be impressed, Sebastian thought as he hung up the phone after thanking the doctor. Of course, she'd also have taken Huff to task about some of his data concerning what men and women looked for.

All the new criteria had intrigued him so much, he doodled his own personal ad.

SWM, who owns a magazine, seeks energetic, fun-loving, managing editor. Must have yards of beautiful, black hair. Must love pencils. Should enjoy volleyball, church, and having every light in the building turned on. Let's put pen to paper and write a happy ending.

Stupid. Sebastian crunched the paper in his fist and tossed it in the wastebasket. Nope, bad idea. Shelby now shared this office. With his luck, the wastebasket would overturn and the personal ad would roll right to her feet.

Either *Agape Today* had been sold and aliens took over or

Sebastian had been up to no good. Shelby tried not to glare at Olive. In a room where the décor no longer looked even vaguely familiar, the woman scrunched behind her computer. Olive's shoulders shook, so Shelby knew laughter waited only moments away. Still, Olive ignored Shelby pointedly, no doubt hoping to avoid confrontation. No problem. Shelby knew who the furniture-moving culprit was.

Olive's old office looked bigger—and for good reason. A wall was missing, giving Shelby a view of Sebastian's too-neat desk. For once, Sebastian wasn't in.

Yeah, right, thought Shelby, *afraid to face me.*

"So," said Shelby, returning to her old office. "Are you going to tell me what's going on, or do I get to guess?"

"According to the boss, you two are now a team. He spent days rearranging furniture."

"I give it one week, three days," offered Alexis.

"I said four days," added Rex Mindell, an accountant who worked part-time.

"And, Olive, are you in on the office pool?" Shelby felt her cheeks burning. What was Sebastian thinking? She'd agreed to help him learn the business, not join with him at the hip.

Olive gave a rare grin. "Oh, I think everything's going to work out fine. He's just what you need."

More than a little annoyed, Shelby headed back to the office and set her cup of coffee on the edge of her old desk. He'd moved the whole entity, complete with piles of things-to-do, to the office. Now she needed to transfer her belongings from the little desk to the big sectional desk. It would take weeks to put everything in its place.

She'd like to put Oz in his place, unfortunately *Agape Today* was his place. Even more than it was Zach's, since Zach was just a brother to the owner and Sebastian, the son.

Shelby didn't know Theodore Maitland. His portrait hung in the foyer. His brown, slightly curly hair looked the same as Sebastian's, as did the determined chin, but the eyes were different. Theodore looked imposing; Sebastian only tried to look imposing.

A stack of messages languished beneath a pile of last month's magazines. Oh, good, Max Williams wanted a meeting. Shelby needed to fly to Oklahoma and meet the man in jail. Apparently, looting wasn't his only less-than-desirable pastime.

Shelby made a note to look into a plane reservation and then checked her to-do list. Time to get busy on the "Singles" issue. Computer dating increased in popularity even as Shelby penciled Max Williams into her day planner. She found two different local avenues to explore. One involved heading for a downtown D.C. address and making a videotape of herself. Reporting the process might prove interesting to readers. The other avenue would take up her Saturday evening. The Datarama Singles Network worked out of a restaurant's banquet room. Their leader, one "Doctor Love," claimed his computer dating network was safe, easy, and affordable.

Shelby took out her notebook and jotted down a couple of sentences comparing computer dating to buying a new Ford. Oh, well, attending a singles outing would be better than watching a rerun on television or going on a date with Sebastian as she'd promised. Surely he'd understand a work conflict.

Shelby's elbow jostled a folder on the edge of her desk. It fell to the floor. Picking it up, Shelby almost tossed it back on the carpet. Closer inspection found three "Dear Lonely Heart" letters and three replies from Sebastian. None looked to be an improvement over last month's effort. Shelby moved some books off her chair, set them on top of the trashcan, and sat. He really was serious about all this. Sunday, at lunch with her family, he'd continuously referred to her as his Gal Friday. Shelby's mother hadn't worn such an enraptured smile since Cynthia's wedding.

Shelby tossed the first letter onto her desk. It skimmed across a full in-box and landed against the vase of now very dead flowers. Zach gave them to her the day he'd told her who'd be taking over his job. She kept them to remind her that hard work wasn't always rewarded. Dead leaf resin blemished her desk. It looked oddly like the pencil markings on the wedding invitations. Funny that Sebastian—the neatnik—hadn't tossed them. Though, in looking at her desk, he hadn't thrown anything away. Not even used Styrofoam coffee cups.

Then, she noticed the fresh flowers. Shelby stood and walked around her desk. They were perched on the edge, but carefully propped up by books.

To my Gal Friday,

I look forward to working as a team.

Oz still traveled down the yellow brick road, and he was as lost as Dorothy. She thought about tossing the whole mess in her trashcan, but it was full and buried under a stack of books.

She picked up his "Dear Lonely Heart" effort and shook her head at his pitiful attempt at prose. Last time, she'd berated him for his calloused brevity. He'd listened. This time, the only thing he'd neglected to do was start with the words *I take my pen in hand to. . .*

He'd chosen a letter vaguely similar to the one he'd answered last month. Both women were dealing with men who had commitment problems.

Dear Lonely Heart,

My boyfriend is wonderful except for one thing. He's kept every photo of his ex-girlfriend, and they are still displayed prominently throughout his apartment. When I mention that it bothers me, he claims that he just hasn't gotten around to taking them down. This has been his excuse for over six months.

Made Miserable by Mementos

Shelby wondered if commitment was the only problem Sebastian could relate to. Did he have a commitment problem? Was that why he didn't have a steady girlfriend or a wife?

Unbidden came the thought: *Do I have a commitment problem*? After all, Shelby admitted, she had no right to judge Sebastian for a way of life so parallel to her own. She put the letter aside and checked Sebastian's response.

Dear Made Miserable,

Offer to clean his house. Men love to be taken care of. Replace all of her photos with photos of you! Better yet, replace all those old photos with photos of you and him together. Just think of the subliminal message you are sending. Get creative. . . .

Shelby stopped reading, although there were many more sentences. Poor girl. If she followed all of Sebastian's advice, the boyfriend's apartment would soon need to be expanded. Of course, Sebastian's advice might work out, and after the wedding they could move to a ten-bedroom Tudor home in the Hamptons. They'd be the proud owners of a portrait studio.

Looking over at his side of the office, she finally noticed the lack of Zach's belongings. They'd disappeared. Replaced by: nothing. Sebastian's side of the office glared in an off-white, empty sort of way. Maybe she should stick her university diploma near his desk. The one that read: Journalism. It proved that she had earned the right to have "Publisher" written by *her* name.

"So, what do you think?" Alexis stood at the door, peering into the office, afraid to come any farther.

It was on the tip of Shelby's tongue to be honest, to say exactly what she thought; but on the drive home from Sage, Shelby had given herself a stiff talking-to. She didn't want to fail at good intentions before she'd been in her—*the*—office a mere hour.

"I think this is a great idea," Shelby said.

Suddenly, she meant it. Sebastian expected her to resist. Maybe if she gave wholehearted effort, loomed at his elbow every moment, gave him no breathing room, maybe he'd do the typical male thing: run!

Chapter 6

They'd taken her car. Shelby insisted; and when he didn't argue, she'd looked surprised. Sebastian liked the look on her face and promised himself he'd be responsible for her wearing such an expression more often. One thing was for sure: If they got together, she'd need a bigger car. No way did he intend to drive around with his knees touching his chin. Camaros were show cars. Shelby needed a real car, like a sport utility vehicle or something a bit bigger than this piece of Plexiglas.

She seemed in a rare mood. Every few minutes, she smiled at him. Twice she'd asked his opinion about which way to turn or where to park.

Located only fifteen minutes from the *Agape Today* offices, the Datarama banquet hall looked more like a warehouse than a social club. Sebastian wondered if his office attire might be out of place; but after looking at the diverse gathering, he realized he could have worn a tutu and nobody would have looked twice. Shelby's black pants accentuated an athletic figure made to look willowy by a silky black and white top.

A young woman with spiked, green hair handed out nametags. An older gentleman, looking like a feisty landowner from a John Wayne movie, took Sebastian's fourteen dollars.

His unlit cigar bobbed up and down as he said, "You could have gotten two dollars off had you thought to bring a couple of canned goods."

Shelby had her notebook out in a minute. Looking over her shoulder, Sebastian watched her scribble:

> *Even in the computer dating world, consumer practices reign. Get two dollars off with a canned good; bring in a flyer promoting Datarama and get a free dating consultation; sign up a friend and you both are eligible to attend a free relationship workshop. Doctor Love promises success and does it with every advertising gimmick known to man.*

"Bit harsh, aren't you?" Sebastian asked, guiding her to a table where a man with long gray hair and wild eyes helped singles pick up stubby, yellow pencils and questionnaires. The man looked eerily like a drawing of John the Baptist from one of Sebastian's childhood Bible storybooks.

Shelby glanced around. "The minute this place starts to impress me, the tone will change."

Taking their pencils and questionnaires, they joined two other singles at a booth.

"I thought you weren't supposed to be biased." Sebastian hunched over his form, thinking he couldn't count the times she'd told him that during the last three days. Every word he put to paper was scrutinized, and she didn't offer to help rewrite, just told him he had to.

"Don't worry," Shelby said. "When I actually put it into article format, you'll see nothing of me in it. These are my notes."

He truly wanted to see the words on her questionnaire, but as if he were the third-grade class cheater, she turned her back to him and held her elbow up—completely blocking the answers she wrote down.

Sebastian finally started his own paper. At this rate she'd be done and circulating before he wrote his name. After his name, he was assigned a number. Number Seventy-three. Sebastian wanted to meet this Doctor Love guy. Using numbers this way was sensible and time saving. Shelby had taken the paper before him; that meant she was Seventy-two.

Age, profession, type of car driven, hobbies, religion, favorite colors and foods, education. . . It was like filling out an elaborate job application.

A few minutes after Shelby, Sebastian took his questionnaire back to John the Baptist. Shelby drilled the man with more questions than Sebastian could come up with in a month of brainstorming. The old man started out answering patiently, but after a few moments, he put up his guard.

Yes, every Saturday night somewhere between fifty and a hundred singles gathered at Datarama.

Yes, Datarama was geared toward young urban professionals.

Yes, Datarama was expanding and could now be found in cities all over the East.

Yes, Doctor Love did keep track of couples who'd wed after meeting through his singles network.

No, this particular employee did not have any information about success ratios of Datarama couples.

No, this employee had not found his mate via Datarama.

No, Doctor Love was not here tonight but could be reached through his personal secretary Monday through Friday.

No, there was nothing else to add.

By the time Shelby finished with the saintly impersonator, their questionnaires had been successfully entered into the computer. The woman with the spiked, green hair handed Sebastian a printout with seven numbers on it. She stuck a large red sticker with the number seventy-three on his nametag.

She pointed to his printout. "You need to find the women with these numbers. They appear to be most compatible to your criteria."

"My criteria?" Sebastian questioned. "I didn't write down what I was looking for in a potential girlfriend."

The girl blew a very pink bubble, which clashed with her green hair. After it burst, she said, "You didn't have to. You wrote down the important information about your life. We match you with females who have similar lifestyles. For example, you were educated in Europe. That eliminated more than ninety-nine percent of the women in this room. You're a nonsmoker. That only eliminated twenty percent. You're a practicing Christian. That made you compatible with twenty-five percent of the females in attendance this evening."

Sebastian started to open his mouth to complain that he doubted his lifestyle was interesting enough to warrant finding a girlfriend with the same interests.

Then, he saw the first number on his list.

Seventy-two.

Mattie, the girl with the green hair, was neither married nor looking. This was a job putting her through med school. She had no time or interest in a mate. Shelby wondered how she found time to do her unique hair.

Mattie wasn't willing to share her opinion about Doctor Love, but the way her lips pursed showed that she didn't think much of him. Neither the man handing out questionnaires nor the woman collecting canned goods cared to comment about Doctor Love, either. The disc jockey looked at her as if she'd lost her mind and turned the music up louder.

Shelby found Sebastian and looked at her list of numbers. "We're no longer people," she complained, "we're numbers."

Sebastian was having a great time, although for the life of her Shelby couldn't figure out why.

He smiled. "I love numbers."

He did, she remembered too late. He loved charts and graphs too. On posters pinned haphazardly around the banquet hall, statistics were quoted. Most of them were jokes, such as: Fifty percent of women who meet their mates in grocery stores are good cooks. Or: Fifty percent of men who meet their mates in grocery stores are looking for good cooks. Another read: One in every four men secretly loves to watch soap operas.

Balloons bobbed against the ceiling, each proclaiming Datarama as the answer to the single's dream.

Shelby took a sip of the water Sebastian had purchased for her. The club's motto *"Looking for a date? Datarama is more reliable than fate."* was printed on the paper circling the bottle.

Sebastian discovered where all the snacks were positioned throughout the room. There were chocolates imprinted with "Give me a call." There were small white bags of popcorn. The bag had a picture of a couple holding hands on it. Underneath the entwined fingers was a place for three prospective phone numbers. Red crayons embossed with "Kiss Me" were on each of the room's round tables. There were even souvenir nail files advertising Datarama as a smooth place to find a mate.

Shelby took another sip of water and stared at the wall where computer printouts were taped. Apparently, after Mattie had collected them, some employee in a backroom typed them into a computer—Shelby really wanted to see this computer, since it had spewed out Sebastian as her number-one date potential—and then, the canned goods lady taped them to this wall.

Shelby looked at her second number, five. Gentleman number five had poor handwriting. Squinting at his information, Shelby wondered how his handwriting could be deciphered enough to enter into the computer. His name was Bill. He delivered papers.

Huh?

Well, she wrote for a magazine, and he worked somewhat for the newspaper; that must be the connection. Shelby crossed his name off her list.

Looking around, she saw Sebastian chatting with a tall redhead. Suddenly, Shelby's two-inch heels didn't seem adequate. The redhead had perfectly coiled hair. She kept touching it as Sebastian laughed at something she said.

Shelby checked out her third choice. Derek Stubbs, number twenty-three. Closing her eyes, she refrained from reading his questionnaire. It would only make her skip to choice number four. If she kept reading their questionnaires, soon she'd be out of choices.

A man bumped into her, then gently turned her shoulder so he could squint at her nametag. "Excuse me. You're Seventy-two. Good. I'm Fifteen, and I've been looking for you."

Shelby almost laughed. Not only was he number fifteen, but he looked about that age.

"Well, you found me. I was just checking out the questionnaires. Where's yours?"

He turned a little red but pointed to one near the bottom.

Shelby had to kneel to read it. Joshua Simpson. He wrote

in print and stayed within the lines.

She touched the spot where date of birth was listed. Yeah, right. If this kid was twenty-three, she'd invest in whatever vitamins he was taking. Pulling out her notebook, she asked, "Do they ever check your ID when you come here?"

If possible, Josh Simpson turned even redder. "Wha. . . Why?"

Shelby smiled. "I'm not really looking for my dream date. I'm writing an article about dating practices and. . ."

The youth had the decency to look sheepish. "You know, I think I see a friend of mine over by the punch. Good luck with your article."

Computer dating has no age limits. Students in high school are just as interested in meeting potential suitors. Why? In an atmosphere of adults, do shy, young men and women feel more at ease?

Josh Simpson disappeared into the crowd before she could grab him for more questions. A few moments later, Shelby watched him consult his list. Looking around, she knew why he'd singled her out. It was mostly a thirties crowd. There seemed to be only a few singles her age, and all of them wore low-hung jeans and exposed lots of stomach.

Oh, well, according to her mother, Shelby had always acted older. Bridget Tate had shaken her head sorrowfully after saying it, as if there was something wrong with being an overachiever.

Where was Derek Stubbs? Shelby located Sebastian. He sat at a table with three women who all leaned toward him as if he were sharing stock market secrets. Shelby mimicked the redhead's deft motion of tucking an errant strand of hair behind her ear and set out.

She found Derek leaning against the wall, holding a bottle of Datarama water. He looked vaguely familiar.

"Hi, Number Twenty-three." Shelby stuck out her hand. "I'm Seventy-two, and this is my first time here."

"Shelby Tate," Derek Stubbs said. "This is the last place I'd expect to see you."

She managed to shake his hand while her brain frantically searched for his history. Used to be, she remembered everyone.

"Derek Stubbs," he reminded. "I go to your church."

Shelby almost choked on her water. "Oh, really." She remembered him now. She'd been away from church too long if she couldn't greet Derek as a friend.

"What church is that?" Sebastian came from nowhere. He leaned against the wall next to Derek.

"The church on Newman Road, right across from the park." Derek shook hands with Sebastian, and then they both looked at her.

"So, I'll bet Shelby makes Bible class interesting," Sebastian said.

"That she does." Derek grinned. "Most of us wish she'd attend more. She instigates the best discussions."

Two hours later, sitting at a scratched table in an all-night diner, Shelby finished her notes. Derek and Sebastian were arguing about the Redskins and downing an order of fries. Shelby hadn't found a date at Datarama, but she did get a front-row seat to male bonding.

Sebastian sat next to her. He'd paid for all their meals and had listened politely while she queried Derek about Datarama. He was a Friday night regular and had been for over a year—not that he'd found the perfect female.

"You need to find her at church," Sebastian advised.

"Right," Derek chuckled. "Do you have any idea the shortage of single women who attend services? Shelby is one of the few, and it's been so long since I've seen her that I thought she moved."

"I attend church," Shelby muttered.

"When?" Sebastian challenged.

It had been months. It hadn't felt like months. Church was a habit, her father always said—one easily broken, apparently. Her family never missed except for serious illness. Vacations were planned around services. School events took second place to Wednesday night sermons. Once Shelby's softball team had lost a key game because she hadn't been there to play second base. She could still hear her teammates' grumblings.

But Shelby believed, and she spoke to God often. Lately all Shelby had done was ask for forgiveness.

"Shelby?" Sebastian nudged.

"It's time to go home. I'm tired." Shelby put her notebook back in her purse and nudged Sebastian's knee. Good-naturedly, he scooted out and said good-bye to Derek.

Once in the car, he said, "I didn't mean to put you on the spot."

"You didn't," Shelby said. *I put myself there.*

Chapter 7

It took Sebastian a few minutes to find the church on Newman Road. It reminded him of Shelby: small, neatly kept, and with plenty of personality. Green vines wove around the frame. A bell, shiny and ready, topped a steeple. There were a few cars in the parking lot. He didn't see hers.

Sebastian's church seated over a thousand, though not that many attended. Twice that number claimed membership. They, like Shelby, just didn't adhere to the necessity of attendance. In Shelby's small church, there were only two classes to choose from: one for adults and one for children. Sebastian took a seat in the back row of a class on the Apostle Peter.

He knew from reading back issues of *Agape Today* that Peter was Shelby's favorite apostle. He knew why too. She thought Peter more human than the others. She liked that he'd gotten angry and cut off the soldier's ear.

"The teacher's name is Smith. He only teaches lessons about Peter." Derek took the seat next to Sebastian.

"Strange," Sebastian said.

Derek shrugged. "I thought so at first, but I have to tell you, I feel like I'm an expert about Peter now. Last time Shelby attended, I thought Smith was going to faint from happiness.

Shelby wanted to know why, if Jesus preached only good will to men, did Peter even have a sword? I guess Smith had never thought about that. He spent the next three weeks talking about ancient sword customs. Even brought in a sword. He says that Peter didn't mean to cut off the soldier's ear. He says Peter meant to cut off the soldier's head. Best lesson I ever heard."

"You know Shelby well?"

Derek shook his head. "I've only been here a little over a year. Moved from Nebraska. She's just the kind of woman you remember."

Sunday school started. At fifteen after, Sebastian thought about asking Derek if Shelby usually ran late.

Regular church service began, and still no Shelby. After the final prayer, Derek introduced Sebastian to the sparse singles group. They all knew and liked Shelby. They worried about her lack of attendance.

Shelby had not gone home for the weekend, Sebastian knew. At the reunion he'd overheard her parents making plans to travel to New York for a vacation. To Sebastian's knowledge, there was only one place Shelby always seemed to be.

The *Agape Today* office should be deserted. Sebastian had seen her signed contract. No one was to work on Sunday. Zach left three months ago. Shelby stopped regularly attending services three months ago. That meant Shelby respected Zach enough to follow her contract. Sebastian decided that meant she didn't respect him enough.

It took barely ten minutes to get to the *Agape Today* headquarters. She was in their office. She'd managed to clear her desk. Her shoes were off and stocking feet were propped on top of two unopened twelve packs of soda. She gripped a pencil as she read what looked to be one of his "Dear Lonely Heart" letters. Her expression was a little more pained than he liked.

"Well?" he asked.

Her feet hit the floor with a plop.

"Ow." She glared at him for a moment, then softened her expression. "What are you doing here?"

"I thought I'd check up on you."

"Why?"

"I visited your church this morning. You weren't there. I thought maybe. . ." He leveled with her. "I visited your church because I wanted to see you. I really enjoyed last night. I was hoping I could take you to lunch or something."

"You were telling the truth the first time. You were checking up on me."

"That too. I hoped you'd be in church. Why weren't you?" He crossed the room and sat at his desk. No papers cluttered the top. His books and magazines were where they belonged, in the bookcase.

"I find peace and quiet here at work." She stuck the pencil behind her ear and laid his response on her desk.

"Church is more important than work. What you do here at *Agape Today* will only bring you temporary happiness. The Lord will give you much more. If you give Him the opportunity."

"*Agape Today* is a Christian magazine. I'm studying His Word when I read over some of the articles."

"It's not the same thing and you know it."

"Spending Sundays here gives me an advantage." She looked so sincere. Sebastian fought the urge to walk over to her. What was she trying to prove? She already worked twice as hard as any of his other employees. Truthfully, she was *Agape Today*.

"What kind of advantage?"

"I didn't work hard enough when Zach was here. Maybe if

I work hard enough for you—"

"For me, what?"

"Then maybe someday I'll publish a magazine."

She hadn't been sleeping. Not in months. Oh, she took catnaps. Four hours at a time seemed to be the max. Her best sleep came when she was alone in her office and just dropped off, but that was impossible now that she shared an office with the Great Oz. Although for some strange reason, during the week they'd shared space, she'd come to enjoy seeing his face first thing in the morning. He'd be drinking coffee and reading a newspaper, but he'd always smile at her over the top of the sports section.

Maybe that's why she told him the truth. A truth he had no response for. He sat at his desk and studied her as if she were one of his graphs. Finally, after about five minutes, he stood and held out his hand.

"Come on, I'm taking you to lunch."

He didn't scold or judge her; he just wanted to take her to lunch. Shelby almost laughed. If he'd stuck his nose in the air; if he'd quoted her Scriptures about putting God first; if he'd threatened her job, then she would have known how to react. But no, he wanted to take her to lunch. She'd intended to pretend that working with him was enjoyable. The pretending never happened. Instead, she found a man she could work with instead of for. And it was becoming more enjoyable every day. She slipped her shoes back on, took his hand, and let him lead her from the room.

His hand was warm. Just feeling the roughness of his palm told her this was not a man who felt at home behind a desk.

"What is your dream, Sebastian?" Shelby asked as the elevator door opened.

"Which dream do you mean? I have many."

With a jerk that almost sent Shelby up against the wall, the elevator began its descent. The light flickered. A grinding noise, resembling a freight train screeching to a halt, had Shelby covering her ears as the elevator ceased moving.

"What's happening?" Her voice was a whisper, but she really wasn't scared.

Then, the light went off.

Shelby hit the ground. Darkness, so satiny that she couldn't see her hand in front of her face, enveloped her. She tried to breathe. It hurt.

His arms came around her before she could start to cry. She hadn't even heard him move. No, she wouldn't cry where he could see her. But he couldn't see her. Still, he could hear.

"Shelby, everything's all right."

"No, it's not." What to say? She hated this. She didn't want to be scared. She wanted to be strong. "I'm fine, just give me a moment."

"Now that's a lie."

In the silence, she could hear him breathing. The scent of him—a combination of peppermint, newspaper, aftershave, and man—kept the tears at bay.

He took his arm from around her, pulled his cell phone from his jacket pocket, and pushed the call button. A tiny light glowed from the cell's screen.

Even knowing the fire department was on its way didn't calm Shelby. She felt like a fool, clutching his arm and trying to still her breathing. Dizziness kept her from moving her head. Her hands were cold, even though the elevator was warm and stuffy.

"Why are you afraid of the dark?" Sebastian whispered, drawing her close. With one hand, he kept pushing the call button on his cell phone, but not dialing in a number. The light barely silhouetted his hand.

Shelby started to deny her fear, but what was the use? He paid *Agape Today*'s electricity bill. He knew how many lights she turned on in the evening. His first month, he'd walked around and turned them off, claiming they must have a poltergeist in the office. The second month, he'd sent out mass memos about conserving energy. Sometime about a month and a half ago, he'd stopped letting it bother him.

It felt good to talk. Her throat was dry, but she still managed. "We were playing hide-and-seek. It was two days after my seventh birthday. I hid in the shed. No one found me. I was a good hider, but I fell asleep; and when I woke up, the shed was locked from the outside."

She didn't tell him about the rustling noises, which she worried might be mice. She didn't tell him about the eerie sound of the wind blowing through the trees.

Truthfully, Shelby found comfort just in the fact she could tell him about being locked in the shed. It hadn't been the dark that had frightened her so long ago. Nowadays, being in the dark simply triggered the memory. She'd been in that shed for hours.

What still haunted her dreams, though, was the memory of her father's voice, calling her name. Over and over, Sheldon Tate shouted. The rest of the family added their cries. But no matter how hard she tried, Shelby could only open her mouth. She couldn't respond; she couldn't make the words come.

Sebastian held her, one rough hand sliding up and down her arm. He spoke of his family, of his first car. He talked about the part-time job he'd held in high school and about going to college in Europe so that he'd be totally independent. He talked about his fear. He worried he might be the first

Maitland to fail. And finally, he spoke about his dreams.

A policeman? Nowhere could be farther removed from the police force than the offices of a Christian magazine.

They heard the noise of the arriving firemen. Disjointed shouts came up the shaft. Sebastian's phone rang; and after a few curt words, he told her the firemen and a maintenance crew had everything under control.

As if to validate his words, the lights came back on. Shelby relaxed, lulled into contentment by both the certainty that she was about to leave the elevator and by the hand that still stroked her upper arm. She opened her mouth. She knew words were possible, but did she really want to break the spell? Maybe there was a time when it was okay to lose the ability to talk.

"So, why do you want to be a publisher?" He straightened, and for a moment Shelby expected him to scoot away. Instead, he gathered her closer.

She felt safer than she had in years. That she could feel this way while trapped in an elevator amazed her. Looking up at him, she wanted to touch that strong chin.

"Are you going to answer me?" he prodded.

"I guess I want to be a publisher because of my grandmother."

"You want to please her?"

"No, it's just that I proved her right one time, and I've never forgotten it." Shelby smiled at the memory. "My grandmother came to spend the weekend. On Saturday morning, she convinced me to stay in from play and we baked in the kitchen. My first batch of muffins tasted a bit like paste with blueberry flavoring."

Sebastian chuckled. "I've tasted your coffee."

"Hey," Shelby bristled, "my coffee is strong, just the way I like it."

"Go on with your grandmother story. I'm interested." Sebastian turned sideways so that Shelby nestled against him.

"We made batch after batch. My father tasted every attempt, and he kept telling me I could live up to his expectations."

"And that's why you want to be a publisher?" Sebastian didn't look convinced.

"No, it was something my grandmother told me. She said I shouldn't live up to his expectations."

"Really." Sebastian said the word slowly, as if he didn't believe her.

"She told me I should *exceed* his expectations. By the time I'd made the fifth batch, they were so good, we could never convince my father that I'd made them."

It took a week for the elevator to function properly. Sebastian doubted he'd ever get Shelby on the contraption again.

The "Singles" issue went to print. Sebastian couldn't say he was proud of his personal ads article, but Shelby seemed to think it showed talent.

He'd flown with her to interview Max Williams. His Gal Friday had been right. It was an excellent piece. Although Shelby had longed for a redemption theme, she'd written an excellent reality story. Max Williams was not a nice man, but he was a man who had gone against his nature when faced with a choice.

Their office was turning homey. The marlin wore one of Sebastian's hats and boasted a number of pencil markings, thanks to Shelby's fine aim.

He liked it at *Agape Today*, but it wasn't where he was supposed to be. He could live up to his father's expectations here; but he'd never exceed them.

And watching Shelby for the last month, spending time with her, showed him what a work environment could be like when someone who truly loves the job is in charge.

He'd told her one dream. Sebastian reached for the phone.

Soon, he'd tell her the other.

Shelby wondered why *Agape Today* had waited so long to do an "Animals" theme. Never had she enjoyed interviewing so much.

There was a minister's wife in Ohio who owned more than twenty boa constrictors. She claimed they gave her a sense of peace after a stressful day. Shelby found a retired Christian schoolteacher in New York who had actually ordered an alligator through the mail fifty years ago. The woman had gone on to author five books about alligators and regularly traveled to Australia.

Shelby shook her head as she hit the start button of the copy machine. Why had she worried about having Sebastian as a boss and a partner? They were a perfect team. He'd taken her out to dinner almost every night for the last three weeks. They talked of everything from politics to religion.

In many ways, Shelby felt ashamed. She'd put temporary happiness before God—only she hadn't been happy at all. She'd been lonely, and she hadn't known why.

She hadn't realized how real a companion He was. It embarrassed Shelby to remember she'd convinced herself she needed sleep instead of Sunday school and quiet time at the office instead of church.

Going to church, sitting beside Sebastian, made her feel complete. Grandmother had said that if God were the third member of a relationship, then the relationship would stand firm.

Gathering her papers, she headed back to their office and acknowledged how she'd been praying for God to change her work environment. She who hated change! God had arranged for the best change of all and his name was Sebastian Maitland.

Shelby pushed open the office door with her hip. Sebastian was on the phone. His voice, deep and resonant, held no trace of humor.

"Yes," he was saying. "I'm willing to sign over control. I never wanted to be in charge of *Agape Today* in the first place."

Chapter 8

"Where's Shelby?" Sebastian began picking up the papers strewn across the floor.

Olive bent down to help him. "She went flying out the door. Must be quite a story."

Sebastian frowned. She had nothing scheduled. They had a little breathing room right now and had been planning on leaving this evening to go to her sister, Cynthia's, for Little Shelby's birthday party. Her next appointment was with the man who made praying-hand soap sculptures, but that wasn't until after lunch.

He went back to the office and sat. Women were unpredictable, that's all there was to it. Just last week he'd watched Shelby, who cringed in a dark elevator, willingly fondle a boa constrictor.

Did he even want to bother with the stack of assignments on his desk? Not really, but his father said it would take at least two weeks before everything was final.

A giant yellow envelope full of "Dear Lonely Heart" letters needed attention. Sebastian grinned. He had a lot to thank "Dear Lonely Heart" for. After all, if Shelby hadn't hated his first attempt, she wouldn't have become his Gal Friday. Now to convince her to become his Gal Monday, Tuesday, Wednesday, Thursday, Saturday, and Sunday.

He pulled out a letter.

Shelby was right, he thought, tossing the letter to the side. Too many women lent money to deadbeat men. Another woman wanted to know how to choose between a man and her cat. He'd give that one to Shelby too. She had a cat.

The third letter stopped him. Its question was as brief as his early answers had been.

Dear Lonely Heart,

How do you know when you are really in love?

Expecting Bells and Fireworks

No wonder Shelby hadn't liked his sparse responses. When a problem really related, there might not be enough room on a single magazine page to fully give an answer.

Dear Expecting Bells and Fireworks,

When you are really in love, that person is with you all the time. She's with you as you drive on the freeway. She's on your mind when you brush your teeth. You're thinking of her while you're selecting the right after-shave. When you are really in love, you have to have a cell phone, because you want to call her from wherever you are. . . .

Shelby would never print this. It had nothing to do with answering a "Dear Lonely Heart" column. It had everything to do with him being in love. A good newsman could separate the two. Leaving *Agape Today* was the right choice.

Shelby hated to cry. Her sisters were all gentle sniffers who carried tissues with elegance. Not Shelby. Her nose ran while simultaneously turning red. It wasn't fair.

Neither was it fair for Sebastian Maitland to make her fall in love with him, then sell the magazine he knew she had a passion for. And without telling her!

Freedom walked over Shelby's stomach. The cat was thrilled to have his owner home in the middle of the day.

"Why can't men be like cats?" Shelby complained. Freedom's tail went in the air, and the cat gracefully strolled to the kitchen for a midday snack. "Freedom, you never disappoint me. You've never lied."

Okay, Sebastian hadn't lied. From the beginning, she'd known that he hadn't wanted the magazine. But he'd made her believe he was willing to try.

Her phone rang. Moments later, Sebastian's worried voice came on her answering machine. Shelby took a sip of coffee and aimed the remote control at the television to turn up the volume.

In a two-hour period, he left three messages. Shelby set up her laptop and updated her resumé.

Typing in references only made her cry more.

The sun was setting when the doorbell rang. Freedom ran to greet the visitor. Shelby peeped out the hole. "Sebastian Maitland, you go away."

"What's wrong with you? Everyone's worried. Are you sick?"

"No. Yes."

"Which is it?"

"Both."

"Let me in."

"No."

"Shelby, I will break down this door."

She could tell by his expression, greatly exaggerated by the peephole, he meant it. She unlocked the deadbolt and walked to the kitchen.

He laid his keys on the counter and followed her. "Aren't we going to your sister's?"

"I'm going. You don't have to."

He tried to put his arms around her. "What?" He honestly looked confused. Confused and innocent.

She swallowed, thinking she should have skipped the fifth cup of coffee. "I heard you."

"Heard me wha—" His eyes widened as understanding dawned. "You heard me, and now you're mad? Why?"

"How can you just walk away? We are doing great. Together we can make *Agape Today* a contender."

"No, Shelby. *You'll* make *Agape Today* a contender. I'm more a hindrance than a help."

"You're getting better every day. . . . What do you mean, I'll make *Agape Today* a contender?"

"I thought you said you heard me on the phone."

"I did. You said you were signing over *Agape Today*. I didn't mean to eavesdrop, but we share an office and—"

"And you didn't hear the whole conversation?"

"Well, no."

"Shelby, I'm signing control over to you."

"Me?" she squeaked.

Sebastian took advantage of her loss of composure. He pulled her in his arms and kissed the top of her nose. "You."

"But your father wants the magazine to stay in the family."

"Oh, I assured him it would."

"Wha—what do you mean?"

"I told him that your last name would become Maitland, eventually."

"You're kidding?"

"No, I figure by the time I'm out of the police academy, you'll be ready to walk down the aisle."

Shelby didn't bother to tell him it wouldn't take that long. Instead, she kissed him.

And not on the nose.

Epilogue

There were four of them, stuck in the right-hand corner of her bulletin board. They were innocent looking, square, each with gold trim. Shelby Tate thoughtfully twirled a pencil as she turned her attention back to the stack of letters on her desk.

Sebastian walked into the office and asked, "You ready?"

Shelby gathered up the letters. "Is it okay if I bring these to lunch with us? I thought maybe you could help me."

"Help you what?"

"Look through all these applications and find the next 'Dear Lonely Heart'!"

PAMELA KAYE TRACY

Living in Glendale, Arizona, where by day she teaches first grade at Southwest Christian School and by night she teaches freshman reading at Glendale Community College, Pamela had her first novel of inspirational fiction published in 1999 by Barbour Publishing's **Heartsong Presents** line. She has been a cook, waitress, drafter, Kelly girl, insurance filer, and secretary; but through it all, in the back of her mind, she knew she wanted to be a writer. "I believe in happy endings," says Pamela. "My parents lived the white picket fence life." Writing Christian romance gives her the opportunity to let her imagination roam.

A Letter to Our Readers

Dear Readers:

In order that we might better contribute to your reading enjoyment, we would appreciate you taking a few minutes to respond to the following questions. When completed, please return to the following: Fiction Editor, Barbour Publishing, Inc., P.O. Box 719, Uhrichsville, OH 44683.

1. Did you enjoy reading *Dear Miss Lonely Heart?*
   - ❑ Very much. I would like to see more books like this.
   - ❑ Moderately—I would have enjoyed it more if ______________

____

____

2. What influenced your decision to purchase this book? (Check those that apply.)
   - ❑ Cover ❑ Back cover copy ❑ Title ❑ Price
   - ❑ Friends ❑ Publicity ❑ Other

3. Which story was your favorite?
   - ❑ *Hope Deferred* ❑ *Mission: Marriage*
   - ❑ *Wait for Me* ❑ *I Do Too*

4. Please check your age range:
   - ❑ Under 18 ❑ 18–24 ❑ 25–34
   - ❑ 35–45 ❑ 46–55 ❑ Over 55

5. How many hours per week do you read? ______________

Name ______________________________________

Occupation __________________________________

Address ____________________________________

City ______________ State __________ Zip __________